Dianne Brennan is having a very bad day.

She thought she was just delivering a foster dog to his new home. How could she know that instead of an eager adopter, she would be greeted by a man holding a bloody knife?

And what happens when she sees in the man's snake-cold eyes his decision to kill her?

Rottweiler Rescue has been the Editor's Choice in the Mystery Category of the Rocky Mountain Fiction Writers Annual Colorado Gold Contest.

ROTTWEILER RESCUE

a Dianne Brennan mystery

Ellen O'Connell

Copyright © 2009 by Ellen O'Connell
www.oconnellauthor.com

ISBN-13: 978-1-45054-610-2
ISBN-10: 1-45054-610-2

Used with permission:
Poem "Baggage" by Evelyn Colbath, now Phoebe Lane Scott, © 1995. All rights reserved.
Rottweiler drawing © 2008 by Geula Resnick.
Cover image is of the author's dog, Schara, from a photograph taken by Randi Bolton © 2010.

Dedication

This book is for all the dogs who have enriched my life—a shepherd mix named Laddie who was the companion of my childhood, Kim and Bear, the dignified Akitas who walked beside me during the early years on my own, and of course the Rottweilers who have graced my life for the last 17 years—my own and those who stayed with me only a short time on their way to new lives.

Baggage

Now that I'm home, bathed, settled and fed,
All nicely tucked in my warm new bed,
I'd like to open my baggage lest I forget
There is so much to carry—so much to regret.

Hmm . . . Yes there it is, right on the top.
Let's unpack Loneliness, Heartache and Loss;
And there by my leash hides Fear and Shame.
As I look on these things I tried so hard to leave—
I still have to unpack my baggage called Pain.

I loved them, the others, the ones who left me,
But I wasn't good enough—for they didn't want me.
Will you add to my baggage?
Will you help me unpack?

Or will you just look at my things—
And take me right back?

Do you have the time to help me unpack?
To put away my baggage, to never repack?
I pray that you do—I'm so tired you see,
But I do come with baggage—

*Will **you** still want **me**?*

by Evelyn Colbath, now
Phoebe Lane Scott, ©1995

ROTTWEILER RESCUE

1

LETTING GO IS THE HARDEST part. The dogs come from shelters, from homes that no longer want them, from vets or kennels where they are left by owners who just disappear.

You take them into your home, love them and teach them, then one day you drive to the new home, make nervous small talk with the new owners, and leave. No matter what else it is, it's a betrayal.

The first time was the worst. Betty was small for a Rottweiler, still thin from the starvation and neglect that had brought her first to a municipal shelter and then to our rescue group. After only a month with me, she believed *I* was her adoptive home.

Dusk was falling when I left Betty. Maybe if I'd never looked back . . . , but I did. The image of her there, clearly outlined through the darkening night by the house lights, nose pressed against the front window of her unfamiliar new "home," has never faded with time.

Other foster homes say this is the best part, the goal achieved, a time of joy. Not for me.

A quick glance in the rearview mirror at my silent passenger diverted my thoughts from Betty and the foster dogs who had come after her. The big Rottweiler rode quietly behind me, gazing calmly out the window.

We were nearing the end of a thirty-minute drive, but he showed no more interest in the children playing in a yard we passed than he had in joggers, cyclists, or even other dogs. The back windows were down several inches, but so far as I could tell he had not reacted to the earthy smell of pastured horses at the beginning of our journey or to the yeasty perfume of a doughnut shop near the halfway mark.

The high school that was a marker in my detailed directions appeared on the left. With an effort I forced my attention away from the dog and concentrated on street signs and turns. The address I was looking for was one of the thousands of new houses in the subdivisions spreading south and east from Denver, making seas of roofs where once there had been seas of prairie grass.

Stonegate had more charm than many other developments, with some variety in house styles and outside finish. The sculpted green belts that wound around the subdivision were studded with pine trees and featured wide sidewalks already in use by early morning dog walkers and joggers.

Spotting the number I wanted, I parked my car across the street from the house so that the shade of an ash tree fell across the front seat. The August day was going to be in the nineties long before noon, and morning cool was already giving way to oppressive heat.

Moving slowly and without enthusiasm, I got out, opened the back door, and snapped a leash on Robot's collar.

"Come on. Let's go see your new home," I said.

He kept his head turned away from me and didn't move until I tightened the leash slightly, then he jumped from the car. Crossing the street, he lagged several feet behind me like a teenager embarrassed to be with a parent.

Opening the gate to Jack Sheffield's backyard finally lifted my mood. The six-foot cedar privacy fence would keep a dog safe, and the lush green lawn shimmering in morning sunlight would hold cool air throughout the day in the tree-shaded areas. A mower roared nearby, filling the air with the sweet scent of new mown grass.

Maybe Susan McKinnough, head of Front Range Rottweiler Rescue, was right. Susan was the one who had dubbed the dog now following me "the Robot" because of his unnatural behavior. She wanted a special kind of home for a dog that had been so abused he had withdrawn from the world, and she considered Jack Sheffield special.

I closed the gate, followed the walk around the side of the house then along the edge of a low redwood deck toward the center steps. The sound of a sliding glass door meant Jack had been looking for me, eager to meet his new dog.

I glanced up and started to greet him. "Hi, I'm Dianne Brennan, I . . . ."

The figure that came out of deep shade near the house into the bright light at the edge of the deck was swathed in black from the ski mask on his head to his ankles. White running shoes stood out under the black apparition. He stopped at the deck's edge, staring at me as intently as I stared at him.

As I stood and gaped, my mind struggled to accept the obvious—this wasn't Jack Sheffield, and something was terribly, dangerously wrong.

Jack was shorter and slighter of build. And he didn't have colorless eyes so cold they made my stomach curl. Because I was staring into those eyes, as mesmerized as any hapless mouse by a snake, I saw the change in them when he decided what to do about me.

The glint of sun on metal broke the spell. I tore my gaze from his eyes and saw the knife, saw him raise the gloved hand holding it toward me.

Before he moved, before I could turn to run, Robot walked forward. He looked up at the figure in black with the same calm indifference he had shown to sights through the car window.

No sound came from him, his hackles were not raised, his posture had none of the stiff-legged signs of canine aggression. He just stood there, a hundred and twenty pounds of unwanted rescue Rottweiler between me and a man with a knife who had just decided to kill me.

The man on the deck was the one who ran, ran across the deck away from the dog and me. He jumped from the deck, crossed the lawn in a few strides and swung up over the fence effortlessly.

Sick and light-headed with fear, I turned and stumbled back toward the gate, toward my car, other people and safety. My hand was on the latch when I realized I was alone. No dog, no leash in my hand. Robot wasn't in the yard. He hadn't chased the man with the knife. The open sliding glass door showed the only place he could have gone.

The smart thing, the safe thing, was to get back to the car and call 911, but what if Robot made whatever had occurred in that house worse?

I didn't waste time calling a dog I knew would not come. I went after him.

A trail of red drops led the way across the wood deck. Only a few steps through the doorway and into the kitchen, Robot was sniffing at the edge of the pool of blood that had spewed from Jack Sheffield's torn throat and countless other ragged wounds. The dog was already leaving bloody pawprints on the white tile floor. Fighting nausea, I stepped on the end of the leash, picked it up, and pulled Robot out the door.

It took three tries to get the key in the car door with my shaking hand. When the lock finally clicked, I shoved Robot into the already broiling back, got in myself, started the engine, and threw the air conditioner on high. After a few seconds, I locked all the car doors again, reassured by the solid thunk.

For the first time since the killer came out of the house, I stopped reacting and started thinking as I looked out at the quiet, empty street. I thought about responsibility, obligation, and duty. I thought about big black dogs in the heat of a day like this one was going to be, about the little I knew of homicide and police procedure, about the prejudice and blind hate too often shown towards Rottweilers as "killer dogs." And I thought about those bloody pawprints now drying near Jack Sheffield's ravaged body.

Finally, with hands still shaking, I dug my cell phone out of my purse and started pushing numbers.

The 911 operator did her best to keep me on the phone, but I disconnected after giving her Jack's address. I had other calls to make and other things to do before the first sheriff's deputies arrived on the scene.

WHEN I FINISHED MAKING SURE both Robot and I would be safe no matter what happened next, I called the dispatcher again.

"Now you stay on the line and stay put until the officers are ready to talk to you," she ordered.

Hours later, I was still staying put. The house and the street around it were a beehive of official activity. Black and white Ford sedans with the blue and gold logo of the sheriff's department lined the street. News vans nosed in wherever they could.

An ambulance had arrived silently and now waited with open back doors for its grisly burden. Men and women in uniform and civilian dress bustled up and down the sidewalks and around the house. Yellow crime scene tape held eager reporters at bay. Curious neighbors stood in small clumps on lawns and sidewalks of the nearest houses.

I sat on a strip of lawn beside Jack's driveway in the shade of a young pine. Hours ago, the shade had shrunk to almost nothing, leaving me thankful for the sun screen I'd slathered on in the cool of morning. Now my shade patch was expanding again.

My sandals, loose-fitting denim skirt, and sleeveless white blouse were not only as comfortable as anything could ever be in the intense summer heat, they were helping me blend in with neighborhood lookie-loos.

An official car pulled away from the curb and disappeared around the corner. Attendants loaded a gurney with a telltale black bag strapped tightly in place into the waiting ambulance, which left as silently as it had come.

A tiny hope bloomed brightly in my thoughts. The first deputies to arrive had taken my name and address before ordering me to stay and wait. Maybe all this massive officialdom would just finish whatever they were doing, pack up, and leave. Tomorrow, or even next week, I would receive an official summons to appear for an interview.

That hope quickly died. The next time an officer in the blue-gray uniform of a Douglas County sheriff's deputy emerged from the house, he headed straight for me. Reporters crowded around, yapping questions like a pack of human terriers.

Under his wide-brimmed hat, the young officer's tanned face was set in a scowl, and he ignored shouted questions with a maturity beyond his years. He gave them nothing, not even my name.

"Deputy Horton, ma'am. Would you come with me please?"

"Of course." I tried to imitate his calm, but the shouting and bodies crowding too close made me hesitate.

As if sensing he might lose me, Deputy Horton took my arm and hustled me through the throng. He let go of me as we ducked under the yellow tape and magically left them all behind.

"It's even worse than it looks on television," I said.

"They're a bunch of vultures. They know we'll talk to them when we're ready, and it will be a senior officer, not me, but they do it anyway." He led the way to the front door.

As I had suspected, the front room of Jack's house was a formal living room done in decorator pastels. One of the uniformed men in a group across the room turned and came toward us. "Thanks, Horton." His tone was dismissive, and Deputy Horton disappeared into the interior of the house.

"I'm Lieutenant Forrester, sheriff's department," he said. "You discovered the body and called 911, right?"

"Yes," I said, studying him as he looked down at handwritten notes in a small notebook. He was like me a few years from forty, but unlike me, I thought, on the far side. A sprinkling of gray hairs salted thick, dark brown hair. His square, strong-jawed face was deeply lined, pleasant more than handsome. Then again, maybe scenes like the one in the kitchen had deepened the lines in his face more than the years.

The lieutenant looked up again, and the intensity in his manner and pale blue eyes cranked my already jittery nerves up another notch.

"Now how about telling me what happened, Ms. Brennan."

I swallowed hard and started my story.

"I had an early appointment with Jack Sheffield, eight o'clock. It was a couple of minutes before eight when I got here, and I went through the back gate, around the side of the house . . . ."

"Why the back, why not the front?"

"He told me to go to the back when he gave me directions. We talked on the phone."

"I see, and what was this appointment for?"

Better just take a deep breath and spit it out, I told myself. "I'm a foster home for Front Range Rottweiler Rescue, and he was adopting a dog from us. I brought the dog he was adopting."

I risked a look at the lieutenant's face, reassessed my previous thought that it was pleasant, and added,

"That's why so early, Rotties have trouble with the heat, you know, big black dogs, so we decided on eight, so it would still be cool."

The silence hung between us for long seconds before he broke it, his voice low and furious.

"You brought that dog here. It ripped a man's throat out, then you made up some story about a man with a knife? You sat out there for hours while every cop in the county looked for a figment of your imagination! Where's the dog?"

"Safe," I said, starting to get angry myself.

After a few seconds of uncomfortable silence, I felt compelled to add, "Jack was dead when I got here. Any doctor will tell you a dog didn't do that to him. I'd be dead too if it weren't for the dog. He got between me and the man, the killer, and that's why I'm still alive. I was so scared I almost fainted, then I dropped the leash, and the dog got in the house and stepped in—made those pawprints before I got him out. He didn't hurt anyone, and I knew it would get too hot to have him waiting around on the street, and so I got someone to—and so he's someplace safe."

None of this had made any impression on the lieutenant, whose mouth was now a tight line.

"Do you know what obstruction of justice is?"

I swallowed hard. "A felony. Most often committed by presidents and those in high office, I believe."

The intensity of the pale blue gaze made me wish I could take the smart words back as soon as I uttered them.

"All right, Ms. Brennan," he said softly, "we'll finish this interview at the Justice Center. Horton!"

2

DEPUTY HORTON APPEARED SO QUICKLY he must have been lurking in the next room. He listened to Lieutenant Forrester's orders silently, then escorted me to one of the black and white Fords with a careful politeness that should have been reassuring but somehow was not.

After a few words from Horton, a second deputy climbed into the front passenger's seat, and I began second guessing myself and the situation wildly. Were there two of them because they thought I was dangerous? Should I have refused to cooperate and demanded a lawyer? But I wasn't under arrest now; would raising hell have made everything worse?

I tried not to think about the purpose of the divider that protected the deputies in the front seat from desperate criminals like me in the back seat. Then I noticed that the car's back doors had no inside handles and almost lost control. Closing my eyes, I gulped in several deep breaths, determined not to let my fear show.

When I opened my eyes, I forced myself to stare out the side window and to concentrate on the scenery flashing by. Neither the blur of rooftops when we started out or the open grasslands beside the highway when we left the developments behind held my attention, but as we approached the Justice Center, I had regained a semblance of calmness. After all, the cavalry was on its way, and everything would work out in the end.

Usually I enjoy any trip to the town of Castle Rock, but this trip was different, and Deputy Horton took a route that avoided the historic town center and its appealing Nineteenth Century homes and businesses anyway. The Justice Center was an ordinary-looking brown brick building northwest of town. Its modern starkness suited my mood far better than the charm of the old town.

Not only that, I thought wearily, the small room where Deputy Horton left me alone with my own thoughts was government-issue dreary, but at least not century-old dreary. Air conditioning was a most welcome modern convenience. I sat and waited. And waited.

When the door finally opened and Lieutenant Forrester walked in, he was accompanied by Deputy Horton and a short female officer who probably didn't look as thick in the waist when she was wearing something more flattering than her uniform. Her brown hair was skinned back into a knot and emphasized the tight lines of her face. There had to be recording equipment built into this room, but she thumped a notepad down on the table. I understood her aggravation at being the one assigned to do the note taking, but my position was much worse.

The lieutenant was either over his earlier anger or had it well in hand.

"It's been a long day for you," he said. "Do you need anything to eat or drink? Restroom?"

I looked at him warily. My thirst was slaked and my bladder was empty. "I'm fine, thank you," I replied.

He threw a hard glance at Deputy Horton, who was busy looking elsewhere. "Just as well," he said. "Saves time. Now, are you ready to talk to us?"

I tried to read something in his face but couldn't. "Am I under arrest?"

"No. You were first at the scene of a homicide, and you saw someone leaving the scene. You're going to give us your statement is all."

"Did the medical examiner tell you that it was a knife, not a dog?"

I expected him to stonewall or to bluster, but he ran a hand over his face and answered quietly. "Coroner. We have a coroner. Dr. Reiker says it wasn't a dog, but that dog still made a mess of the crime scene, and you're going to have to give him up. We could bring charges for tampering with evidence or hindering an investigation. Now, do you want to cooperate, or do you want us to find something to charge you with?"

If he was going to be halfway forthcoming, I would do the same. "I'm willing to talk about anything except giving you the dog. We can fight over that when my lawyer arrives."

The lieutenant's eyes narrowed very slightly, but he kept his voice even. "So you ran out of that house, you called somebody to hide the dog, then you called a lawyer, and then you finally called us. You're a good citizen, Ms. Brennan."

I couldn't help smiling at him. "Actually, I called you first. You can ask your 911 dispatcher. She tried to keep me on the line the first time and couldn't. I hung up on her and called someone about the dog. I never really called a lawyer—I don't know one to call—but I do know Judge Cramer in Arapahoe County because he and his wife adopted a dog I fostered last year, so I called him. And I didn't call him until your officers were already there."

"And you didn't worry about the risk of our first responders showing up before you handed off the dog?" he asked.

"I've lived in Douglas County for a long time. I figured it was a good bet you wouldn't show up until he was safe."

His frown told me I'd just risked our new found détente, so I added quickly, "I'm not being critical. I live here, and I know how big the county is."

"Eight hundred forty-four square miles," he growled.

"Exactly, and our county commissioners have never heard of a development they didn't like. Your department must hire a new deputy every other month to try and keep up."

Admitting that the response time of the sheriff's department hadn't concerned me because I'd driven Robot back to the school that had featured so prominently in my directions and met Carey Inman there didn't seem prudent right then. Carey was a rescue adopter who lived only a few miles away, and she'd been willing to provide a safe haven. I'd parked in front of Jack's house again and reestablished my connection with the dispatcher at the sheriff's office only minutes before the first deputies arrived.

Our preliminary sparring was over. Lieutenant Forrester dictated time, date, names of those present, and a case number clearly for the recording equipment. I took note of the fact that he didn't recite a Miranda warning.

At first knowing I was being recorded and the sight of the deputy taking notes made me stutter self-consciously, but soon the horror of the morning wiped out such small concerns. No one interrupted, but as soon as I finished, the lieutenant's questions started.

"You're sure it was a man?" he asked.

I was sure, but had to think why. "Yes. His size, the way he looked at me, body proportions, the way he went over the fence. Yes, I'm sure."

"And you think he was a big man? You're what, five foot five? What's big to you—six feet?"

"Usually, yes, but he was above me on the deck, and I was so scared . . . . So maybe he wasn't that tall, but my first thought was that he was bigger than Jack, and Jack was maybe your height, but smaller looking, fine boned, really thin, not that you're . . . ."

"I get it. Sheffield was scrawny, delicate even. I'm not. And the killer was definitely more than five foot ten. You call Sheffield 'Jack.' How well did you know him?"

"Not well at all. He's—was—a professional dog trainer. Dog handler is what he'd call himself, I guess. He showed dogs for a living. I go to a dog show maybe once or twice a year, just to look sometimes, to help at the booth our rescue group sets up sometimes. I knew who he was. He probably couldn't have put my name and face together."

"Tell me more about this rescuing business."

"Okay, rescues are groups, or sometimes individuals, who take in homeless dogs and find new homes for them."

"Yeah, but you called it 'Rottweiler Rescue.' You don't take any Benji types, right?"

"Well, no. Rescue usually means purebred dog rescue. Fanciers of one breed work with that one breed. The theory is that people familiar with a breed can evaluate their own better and know if a certain dog is adoptable and what kind of home it should have, and that if each breed takes care of its own, the shelters would have more time and money for the Benjis."

Lieutenant Forrester wasn't buying my explanation. "Sounds like a bunch of dog snobs to me."

I wasn't going to deny what I knew to be true. "There's an element of that in it. The reason people are fanciers of one breed is that they think it's the best. And while most dog people care about all dogs, they tend to care most about the kind they live with."

The lieutenant changed the subject slightly. "So if Sheffield dealt with show dogs, why was he getting one of these homeless leftovers from your group?"

"I don't know."

His look told me he heard more than my words. "Tell me what you do know."

"What I know is all from Susan McKinnough, the head of our rescue group. She told me Jack always said he couldn't have a dog at home because his boyfriend—his, um, partner—was allergic." Here I searched the lieutenant's face to see if he understood my full meaning. He did.

"The neighbors told us about the boyfriend. He's out of town on business."

"Yes, well, all of a sudden Jack called Susan and said he wanted to adopt a dog. He said his friend was moving out soon and until then they had agreed that the dog would be in only part of the house, and . . . ." I tapered off, unsure how much to say.

"So Ms. McKinnough believed it, and you didn't."

Perceptive. The lieutenant was all too perceptive, but I couldn't see how telling him about Robot could do any harm.

"Susan's been breeding and showing Rotties for over thirty years. She started before most people even knew what a Rottweiler was. She's really at home with the breed people, the people whose whole lives revolve around dog shows. She didn't want to adopt Robot— the rescue Jack was adopting—to the kind of regular family that adopts most rescues. She thinks, thought, an experienced dog handler like Jack was perfect."

"What's wrong with the dog?"

"Nothing's wrong with him."

"Okay, what does *she* think is wrong with him?"

"He's been abused, abused so badly he's like children get, I guess, when they just withdraw. Most abuse cases are so delighted to have anyone be kind, they're all over the first person who feeds them. We test all the dogs before we adopt them out, and Robot flunked the sociability part of the test. On a scale of one to ten, he's a zero. In any area he's in, he'll get as far from people as he can. For that matter, he doesn't react to most things like a normal dog. It's like you have this living, breathing dog, but there's nothing inside."

"I'd think people would be standing in line for one like that. He'd be easy to take care of."

"People love dogs because dogs love them back. This one isn't going to. People don't want to adopt a dog that won't have anything to do with them. Susan thought if Jack knew what the dog was like and still wanted him, it was an ideal solution."

"How long have you been fostering the dog?"

"A little more than a month."

"And you didn't think Sheffield was good enough for him, and you were willing to go to jail to keep him away from us."

I just nodded my head, admitting the perceptive lieutenant was right. He said nothing. His expression made it clear he didn't think much of my priorities.

"Jack didn't suddenly want a pet after all these years. He told me to come to the back because he didn't want the dog in that fancy living room. He was going to make him a yard dog, and we don't adopt to people who keep dogs outside. I couldn't imagine what he did want, but now—I bet it was protection. He thought a big dog would keep exactly what happened from happening. Only I'm the one who was protected. It was too late for Jack. And if I hadn't gotten scared out of my wits and dropped the leash, Robot never would have gone inside, and you wouldn't be so keen to kill him and stuff him as Exhibit A in a murder trial when you may never even catch the guy."

My voice was rising with emotion, and the lieutenant replied to the part of my fear he had no problem with, in fact probably considered rational.

"We'll catch him."

"Oh, sure. From my great description. If he had shorts and a T-shirt underneath, he could pull off the black clothes, stuff them and the knife in a fanny pack, and just jog away. No one would remember him, and he'd be long gone before you ever arrived. And covered up like that he didn't leave so much as a flake of skin for you to find at Jack's place."

Some subtle change in his face told me I'd hit a nerve, but what he said was, "You watch too much television, Ms. Brennan."

Maybe so, but I was right about this. "So did any of those people jogging and biking through Stonegate see a man in black clothes?"

"Ms. Brennan, I ask, you answer. We're not sharing information here."

He'd already shared the information, and we both knew it. No one had seen the killer. Had the investigators found anything at all? I glanced at Deputy Horton thoughtfully, and the lieutenant caught me.

"Don't even try it. He likes ladies, and you all like him back because of his pretty face, but he's not that young, and he's not that dumb. He likes working here."

Not only would Deputy Horton give Brad Pitt a serious run for his money in the looks department, he was years younger and inches taller. I tried to look like I hadn't the foggiest idea what Lieutenant Forrester was talking about. So did Deputy Horton.

"Now, it's going to take a while to get a statement typed up for you to sign. So suppose while that's going on, you and your friend Deputy Horton there go and get this dog."

"Not without assurances from your department and from the county attorney."

He sighed heavily and leaned back. "What kind of assurances do you want?"

I'd had a lot of time alone to think about that and reeled it right off. "No confiscation, no impoundment, no quarantine except at my home, and no invasive tests."

"What's an invasive test?"

"Oh, cutting off a foot to preserve the pawprint, or removing his stomach to keep the contents, like that."

He got up and went to the door. The muttered reference to a female dog I thought I heard just after he yanked it open and before he slammed it behind him had to be my imagination. It had to be.

3

WHEN THE DOOR TO THE interrogation room where I had once again been left alone with my thoughts opened, a tall man peered at me uncertainly through gold-rimmed glasses perched on a beaky nose. His body was thin and his hair was thinner.

"Are you Dianne Brennan?" he asked.

I nodded, wondering why anyone with such a diffident manner would choose a career in law enforcement.

"My name is Owen Turner. I'm an attorney with Simon, Perry & Simon. Judge Cramer asked me to see if I can help you out."

This was the cavalry that was going to rescue me? My spirits sank to my sandals and ran out onto the floor through the open toes. Sternly telling myself that the Honorable Horace Cramer wouldn't have sent anyone less than qualified, I poured out the story of the events that had brought me to this chair in the Justice Center.

Turner listened intently without interruption, making notes in a cramped hand on a yellow legal pad.

When I finally wound down, he stopped writing, looked me in the eye, and proceeded to give me a lesson in not judging lawyers by their looks.

"Do you understand why they brought you here, kept you, and didn't just agree to have someone in Animal Control look at the dog and let you go?" he asked.

"Because I won't let them see the dog unless they agree not to hurt him and to give him back, I guess."

"Only partly. The fact is you committed what they consider to be a major crime, even though it isn't on the books—you dissed a cop, refused to back down, mentioned friends in high places, and had a lawyer on tap so they couldn't even give you a really hard time."

His language alone made me do a rapid reassessment of Owen Turner, but what he was saying was even more striking than how he said it, and I wasn't convinced.

"Half the world doesn't cooperate with the police any more," I said, "and everyone knows to say they want a lawyer."

"The reason the police do profiling is that profiles are usually right, and the profile for a woman like you would be someone eager to cooperate and slightly intimidated by the police," he said. "They realized you were unusual at exactly the same time they realized you weren't going to cooperate."

Turner was telling me I should fit in a profile labeled "Ordinary Woman in Her Thirties." Did all the fellow members of my group have ordinary brown hair cut short for wash and go, ordinary blue eyes, and an ordinary figure, neither noticeably svelte nor plump? Was there room in my profile for blondes and redheads?

Were we all fair-skinned? Considering the wrong conclusions I'd leapt to about Turner himself based on
appearance, his conclusions as to my ordinariness
served me right, but that didn't occur to me at the time.

"And so what made them realize I'm not entirely
ordinary?" I asked tartly.

"You're a foster home for Rottweilers, and you're
suspicious enough of the police you hid the dog from
them rather than take a chance they'd call Animal
Control and haul him away. They don't believe that
excuse about the heat any more than I do, you know."

"I was afraid they'd *shoot* him," I said. "All it would
take was one deputy who's afraid of dogs. Jack was all
torn up, and there was blood everywhere, and Robot's
pawprints were in the blood."

Turner nodded. "Well, whatever they might have
done, we're past that now, so what are you willing to
agree to? What if they want stomach contents, for
instance?"

My answer was ready, of course, but I couched my
reply more politely than I had to Lieutenant Forrester.
"I have no problem with that. I really have no problem
with any test that doesn't hurt him, but I'm not willing
to let them keep him locked up somewhere. I've been
fostering him for over a month. I'll keep him."

"Even if they make an arrest, a trial and appeals
could take years. Are you willing to keep the dog that
long?"

"I've already accepted that this means I'm as good
as adopting him. Yes, I'm willing, although I don't see
why I'd have to keep him through all that. He just
made a few pawprints. Why couldn't any adopter make
him available?"

"They're worried about what some slimy defense attorney might make of those prints," said Turner with a hint of a smile, "and there's the question of identification of the right dog. By hiding him, you've already brought that into question."

"He has a microchip for identification. All our rescues are chipped before they go to new homes."

"Ah, that's going to make things easier, I think. Let's go talk to the county attorney."

An hour later, after signing my official statement, I also signed my name to an agreement with the county attorney as a representative of Front Range Rottweiler Rescue with only a small twinge of guilt. I am merely a volunteer, a foster home for the rescue group, which is a Colorado nonprofit corporation, but somehow Turner and the county attorney both got the impression that I was a member of the board of directors.

Susan would go along with the arrangement, I told myself. She would just take more convincing than I was willing to try doing by phone right then.

My new attorney had some more advice for me.

"You need to decide what you're going to do about the reporters outside," he told me.

"Oh, yuck," I said. "Can't I just sneak out of here and avoid them?"

"Yes, you can. But if you avoid them now, they'll be on your doorstep in the morning, or even late tonight. They probably already have your name and address. I'd advise dealing with them now. If you're careful you may be able to get away with telling them just enough so that they'll leave you alone, at least for the near future. A lot depends on whether there's better and more exciting news tomorrow and next week."

"If they hear the word 'Rottweiler,' they'll go crazy. If a Chihuahua bites someone they always put a picture of a snarling Rottweiler in the newspapers. They'll want to see Robot and take pictures."

"So don't say the word 'Rottweiler.' Nothing says you have to bare your soul. Tell them as little as you can." He seemed to consider for a moment, then went on. "Crying can help sometimes. Especially with the television people. They like visual emotion."

No wonder people paid attorneys huge sums to help them deal with situations like this. For the first time thoughts of attorney's fees skittered through my mind.

"Do you want me to stay with you?" Turner asked.

"Um, how much am I paying you?" I said.

Once again he gave me that controlled hint of a smile. "That should have been the very first thing you said to me, you know. But you're in luck. Judge Cramer talked me into donating today's time to your rescue group, which I understand is a tax-exempt charity." He paused for just a second before adding, "My wife and I have two greyhounds."

Greyhounds. One of the most abused and badly used of all breeds, greyhounds are killed by the thousands, sometimes in ways that don't qualify as "euthanasia." Dogs too old to race, dogs too slow to win—their bodies make pathetic mountains. Greyhound rescue is one of the oldest and most effective of all dog rescue groups, and if someone has a pet greyhound, they almost always have a rescue dog.

"My usual fee is three hundred dollars an hour."

Turner pulled a small leather case from his breast pocket, extracted a business card, and handed it to me. "For next time."

"There won't be a next time."

"Mm." His polite murmur was the essence of disbelief. "So suppose I help you face the press, and then if you'd like to ride with me, I wouldn't mind meeting this dog."

And I would like to ride in the front seat of whatever he was driving instead of the back seat of a sheriff's car.

Turner was right. The pack of reporters outside the Justice Center already knew my name. As soon as we walked outside, they proved it at the top of their lungs.

"Ms. Brennan, are you a suspect in Jack Sheffield's murder?" shouted one.

"Dianne, Dianne, why are you here at the Justice Center?"

The pack was smaller than what I'd seen on those tv crimes shows Lieutenant Forrester was sure I watched too much, but even so the group was intimidating, bristling with microphones and cameras, and I was grateful for Owen Turner's steadying presence at my side.

Taking a deep breath, I tried to look as if talking to reporters were the highlight of my day, and began answering their questions. I was at the Justice Center to give a formal statement to the investigating officers, I told them. Since I'd seen someone leaving Jack Sheffield's yard and through the open door seen blood on his kitchen floor and called 911, the sheriff's office wanted to be sure what I'd seen.

So did the reporters, and I told them. Sort of. As soon as I finished describing how little I'd seen, they shouted more questions.

A black-haired woman with lipstick so red the color dominated her pale face had elbowed herself to the front of the pack.

"Were you afraid?" she asked. "Did you think he might attack you?"

Her voice was shrill enough that her questions were clear through the din, so I chose to answer her.

"Yes, I was afraid," I told her. "For a few seconds I thought I might pass out. Then I ran back to my car and called the sheriff's office from my cell phone."

The voice of the woman in the front row carried over the rest again. "Why were you there? What were you doing there at Sheffield's house?"

"I had an appointment with Jack Sheffield this morning to talk to him about adopting a homeless dog," I said, choosing words with great care. "You must know by now that Jack was a professional dog handler. I went there to see him about a dog."

So those reporters got the impression that I never went into the house, never saw Jack's body, didn't have a dog with me but only wanted to talk to Jack about a stray I'd found. Maybe I'd missed a calling as a politician because Turner was right—misleading the reporters was only a matter of choosing which questions to answer and answering carefully. Just let tomorrow bring some juicy scandal, I thought. Nobody hurt or killed, just a scandal so they never follow up with me.

When the shouting erupted again, I felt Turner's arm around my shoulders. "Very good," he said in a low voice. "They've got enough for now. Let's get out of here."

He hustled me through the crowd. The reporters trailed us across the parking lot to Turner's Lexus. I sank back into the leather seat and closed my eyes with relief.

The deputies assigned to go along with me to get Robot led the way back to where my car was parked on the opposite side of the street from Jack Sheffield's house. The drive seemed much shorter than it had when going in the opposite direction all those hours ago. The bustle of activity was over, but crime scene tape still marked off the front of the house, and two sheriff's cars were still at the curb.

I left the air-conditioned luxury of Owen Turner's SUV with reluctance, got into the oven of my own car, and led the way to Robot's safe house.

The steering wheel was barely cool enough for me to leave my hands on it when I pulled up in front of the Inmans' home and waited for Turner, Deputy Horton, and Deputy Carraher, who looked only slightly less sour than she had when taking notes back in Castle Rock, to join me on the doorstep.

Petite, blonde, and too pretty to be considered ordinary by anyone, Carey Inman answered the door as if she were used to welcoming such motley groups. Greta, the small Rottie she had adopted more than a year ago, stood at her side, well behaved and watchful.

Carey didn't wait for introductions. "I'm so glad to see you," she said. "I didn't know whether to feed him or what to feed him."

I didn't tell Carey why it was a good thing she hadn't fed Robot, but just introduced everyone. Carey disappeared for a moment to shut Greta in a bedroom.

"She isn't too happy with a strange dog in her crate," she explained. "I moved it out of our bedroom and into the family room, but she still doesn't like it, and since he isn't staying, there didn't seem to be any reason to introduce them. You said he should stay in the crate."

"That's perfect," I assured her as we all followed her down steps into the family room and over to the plastic Vari-Kennel crate, which I suddenly realized, was roomy for Greta but really too small for Robot, who had been squeezed in there for hours.

"It's a tight fit," Carey apologized again, "but you said . . . ."

"You did just fine," I told her. "Believe me, he was better off here with you in an air-conditioned house than in the heat for hours with me."

I uncoiled the leash from where it rested on top of the crate, reached down and unlatched the wire door on the crate and swung it wide. Robot stepped out as quietly as he did everything else and then stood there, waiting to see what the humans who controlled his life would do next.

For me, the moment was one of those rare ones when the reactions of others take you back in time and let you see something familiar as if for the first time. I was looking down at Robot, but saw Turner's gray-clad legs as he took a step back. At the same time I heard Deputy Horton inhale sharply. I never saw Deputy Carraher move, but when I looked up, her right hand was at her holstered gun. Their combined reactions brought back the memory of the first time I'd walked up to a full grown male Rottweiler, how my mouth had gone dry and my pulse had quickened.

Contrary to urban legend, Rottweilers are not giant dogs, and Robot was a proper twenty-six inches at the shoulder. He tipped the scale at my vet's office at one hundred and twenty pounds, a good weight that included little fat and showed off sleek, powerful muscling. He had come to rescue with no known background, but Susan estimated he was between two and three years old, a mature male with the typical substantial bone, strong level back, and deep chest.

In his time in foster care, Robot had shed a lot of dull, dry hair, and now, after the bath I'd given him the day before, his short black coat had a healthy shine, and the mahogany markings on his legs, chest, and face had a rich glow.

Still, it is undoubtedly the head that leaves so many people in awe of these dogs. Broad in the skull, with ears folded close to his head in a way that emphasized the breadth, Robot also had the developed cheekbones and shortish wide muzzle that all add up to impressive. His eyes were the proper medium size and almond shape, but instead of the dark brown, almost black color, the breed standard calls for, Robot's eyes were a topaz that made them stand out eerily in his dark face.

I pretended not to have noticed the reactions of any of my companions and snapped the leash onto his collar. My thanks to Carey were all the more prolonged and profuse because of my new insight into exactly what this small woman had done for me in putting a strange big dog into her car, taking him home, and stuffing him into a too small crate in her home.

Carey refused to let us leave until Robot had a drink, and I refused to put him in my car until he had a walk down the block. I even offered Deputy Horton the full plastic cleanup bag after our walk, but he insisted in a most gentlemanly fashion that I keep custody of the "evidence."

Turner and I followed the sheriff's car to the emergency veterinary hospital the county had decided to use to examine Robot. The hospital was a new one, open nights and weekends and closed during ordinary business hours. I was not familiar with the place, even by reputation, but as the heat began to fade with evening, and fatigue began to creep up my spine, I was grateful for an agreement on anywhere that didn't mean much more driving.

The staff was expecting us. As soon as we arrived, a wide-eyed vet tech led us to a large examining room. There was only one chair in the room, and I sank into it without asking, holding Robot close to me. No one spoke in the few minutes we waited before the vet appeared.

Dr. Jaeger was a small, round man who looked too young to have many years of practice behind him, but he had an easy way with Robot and showed none of the fear of big dogs too common in veterinarians these days. He asked me once if a muzzle would be necessary, and simply accepted my negative answer.

He started by running a handheld scanning device over Robot's shoulders until the microchip implanted there registered in the scanner window. He wrote the number at the top of the record he was starting for Robot, and both deputies verified the number on the scanner and initialed the record. He accepted the full plastic bag from me without comment and placed it on the counter. He used a small sharp instrument to scrape around each of Robot's nails. The rust color of some of those scrapings made me glad to be sitting down.

I watched as if from a great distance as Dr. Jaeger and Deputy Horton discussed the best way to get prints of Robot's paws. In the end they unrolled what looked like a large piece of wrapping paper on the floor, dipped each of Robot's feet in a blue liquid and walked him across the paper. The blue pawprints looked all too much like the red ones I'd seen so much earlier in the day. A wave of nausea rolled through me, and I leaned forward, elbows on thighs, head down.

"Are you all right?" Owen Turner asked.

"Yes. As soon as this is over I'll be fine," I assured him.

"Just a little bit more." Dr. Jaeger rubbed Robot behind one ear. "This good boy is making things easy," he said, earning a new client for his emergency services, even though I hoped never to need them.

"What is this?" he asked, his fingers still on the ear, but now moving over the entire length.

"Scars," I said. "He has a lot of scars all over."

I watched the vet's skilled hands move over every inch of Robot and saw from the look on his face he didn't like what he found any better than I did.

"Where did this dog come from?" he asked.

"A Good Samaritan found him more dead than alive on the side of Highway 85 north of Greeley. They took him to a vet up there, and the vet called our rescue group."

"Were these open wounds?"

"No, they were healed over already. The only fresh wound was from a bullet that almost killed him. Evidently it came close enough for whoever dumped him. Maybe they thought he *was* dead."

"And maybe he didn't care enough to make sure," Jaeger said angrily.

"He?" Owen Turner asked. "You know who did it?"

"No," I told him. "We just know the kind of person who did it, and it's almost always men. They try to fight Rottweilers, but Rotties aren't fighting dogs, and when the dogs don't work out, they dump them, and sometimes they use them as bait for real fighting dogs before they dump them. The scars on Robot—he would have made somebody like that really mad, he's totally non-aggressive towards other dogs." And towards all people, but I didn't bother saying that, as everyone in this room was seeing that first hand.

The rest of the exam didn't take long. Robot endured having blood drawn out of him and an emetic poured into him. He vomited promptly and saved himself a second dose.

I thanked Dr. Jaeger sincerely and left him labeling various samples.

In the parking lot, Deputy Carraher shut herself in the cruiser without a word, saving both of us any false politeness. I thanked Owen Turner and Deputy Horton and assured them that I was capable of driving home by myself.

I lied. Instead of starting the drive home, I detoured to the drive-through line at the nearest Arby's. Robot might not like people, but he was a fan of people food. Sharing a roast beef sandwich and potato cakes with him made me feel better. After all was said and done, the day was ending for both of us the same way it had begun, going down the road together. All considered, it could have been worse. For Jack Sheffield it had been a lot worse.

4

THAT FIRST MALE ROTTWEILER THAT I'd ever met was my ex-husband's dog Butch. Butch was only one of the surprises John Brennan brought into our marriage. Like many young men, John had gotten himself a Rottweiler puppy on a whim.

Of course, unlike a Harley, a pickup, or a tattoo, the living breathing masculinity symbol John chose grew into an unruly adult dog that he dumped on his mother, who kept Butch tied in her yard until her son married me and she saw her chance. On her first visit to our new home, "Mother" Brennan brought Butch with her and tied him in *our* yard.

"Now that you have a home of your own, you need a watch dog," she said, almost unable to contain her glee.

Butch was only one of the many things John and I disagreed about with increasing vehemence over the course of our short and unhappy union. Our divorce settlement did not address the dog because neither of us wanted him. John was out of the house by then and never responded to any plea to take his dog. His mother had moved to another state. With no little bitterness, I suspected she'd deliberately made herself unavailable for involvement with any debris from our failed marriage, particularly Butch.

"Just take him to the pound," John told me blithely. "He's a great dog. Someone will adopt him."

As a matter of fact, I did take him to a shelter, the politically correct term for pound, but I never took him inside. Even without knowing the statistics, I suspected John's "great dog," so totally untrained that getting a leash on him and battling his filthy self into my car had taken all my strength and wiles, would not attract a line of eager adopters.

I watched several other people take dogs into the building. No one took any out. I wondered what Butch's odds would be in that place. I wondered how they killed—euthanized—the unwanted.

Butch never went in that building, but in the end, I did. The staff was quite willing to tell me about an alternative for Butch. Rottweiler Rescue. It sounded grand. It sounded safe. I called the number they gave me with great relief and got—Susan McKinnough.

The reason Susan is fond of me, I suspect, is that I'm one of the few callers wanting to "find a new home" for an unwanted and hopelessly unadoptable dog who ever listened to her.

Susan told me the unvarnished truth she tells all callers like me.

"Most adopters want young dogs. The few people who will adopt a dog as old as four want one that's housebroken, trained, good with children and other animals. If you find someone to take him, they'll keep him exactly the way your husband kept him, on a chain in the yard. Do you think that's any kind of life for a dog?"

No, I didn't, which was why John and I had argued about Butch on and off for the entire two years of our marriage. It was also why I felt guilty. I had argued but had never done anything about it, in part because I didn't know *what* to do.

Susan also told me about the other things that could happen to an intact male Rottweiler like Butch, things that were worse than living on a chain. She explained that sometimes euthanasia is the only decent thing that can happen to a dog.

"He's only four years old," I argued. "Surely there has to be something better for him."

"He's your dog," she said. "If you aren't willing to give him what he needs, why do you think someone else should?"

He's not my dog! I wanted to shout. *He's John's dog!* But John was already long gone on his merry way. Butch was mine, like it or not. So I asked Susan what to do, and she told me, although our voices reflected our mutual lack of confidence in my ability to bring about any change for the better in Butch.

Our pessimism proved unfounded. I wasn't totally without experience with dogs. I just didn't have any experience with a dog that could pull me off my feet without half trying. However, one area in which I was not and never had been "ordinary" was in my level of sheer cussed stubbornness. Just ask anyone who knows me, especially my mother.

Enrolled in a basic obedience course, the freshly neutered Butch terrorized all the other students and their handlers for only about the first five minutes of the first class before we were expelled. After several months of weekly private instruction, we were allowed to rejoin a class and proudly graduated with half a dozen others at the end of the eight-week course.

Butch was one of the two good things that came out of my marriage. The house that I refinanced to get the money necessary to fence every one of the five acres around it was the other. Once the property was fenced, Butch was never tied anywhere again for the rest of his life, and as soon as he was housebroken, he slept every night on John's side of the double bed, providing considerably more comfort than John ever had and snoring less.

Five years later, when Butch was diagnosed with the cancer that took a year to kill him, I talked to Susan a second time. She remembered me, and finding out what had happened to that unruly four-year-old yard dog pleased her enormously, which was why she adopted my current Rottweiler, Sophie, to me.

Sophie was released to rescue at four months old by owners who claimed they hadn't realized puppies chew. Healthy puppies with little baggage from neglect and mistreatment don't come to rescue often, and I took my puppy home feeling particularly fortunate. I paid the adoption fee and didn't wake up to the fact Susan planned to extract another kind of payment until months later.

Susan kept in touch the way she keeps in touch with all her adopters. She also set her careful rescue trap. First she made just the occasional phone call, could I keep one nice dog for a day or two? Could I do a short transport run?

I can't claim that when I finally tumbled to what Susan was up to, I couldn't have refused to go along with her plan. I let her knit me into her rescue net willingly enough, and now here we were the morning after Jack's murder, sitting in the same kitchen where John and I used to argue over Butch, arguing over Robot with equal intensity.

When the argument started, Robot and Sophie were sprawled on their respective mats in opposite corners of the kitchen. Robot still was, but our raised voices had Sophie alert, keeping a wary eye on us.

"I can't believe you did it!" Susan said for at least the tenth time. "I never should have let you take that robot of a dog to foster in the first place. You know perfectly well I've been looking for something special for you for months."

Yes, I knew. At seven, Sophie was getting up there in years for a Rottweiler, and getting a younger male dog now so that I wouldn't be without a dog when her time came seemed sensible. But it was Susan's ambition to find me another dog like Sophie, young and easily trainable, with no history of abuse or neglect.

She wanted me to do what she would have done—train him right from the start and compete in obedience, agility, or herding. The fact that she had failed to push or lure me down that path with Sophie hadn't discouraged her in the slightest. She was quite ready to try again. My enthusiasm for canine competition was distinctly less than Susan's, non-existent in fact, and she simply refused to acknowledge it.

"Maybe they'll make an arrest soon," I said, also repeating myself.

"Hah," Susan actually snorted. "If they arrested him tomorrow, it would be years of trials. They sit on death row for decades, appealing and appealing. You've basically adopted that lump of a dog yourself. I should go to the county attorney and tell them you had no right to sign that agreement. I'll tell them they can have him. They'll kennel him. He'll be fine."

We had been going round and round over the situation for more than half an hour, and suddenly I was fed up with it. If you started counting from that first phone call about Butch, I'd known Susan for over a dozen years, and in all that time when it came to dogs I'd always deferred to her judgment.

Susan is twenty-five years older than I am, about the same height, and at least ten pounds lighter, one of those women blessed by the gods who can eat anything and stay slim. Her hair didn't turn gray, it turned silver, and it always hugged her head in a gleaming cap. Her elegant, classy look and reasonable way of clearly stating her most extreme positions let her regularly steamroll her way over us lesser beings with impunity.

I for one had always docilely done exactly what she told me with the foster dogs, even when I disagreed with her as violently as I did about the wisdom of adopting Robot to Jack Sheffield. The dogs actually belonged to Front Range Rottweiler Rescue, and she was the corporation's president, but it was the fact that she knew more about dogs than I ever would that had always made disagreeing with her seem foolish.

All that had changed yesterday. I knew it, but Susan didn't yet. If our friendship was to continue it was going to have to change. I looked straight into her angry eyes that were as dark as could be desired in a champion show dog.

"Susan, I've taken in every dog you've ever brought here without a quibble and never asked for favors. I took Robot to Jack's because you said to, even though I didn't want to, and you knew it. The dog saved my life . . . ."

"By accident! You admit it was an accident!"

"I'm just as alive as if it were by design or on command! If you go to the county attorney, I'll fight you. I'll use Judge Cramer. I'll use Owen Turner. I'll use every penny of equity I have in this house fighting you, the county and anyone else I have to, but this dog isn't going to spend his life in some little cement-floored run. I'm keeping him!"

For a moment I thought she was going to take up the gauntlet I'd just thrown down, but the moment passed. She sighed, and tension drained out of her.

"All right. If it means that much to you, he's yours. I'll bring an adoption contract the next time I'm out this way."

"Thank you," I said, trying for a conciliatory tone. "How much is the adoption fee?"

"Same as for anyone else! No favors, right?" After a small pause, she said, "That's really silly, isn't it? No, of course not. A dollar to make it legal, that's all."

"Thank you," I said again. "And I'm changing his name to Robo. Just that little change to soften the sound a bit." And to take away Susan's derogatory meaning, but I wasn't going to tell her that outright.

"So since it's too early in the day to celebrate my new dog with a beer, how about some coffee? Have you had breakfast?"

"Not really," she admitted. "I came over as early as I dared, and breakfast was the last thing on my mind. You were all over the news last night in the story about Jack's murder, and I couldn't get you on the phone. I'm sorry I got you up."

"You didn't quite get me up." In fact, I'd been up just long enough to let the dogs out and listen to the many increasingly frantic messages from Susan on my phone before she showed up at my front door.

I busied myself starting coffee, then took straw-berries that should have been eaten the day before out of the refrigerator. As I picked through the berries, discarding some, cutting soft spots out of others, I wondered as I had many times before why Susan, who had so many demands on her time, almost always turned down my offers to drive to her house and in-stead drove to mine.

Of course at home Susan had a husband, show dogs, never less than two rescue dogs, and a phone that never stopped ringing. She had three grown chil-dren, the youngest of which was a son who was to my knowledge her single weakness.

Divorced and chronically unemployed, Wesley was a bum who dumped his small children on Susan every time he had visitation with them.

As I finished with the berries and popped frozen sweet rolls into the oven, I once again came to the con-clusion that for Susan, time spent visiting me was restful. At least it had been until this morning.

I poured coffee, put bowls of berries on the table, and sat down again. "Was Jack the kind of man some-one would want to kill?"

"Mmmf," Susan said around a strawberry. Then, "Do you think Jack was killed on purpose—he didn't just interrupt a burglar?"

"Yes, I do. Think about it. What burglar would be in a house that time of the morning? And why did Jack want a dog all of a sudden?"

"He said his boyfriend, who was the reason he never had a house dog, was moving out."

"But the boyfriend wasn't out. He still lives there."

"He was going to leave, and he'd agreed to a dog being only in the kitchen until he was gone."

"Why wouldn't Jack just wait until he was gone? Why wouldn't he bring one of the show dogs home?"

"He wanted a dog of his own that didn't have to be kept up. He wanted to know he was helping a dog that needed help, just like any other adopter. Why do you have so much trouble with that concept?"

"I guess because it's not what I'd do. I'd never live with anyone so allergic I couldn't have pets to start with, but if I did live with someone like that for years, I'd wait till he moved out to bring a dog into the house."

"Not everyone is the same," said Susan, a woman who imposes her own beliefs on everyone she can without mercy.

"No, but even so . . . . Did he say anything that would make you think he wanted some protection, even just as a minor consideration?"

"Absolutely not," said Susan with confidence. "And if that's what he wanted, he'd have been better off bringing home one of the dogs in his show string. Rescues are a poor choice for protection. They almost always have too much baggage to have the confidence a protection dog needs." After a pause, she added, "Of course the mere presence of a big dog can be a deterrent. You saw that yesterday, thank God."

Thank Robo, I thought but didn't say as I pulled the rolls from the oven and set them on the table. Sitting down again, I went back to the subject of Jack Sheffield's personal life. "Lieutenant Forrester said the boyfriend was out of town. Did you ever meet him?"

"I'm not sure—not at shows—he's allergic. What's his name again?"

"Warmstead. Carl Warmstead."

Susan finished her berries while she thought it over.

"Carl. I do remember. At the committee meeting for trophies for last year's specialty show. I remember thinking he and Jack were like salt and pepper. Jack so dark, dark hair, always a deep tan, and this Carl was very blond. He was taller than Jack, just a little, but taller."

"The man I saw could be almost any height," I said. "He was a couple of feet above me on the deck. He seemed tall, taller than Jack, but I was so scared. And I have to be wrong about the eyes. Nobody has colorless eyes."

"An albino?" Susan said doubtfully.

"No, not like an albino. Just . . . not like that. Like water in a clear glass. Like ice. You know what they say about eye witnesses. I'm hopeless."

"Maybe not. Gray eyes could look like that in certain light, and when you're frightened to start with."

"Did this Carl have gray eyes?"

"Blue. You wouldn't think I'd remember, but I do. I remember thinking he looked like a Scandinavian doll, very blond, very blue eyed. Quite handsome, really. Jack was so, so proud to be with him. I was almost embarrassed for him."

"Well, if he was really out of town, Carl isn't a possibility, and a Rottweiler in the yard wouldn't protect against anyone who lived in the house anyway."

"The dog was *not* for protection, and he was going to be in the house," Susan said forcefully. "I told you that, not all over the house, but in the *house.*"

Yeah, right, I thought, remembering the designer living room done in pastels, but out loud I said, "Of course," as if she'd convinced me.

We left it there.

5

THE NEXT SEVERAL WEEKS PASSED peacefully. The customers who counted on me for help with their computers and networks had enough problems to keep me busy, but not enough to make me frantic. I finished customizing report forms for an accounting firm in Denver, and by the end of the month had set up a small network for three architects leaving a large firm and going out on their own.

A few days later, Susan brought me a small female Rottweiler named Millie who had been abandoned at a local vet clinic with injuries from falling out of the back of a pickup truck. The vet had done the surgery to repair Millie's broken leg, and after she finished healing, he adopted her out himself to a young couple who returned her in a week. At that point he called Susan.

Millie was a cutie with what I call "rescue ears," that is, her right ear had the proper Rottweiler fold, and her left stuck up a bit. Neither Susan nor I could figure out why anyone lucky enough to adopt her wouldn't be totally charmed. Yes, she jumped on any human she got close to, and yes, she pulled like the little train who could on a leash, but a bit of training would fix that.

Susan and I cursed the irresponsibility of the pickup owner and lamented the lack of vision of the failed adopters while introducing Millie to Sophie and Robo. Millie was hardly more than a baby at a year old and was properly deferential to Sophie, who accepted her with resignation, and to Robo, who ignored her as if she were human.

When Bella, my all-too-fearless calico cat, put in an appearance, Millie showed far more interest than the vet had promised, but none of the true cat killer's intensity. Susan helped me set up a crate in a corner of the kitchen and settle Millie in with chew toys to keep her busy.

With Millie taken care of, Susan picked up her purse, but made no leaving motions. Instead, she pulled out folded papers and held them out. "Here's your adoption contract on the robot," she said.

I took the papers from her readily enough, but felt a wave of suspicion rising. As I dug a dollar bill out of my own purse, I considered the situation. Susan had avoided giving me that contract for weeks. When she visited me, she forgot. When I visited her, she was too busy with chores that made booting up her computer and printing an agreement an insurmountable task.

I hadn't made an issue of it. In a secret corner of my heart I wished things were different as much as she did. In a perfect world I would adopt a second dog who loved me with Sophie's passion. In an even slightly less flawed world I could adopt a dog who at least *liked* me. Of course in that better world there would be no rescue dogs, no fools transporting dogs in open bed pickup trucks, no sadists making the wounds that had left Robo so scarred inside and out.

Regret about the dog and the adoption had nothing to do with my sudden wariness, though. That came from my knowledge of Susan herself. She had spent a lifetime manipulating dogs and people into doing what she wanted them to do. Robo's contract was today's bait, and I was already in the jaws of today's trap.

By the time I had it worked out, Susan was talking me into helping her with the rescue booth at the local breed club's annual specialty show. A specialty is very much like any other dog show, but is for only one breed. This Rottweiler specialty was scheduled for the Friday before the last weekend in September, an outdoor show in Greeley, a two-hour drive north of my peaceful little house, which might not be air conditioned, but was quite comfortable with a swamp cooler and fans running. Even knowing resistance was futile, I resisted.

"Patricia always helps you at shows. Patricia *likes* shows," I said, as a way of reminding her that I didn't like them that much.

"Patricia is doing obedience with Gunnar. You know, that cute male she adopted last year. She got an ILP on him as soon as she adopted him. Well, they call it something different now—PAL. Purebred Alternative Listing. And if you'd just adopt a nice young male, you could get a PAL number and you could help Patricia show everyone what rescue dogs can do. If obedience competition isn't your cup of tea, you could do agility. You'd *like* agility. It's loads of fun for people and dogs."

"*Competition* isn't my cup of tea. I had enough of that in my teens with horses. I've told you the kind of things I saw people doing to horses in pursuit of the almighty blue ribbon."

I cut her off fast before she started her usual sales pitch about PAL numbers, AKC—the American Kennel Club—and canine competitions. Susan really believes that since I succeeded in civilizing Butch, I have undeveloped talent as a dog trainer, and it is one of her many missions in life to develop it.

"You help every dog you foster, you know. You could make people sit up and notice the potential of rescue dogs if you'd just work with a halfway decent candidate." She threw a disapproving look at Robo where he slept in his corner, reminding me without words how very unsuitable a candidate for anything he was.

"There are people who put titles on rescues all over the country. They don't need me to make a difference."

"Patricia's dog is the only rescue Rottweiler competing in Colorado," Susan said. "You could make a difference here."

This was another argument we'd had before, and I didn't want to have it again. My horse show experiences had turned me off competition, and watching news reports of human athletes who took drugs that would render them sterile and shorten their lives just to win a race, a game or position on a team had reinforced my aversion regularly.

"Okay, I'll help you in the rescue booth, but only for that one day of the specialty," I said. There would be an all breed show at the same fairgrounds on Saturday and Sunday. Being very clear about the limits of my commitment was only wise.

"Of course," said Susan. "I'll only have the booth on Friday anyway. On Friday, everything is slower paced, and Rottweiler people are more inclined to feel generous to their own breed. Setting up at the all breed shows over the weekend is a waste of time. I learned that years ago."

When I realized how early in the morning I'd have to meet Susan to be in Greeley on time, I almost balked, but it was too late, I'd been had.

Two weeks later, sitting in Susan's makeshift "booth" that was really just an area set off by a folding table under the shade of a tent canopy, I had to admit to myself I had been wrong. My only other venture to an outdoor dog show had been one held in the Denver area in mid-summer on a barren, dirt-surfaced area. The shallow shade from canopies had been little help against the intensity of the sun that day, even before a sudden windstorm tore them all apart.

The previous outdoor show had long stood out in my mind as a hellish experience, but this one was quite the opposite. The day was clear with a deep blue, cloudless sky, but the temperature was only in the seventies and the air was still. Greeley's Island Grove Park was full of huge old cottonwoods that dappled freshly mowed grass with deep shade.

Several other breeds were also holding specialties in the park, so many dogs, their owners, handlers, and spectators milled around. Vendors' booths were covered in canopies of bright reds, blues, and greens. Sections of portable white fence set off the show rings. In the Rottweiler ring, one shining black and tan dog after another strutted across bright green grass for the judge, then all but disappeared into a shady spot while the next dog took its turn.

Susan, elegant as always in a sleeveless cotton blouse of ice blue and white slacks that emphasized the silver of her hair, was one of many who added more color to the festive scene. Even so, my jeans and white T-shirt were the uniform of choice for enough people that I felt right at home.

Not only that, but for the first time, even though I didn't have a show dog or aspire to acquire one, I didn't feel like an outsider at a dog show. Having been the one to see Jack Sheffield's murderer leaving the scene was a sad reason to be so popular, but the fact was one exhibitor after another introduced himself or herself and wanted the vicarious thrill of hearing my story. And I exchanged that vicarious thrill for a five or ten dollar bill stuffed into the donation jar sitting on the table. By the time the judge declared a lunch break, Susan was beaming, and it seemed everyone on the fairgrounds had heard my story. I'd certainly told it often enough to be sick of it.

"Will you be all right if I walk around a bit and visit some of the vendor booths?" I asked Susan.

"Of course I will. Don't spend money on food. I have plenty of sandwiches and drinks in the cooler."

"With any luck I won't find anything to spend money on. I mostly just need to stretch my legs."

The vendor booths set up for the specialty were fewer in number and far more specialized than those that would surround the show rings during the all breed shows over the weekend. Rottweiler images peered at me from T-shirts and tea towels, from tiny earrings and from four by six rugs. The display that made me stop and consider pulling out a credit card, though, was of customized collars. Bands of colorfully patterned cloth were sewn onto plain nylon collars. My hand was reaching for a black collar trimmed with a maroon ribbon patterned in gold when grasping fingers locked on my forearm.

"Dianne," shrilled Marjorie Cleavinger. "You just have to tell me all about your horrible experience. I hear you saw Jack's body. Did he suffer?"

Usually the sound of that voice made me find somewhere else to be. With Marjorie's talons embedded so deeply in my flesh that flight was impossible, I panicked and knocked over the rack of collars. It was an accident. Even though apologizing to the vendor and helping to pick up her merchandise bought me enough time to gird myself to deal with Marjorie, it really was an accident.

I was acquainted with Marjorie because she often turned up at the events where we set up a rescue booth and spent time driving Susan crazy. Susan tolerated her because she also often left a donation, although in Susan's place I'd have done without the small amounts and run every time Marjorie showed her face.

A short, heavy-set woman with bleached hair that contrasted badly with her pasty complexion and heavy, dark brows, Marjorie had on a white blouse that was stretched so tight across her ample breasts that a large section of yellow-tinged bra showed in the gaps between buttons. Orange culottes emphasized the breadth of her hips and showed way too much of thick legs webbed with heavy blue veins and dotted with dark stubble.

Marjorie showed dogs with dull coats that trotted unevenly around the ring and had never to my knowledge won a ribbon. The condition of her dogs put me off, her shrill voice made my skin crawl, and her know-it-all attitude made treating her as a valued supporter of rescue a chore.

"Marjorie, how nice to see you," I said, hoping the lie wasn't written all over my face. "It sounds to me as if you've already heard all about what happened."

"I talked to Susan, but that's not the same as hearing all about it straight from you. She says you had to go right in the house to get the dog out. Was it terrible? Was there a lot of blood?"

Susan was going to have a lot to answer for. In all my telling and retelling of the events of that morning I hadn't mentioned going in the house or seeing Jack's body to anyone. Arousing this kind of ghoulish curiosity was exactly what I didn't want to do, and dealing with someone like Marjorie hadn't even crossed my mind.

"I'm sorry, but I don't want to talk about it," I said. "I'm still getting nightmares about that day. I can't bear to relive it."

"Oh, so you did see the body." Her voice dropped a few decibels to her version of a whisper. "I bet the dog was right in the blood, wasn't he? I mean, we all love our dogs, but we know how they *are*."

"The dog barely got in the door, and I was too scared to take in anything I saw," I lied. "What gives me nightmares was seeing the killer, and I didn't really even see him. He had a ski mask on."

"Oh, but there are things you can tell, even with a mask. You saw his eyes—and his mouth. Don't those things have nose holes for breathing? You saw his build. Did you help the police with one of those drawings? Do they do that on computer now, or was it an artist?"

At least I'd diverted her from blood. "I didn't see enough to identify anyone, and the police know it."

We had stepped back a bit from the collar display, and now another shopper was browsing through the rack. Inspiration struck me. "Marjorie, excuse me, but I saw a collar I really want. It's so pretty I don't want to stand here and watch someone else buy it."

Without giving her any time to object, I stepped away quickly. With an apologetic smile at the woman looking at the rack I reached past her, grabbed the maroon collar and took it to where the vendor had her cash box and credit card machine set up.

Marjorie followed, unwilling to let me get away so easily. If she wanted to wait for me, she was going to have quite a wait.

"Do you make these collars yourself?" I asked the gray-haired saleswoman.

"Yes, I do. Every single one," she said pleasantly.

With that opening, I set myself to learning everything possible about her collars. She patiently discussed the quality of the basic collars she bought and then customized, their sizes and adjustment. She explained how she applied the cloth inserts to the nylon collars and how long I could expect the collar to stay new looking if left on every day. When my questions led her to pull a book of sample fabrics out from under the table, Marjorie finally drifted away.

The collar lady was no dummy. "Your friend got bored and left," she said. "I think the least you can do is buy that collar, don't you?"

I bought two.

My trip to the restroom was supposed to be a quickie before getting back to the rescue booth, but I had just opened the stall door to leave when the outer door to the restroom opened. Marjorie's distinctive voice echoed through the tiled room. Gritting my teeth, I slammed the stall door shut and for a brief moment actually considered sitting down and pulling my legs up.

Instead I just stood there, listening with horror as Marjorie went on and on, entertaining whoever was with her and everyone else in the ladies' room with her very own version of my encounter with Jack Sheffield's murderer.

"She saw him right up close, and as soon as the police have a suspect, she'll get to pick him out of a lineup," boomed Marjorie.

"That's not what she told me," said a far less distinctive voice.

"She probably told me more because we're friends. I've been helping with rescue for years, you know," said Marjorie.

I leaned my forehead against the front of the stall door fighting the urge to shout. *You're not my friend and five dollars a couple times a year isn't much help.*

Stall doors closed and Marjorie continued her version of my story. Her voice, slightly muffled by the enclosure, still carried as if she had a bullhorn. "The worst thing is that she let the dog she brought with her loose and it went in the house. There was blood all over and you know how dogs are about that! By the time she got him out of there he was covered with Jack's blood, and I bet she was too. I'd put that dog down, a dog that's been in human blood like that. That's what I'd do, but you know how those rescue people are."

I was going to *kill* Susan. And if Marjorie didn't shut up I was going to stop hiding in this toilet stall like a coward and storm out and put an end to what little support she gave rescue forever. By the time Marjorie and her companion finished and left, I was shaking—furious with myself for hiding, furious with Susan for telling that horrible woman things she shouldn't have, and furious with Marjorie for shouting her ignorant exaggerations all over the show grounds.

When I got back to the rescue booth, Susan didn't let me get a word out before she started apologizing.

"I'm really sorry, Dianne, but Marjorie Cleavinger showed up here a while ago. She was picking at me the way she does, and I really said too much to her about what you saw at Jack's that morning. It was like throwing meat at a lion hoping you can fill him up and he'll leave you alone for a while."

Susan paused, took in the look on my face, and hurried on. "Oh, dear, it worked for me, but she left here looking for you, and from the look on your face, she found you. I'm so sorry. Go ahead and ream me out. I deserve it."

I threw my purse and the bag with the collars out of sight under the table. Susan was taking all the steam out of my anger. "Did she mention to you that she thinks Robo ought to be put to sleep because he's tasted human blood?"

"Oh, no," Susan said. "Nothing like that. Did she say that to you?"

"No. I was in the ladies' room and heard her going on about it." I collapsed in one of the lawn chairs we'd brought to the show. "Part of why I'm so mad is that I'm ashamed of myself. She'd caught me earlier and I managed to give her the slip, and then when I heard her voice later in the restroom, I hid in a toilet stall. If she shows up here again today, I'm sorry, but I'm not running or hiding again. I'm going to tell her exactly what I think of her."

"Don't hold back on my account," Susan said. "Enough's enough. You *hid* in there to avoid her?"

I could see the laughter starting in Susan's eyes. "Don't you dare laugh!" I snapped.

Susan's lips twitched, and all of a sudden we were both laughing.

"It is funny now," I admitted once we'd wound down, "but it wasn't at the time. Part of me wanted to jump out of there and smack her, but part of me didn't want to have anything more to do with her, and the cowardly part won."

"Don't be so hard on yourself," Susan said. "Think of it as prudence, not cowardice. Telling her off wouldn't have any more effect than beating on a rock. So what did you buy?"

I pulled my sack back out and showed her the collars. The second one I'd purchased had a floral insert on pink nylon.

"Very nice," Susan said. "That maroon will be good for a male dog, fancy but not too fancy. Now, how about some lunch?"

The show was over by two, and Susan and I had packed up and were heading home by three, feeling pleased over the successful fundraising. Except for the incident with Marjorie I'd enjoyed the day, and after all, what did Loudmouth Marjorie matter?

6

THE WEEKEND AFTER THE SPECIALTY show was quiet. Millie was already housebroken and learning that chasing Bella was unacceptable entertainment. Why anyone would not jump at the chance of having Millie in their home was beyond me. When I'd angrily told Susan I'd fostered every dog she'd ever brought me, it was technically true, but the ones who wanted to kill Bella only stayed until Susan could place them in a foster home that had no cats.

Starting early Monday morning, however, I entered a freelancer's nightmare. Not one but two clients had emergencies. I put in long hours cleaning up the mess a virus made of one system. The client admitted to an addiction to clicking on pretty much any offer that popped up on her screen and had finally found a virus that her anti-virus software couldn't catch. Her excuses and regrets didn't fix the system. I did. My other client had promised one of *his* clients work his current system couldn't produce and needed an upgrade *right now.*

Crises like these were my bread and butter. If only they were considerate enough to come one at a time and on a regular schedule. By the time everyone was happy, I was a frazzled mess. I spent my first free morning on neglected household chores while the washer and dryer in the basement earned their keep.

My house was a small plain box with two bedrooms and a bath upstairs and living room, kitchen and half bath downstairs. I didn't really need more space, but sometimes I dreamed of airy, open rooms. Mostly I was happy with what I had and contented myself with applying a new coat of paint in a slightly different shade of eggshell every few years.

The carpet was still the same nondescript tweedy combination of shades of beige that John had picked out without consulting me more than a dozen years earlier. You'd think the day after he left for good, I'd have replaced anything that caused a fight of the magnitude that carpet had caused, but it was still there, a bit worn in places, but still there.

The kitchen was my very own, redecorated only the year before. The failing harvest gold appliances had left on the same truck that delivered cream-colored replacements that made the light oak cabinets, kitchen table and chairs look almost as good as new. Almost.

The tile pattern on the linoleum would only fool someone very nearsighted who didn't have glasses handy, but I'd put up wallpaper with cheery red, pink, and yellow flowers on a cream-colored background that matched the appliances, and all in all it was a cozy room in the winter and at this time of year, light and airy.

If I wasn't totally in love with my house, I was with my home. That's how I thought of the entire place, the house, the five acres it sat on, and the barn at the back of the property. The original owners had cleverly positioned the house so that it seemed to nestle into sloping land and a covey of Ponderosa pines.

Then they landscaped the hill in front of the house with drought resistant ground covers and plants that bloomed all spring and summer and managed to give a hint of color well into the fall. The pale gray house with its dark blue trim and hillside of front gardens looked like an enchanted cottage at all times of the year.

The gardens were not high maintenance. An automatic drip system gave them their small ration of water with no help from me, but after lunch I headed outside to continue my never-ending battle with the weeds. By the time the sun began setting over the mountains, filling the western sky with a glory of deep orange behind peaks purple in the fading light, I was physically tired and restored in spirit.

I stood under the shower deciding whether to make a trip to town that night to replenish my empty larder or put it off and have soup for dinner. Two things tipped the scales towards a nighttime shopping trip— Bella had finished the last can of cat food that morning and wasn't going to be happy with just dry food, and if I shopped in the cool of the night, the dogs could come along. At least Sophie and Robo could. Sophie was fairly tolerant about another female dog in her house, but squeezing her into the back of my Toyota Matrix with both Robo and Millie was asking too much.

Stepping out of the shower, I almost tripped over Sophie, who had a sixth sense for when a shower meant imminent departure. She stuck to my side like a velcro dog, barely giving me enough room to pull on jeans and a T-shirt, hoping the power of her presence would convince me to let her come along.

Why dogs love going in the car when it means long boring waits while their human shops and runs errands, I don't know, but there's no mistaking the fact that they do love car rides.

As soon as Sophie realized her quest had been successful, she left my side and stood intently at the door leading from the kitchen to the garage. Robo followed us out to the car without showing any enthusiasm, but he didn't leave room for any doors to shut in his face either.

I parked in the out of the way spot I always use at my favorite King Sooper's on Lincoln Avenue. Long ago, after a particularly aggravating and embarrassing search for my car in a crowded parking lot, I'd come to the conclusion it was better to walk a little further to the store and always know where my car was.

The night was clear and pleasant with just the barest hint of a breeze. The dogs would be comfortable in the car with every window lowered enough to let in cool evening air but not enough for more than a nose to fit out.

Half an hour later I rolled my grocery cart full of plastic sacks through the well-lit parking lot toward my distant car, lost in speculation about the new client I was meeting the next day. As I walked into the shadows cast by a van and SUV parked side by side, a dark figure jerked me between the vehicles with a muscular arm around my throat. An involuntary yelp of pain and fright escaped from me.

"Shut up," he hissed in my ear.

One black-clad arm was tight around my neck, dragging me backwards, the other was free to use the knife he pressed into the side of my throat, almost under my chin, forcing my head back into his chest. A thin warm line of wetness ran down my neck and soaked into my shirt.

Each breath I took was a small violation of his command for silence. He said nothing else. Maybe he never heard the little sounds that seemed so loud to me. Maybe they were drowned out by the thunderous non-stop barking echoing through the lot from my car.

Sophie had heard my first cry. Her barks were so furious they were blending together into a roar. The man kept dragging me backwards, and I instinctively knew he had a vehicle close by, and once inside it, I was dead.

A loud crack exploded in the night. A gunshot? The barking stopped. *No! Oh, no!* But immediately there was a shout, "What the hell . . . look out for those dogs!"

I couldn't look, couldn't turn my head, but the man behind me inhaled sharply. His left arm tightened around my neck, and he thrust the knife forward into the air as if he could ward off the charging dogs.

Then the black forms appeared out of the shadows. Their eyes reflected red in the night and their teeth gleamed white. My captor gasped again, froze for a split second, and threw me toward the dogs.

I skidded on my hands and knees and fell into Robo, clutching him around the neck with all my strength. The distinctive slide then slam of a van door sounded nearby, then the roar of an engine.

Fear gave me the strength to lift and turn my head. Sophie was running after a dark van like a vengeful fury. At first she was clearly visible under the parking lot lights. When she turned onto the sidewalk dividing the parking lot from Lincoln Avenue, following the van west, only the headlights of cars speeding by at dog-killing speed illuminated her dark form.

"Sophie, Sophie, come!" My attempt at a scream came out of my bruised throat as a painful, hoarse croak. Would she recognize the voice as mine? Could she hear me at all?

She kept running, didn't seem to slow. Holding Robo, who wanted to go after Sophie, trying to struggle to my feet to go after her myself, I fell again and settled for calling Sophie's name again and again as loudly as I could. She didn't do the trained obedience dog's instant, skidding halt. She slowed reluctantly, and finally stopped without turning, the urge to go on clear in every line of her body.

Looking tiny in the distance, her silhouette appeared then disappeared in the flashes of the headlights, yet the intensity of the way she stared after the van radiated through the night. When I called again, sobbing with relief that she had listened at all, she turned and started back to me at a trot.

A babble of voices sounded around me.

"Lady, are you all right?"

"My God, that dog attacked her."

"She's bleeding. Somebody get the cops."

"I called 911 on my cell. They said I was the third one that called."

"We've got to do something about the dogs. Has anybody got any rope or anything?"

That last made me take my eyes off Sophie long enough to straighten out the people around me.

"The dog didn't bite me. There was a man with a knife. He escaped in that van. Don't even think about hurting my dogs!"

My voice, which had been so hoarse when I had been calling to Sophie, now started out squeaky and rose to half-hysterical. As Sophie trotted up, the circle around me parted, making a wide path for her. I grabbed her collar and sat there, holding both dogs, unsure what to do next.

One brave soul finally broke out of the circle of concerned shoppers surrounding me. "Okay, lady, okay. Are you all right?"

"No. Yes! My car is over there. I want to put my dogs in it. I want to go home."

"Can you stand up?"

"I-I'm not sure."

"Those dogs going to be all right if I touch you?"

"Yes! They're good dogs. They were in the car. Something happened. There was a gunshot. They chased him." In truth I wasn't so sure of Sophie's mood right then, but I wasn't admitting it to any of these people. With the Good Samaritan's help, and using the dogs' sturdy bodies, I managed to get to my feet.

My sensible savior was a thick-bodied, middle-aged man with a kind face. He gave me his belt to use as a leash and talked another shopper into doing the same. Sophie stayed pressed so close to me I could feel the heat of her through my clothes. It was the only thing I could feel that was pleasant. I hurt all over. My throat was crushed and bruised, and my knees were on fire where raw flesh was exposed to night air through the gaping holes torn in my jeans. The palms of my hands were only slightly better off than my knees. The cut on my neck was starting to throb.

Seeing that it was safe to approach, more people crowded around me. Helping hands pressed a wad of tissues into mine. When I began to wipe my neck, the amount of blood shocked me. Gingerly I explored and realized in addition to the original cut on my neck there was a long shallow slash that extended around under my ear then into my hair. Since I was standing and breathing and feeling stronger than a few minutes ago, I decided the wound couldn't be serious.

Dennis Conrady introduced himself and his wife, Karen, who was equally concerned about me but unwilling to get close to the dogs. He let me keep hold of the belts and the dogs, but steadied me by the arm and helped me toward my car.

We all stopped as we got close enough to really see it. A back window lay in two pieces on the ground. Slowly it dawned on me that the loud crack I'd taken for a gunshot was the sound of the window exploding outward from the car. There had been stories of Rottweilers taking out car windows on my email lists, but could a dog Sophie's size slamming every one of her eighty-five pounds into the window do that? If Robo had caught her excitement and somehow hit the window simultaneously? An explanation for their saving presence hadn't really occurred to me, and now faced with one, I could barely credit it.

The dogs jumped willingly enough into the back, and this time I used their own leashes to fasten each one loosely to a seat belt anchor. Dennis took his belt back and gave the other to its owner, who disappeared into the night. Both Dennis and Karen relaxed visibly with the dogs away from them and restrained.

I left the back door open and sat on the floor of the back of the car. Sophie leaned against me, her solid body a comfort. "Thank you," I whispered. "I'm sorry the dogs scared you. They really wouldn't hurt you."

"When we first saw them they were charging across here like the hounds of hell," Dennis said. "Small wonder that son of a bitch let you go and ran."

Karen rescued my groceries from where they sat abandoned and unloaded them into the passenger's side of the front seat for me.

"At least he didn't get your purse," she said, putting it on the driver's seat.

In spite of my assurances that I was all right and they didn't have to stay, the Conradys waited with me and stayed even when the paramedics arrived, closely followed by two police cars.

The paramedics were gentle and sympathetic until they realized my insistence that I was fine and wasn't going to a hospital was for real. At that point the slim young Hispanic who had been cleaning the wound on my neck disappeared. His older Anglo partner continued to argue with me until I mentioned just using some Super Glue on my neck myself when I got home. At that point he stomped into the back of the ambulance, came out with a tube of medical glue, and used it to close the cuts with a marked ungentleness.

"Our report's going to say you refused treatment," he said.

He ignored my thanks and joined his partner in the cab of the vehicle. They roared off in a cloud of disapproving exhaust.

Their departure left a few members of Parker's finest as the only barrier between me and home. The Town of

Parker has its own police department, but most of the area known as Parker, including my own address, is not in the town limits and is served by the sheriff's department. One of the small blessings of the evening's events was that the grocery store *was* in the town limits, so the officers I faced were strangers, and not Lieutenant Forrester, or, worse, Deputy Carraher.

One of the officers talked to Dennis and Karen Conrady and a few of the other shoppers. When the instinctive human desire not to be involved melted the rest of the watching crowd away, he dragged the pieces of my car window out of sight behind the store.

I gave the officer questioning me a straightforward account of exactly what had happened without mentioning my previous encounter with a man in black and refused to speculate on motive. After promising to sign a sworn statement at the station the next day, I was ready to force my stiffening body to move, when the officer spoke again.

"You need to be careful with those dogs, you know. It could get nasty if they took off after some innocent citizen."

"Sophie is seven years old," I said icily, "and she's never 'taken off' after anyone until she met a criminal the police obviously haven't caught and locked up."

The only answer to that was another car door slamming as the officer joined his partner in the cruiser and they left the parking lot.

"Well, it looks to me as if you've got enough starch left to get yourself home safely," Dennis Conrady said with a chuckle.

He and Karen watched me move slowly and stiffly into the driver's seat and insisted I lock the doors on my car in spite of the gaping hole where the driver's side back window used to be. They waved off my sincere thanks and watched me drive away.

Dennis was right. I made it home, got the perishable groceries put away, fed Bella and the dogs, checked the lock on every window and door twice, and swallowed several Advil. Then I crashed.

7

EARLY THE NEXT MORNING, AS I soaked away some of my stiffness in bath water aromatic with lavender essential oil and frothy with bubbles, I decided that no matter how much pain killer it took, I was keeping my late morning appointment with the new client. Canceling would invite him to shop around for tech help.

That decision was easy. What to do about last night's attack was not, and I was still worrying at the problem when I realized the water was cool and my fingers and toes were starting to look like pink prunes.

Clean and dry, I pulled on a baggy T-shirt and cutoffs that ended mid-thigh and didn't rub on my sore knees. The deep cut under my chin didn't show unless I lifted my head, but the raw red line that ran across half my throat and behind my right ear before disappearing into my hair was a different matter.

I decided makeup could wait until I was dressing for the client appointment. Searching through my closet, I found a knit blouse with a high neck that would cover most of the wound and decided to dress for my meeting like a Katherine Hepburn wannabe. The damage to my hands was all to the heel of the palm, so I should be able to hide the wounds. Maybe.

Limping around the kitchen starting coffee, I continued thinking over the events of the night before with increasing dismay. For weeks, Jack Sheffield's murderer had quite rightly ignored me as no threat to him. What had changed his mind? I didn't like the answer I came up with.

When the doorbell rang, I followed the dogs to the front door and peered out with unusual caution. The man on my doorstep wasn't tall, masked, or dressed in black. His arrival resolved at least one of my early morning dilemmas and was more of a relief than I wanted to admit. After making all three dogs sit behind me, I opened the door.

"Good morning, Lieutenant," I said.

"Morning, Ms. Brennan. I hear you had an interesting time last night." Lieutenant Forrester's perceptive gaze swept over me, taking in the evidence of my interesting time.

I crossed my arms and leaned against the doorjamb.

"Is my name on some kind of a list?" I asked suspiciously.

"No, but I try to keep an eye on what's happening in the county, and there was your name staring up at me, spelled right and all, on a report out of Parker. And surprise, surprise, dogs were involved. Are you going to tell me what happened, or can't you resist the pleasure of slamming the door in my face?"

"Oh, come on in," I said, moving back out of the doorway. "I've been debating whether or not to call you."

Without thinking, I led him back to the kitchen, poured us both mugs of coffee, and sat down across from him as if he were a friend on a social call. "I didn't tell the Parker cops it was the same man because I didn't want to be there all night. I hurt and I wanted to come home."

"I figured it was something like that, and of course the paramedics wouldn't have let you take the dogs in the ambulance."

"Exactly." I studied his face for any trace of condescension but didn't find any.

"So it was him."

"It had to be. He grabbed me from behind when I walked into shadows and had me around the neck right until he shoved me away so hard I fell, but he was the right height, I think, and dressed all in black the same way. It had to be him."

"Ski mask again?"

"I think so. The way he had hold of me I couldn't see his face anyway, but there was something, something that gave me the impression of a mask again. He couldn't risk being seen. He meant to kill me."

"So why didn't he?"

"I've been sitting here thinking about it, and I think he meant to drag me to his van, kill me there, and maybe dump my body somewhere it wouldn't be found for a while. He didn't count on the dogs, and when they came at him he panicked and threw me at them. He took a wild swipe at my throat, but I was already falling, so he missed. Sort of."

I lifted my head and showed him the deep cut under my chin and gave him a good look at the shallower line running from there into my hair.

Forrester whistled. "He couldn't have come much closer and not got the job done."

"No, but he was scared of the dogs."

"From what I hear any normal human being would have been scared of those dogs. I stopped in Parker and read some of the witness statements."

Forrester himself showed absolutely no sign of being bothered by the dogs. At that moment, Millie had her head on his thigh, as close to purring as a Rottweiler can get as he massaged her ears. I got up and pulled out the coffee cake I'd bought the night before, cut two slices and put a plate on the table for each of us, ignoring Forrester's protest.

"You don't have to eat it, but I'm hungry," I told him, sitting back down and starting on my breakfast. After savoring the first buttery, cinnamon-laden bite, I went back to the subject at hand. "He could have just killed me the minute he saw the dogs and still beat them to his van. He made it way ahead of Sophie. The thing is, he shouldn't have been that scared. He should be a dog person. He has to be."

Forrester just cocked his head at me and waited.

"It's been weeks and there's been no sign that he was worried about me. He knows I only saw his eyes. Then I went to a dog show I wouldn't usually go to. Everyone there made me tell all about what happened and what I saw over and over. And I heard this one woman exaggerating what I said wildly, making it sound like I might be able to identify the killer. So in about the amount of time it would take someone to decide what to do and plan how to do it . . . . Well, there he was."

"So you think it's someone who was at that show."

"Or even someone who wasn't at the show but who heard about it from someone who was. The loudmouth

I heard exaggerating probably wasn't the only one who did it, but why would he care? Why would he do anything? He knows I can't identify him. If he sits tight, he's safe. If he comes after me, he might get caught."

"You're thinking rationally. If he was rational, he wouldn't have killed Sheffield."

"Maybe so." I got up and refilled our coffee mugs, needing the activity to hide my reaction to his words. My mental picture of the killer as vicious was bad enough. Adding crazy to that picture made my hand tremble slightly as I poured the coffee.

Sympathy was clear on the lieutenant's face, and I didn't like it. "You haven't made any progress in your investigation, have you?" I said.

"We have leads we're pursuing. We've eliminated a few suspects. Warmstead has witnesses. He was out of town."

"Did he really agree to Jack having a dog in the house?"

"No, you were right about that. He thinks Sheffield was doing it to push him out and keep the house. They bought it together, but they weren't getting along, and Warmstead admits they were both maneuvering for the best position asset-wise. He says he wouldn't have let that dog set foot in the house and would have had a fit about it in the yard."

"He," I said.

"Yes, he, that's what I said," Forrester repeated, puzzled.

"Not he Carl, he Robo. Robo may be neutered, but your sex is in every cell of your body. He's a he, not an it."

"Uh huh." Forrester didn't quite roll his eyes.

"If a dog like Robo was in the house when he got back from that trip, would he have been able to do anything about it other than move out?" I asked.

"To hear him tell it he'd have grabbed Sheffield and the dog by the scruffs of their respective necks and thrown them both out in the street." Forrester actually smiled at me as he said this. Then he sobered. "So you think we're looking for a dog person who's afraid of dogs, or strange dogs."

"That's the hard part," I said. "I've been thinking about it all morning. All I can come up with is that it could be someone who has a different breed and is afraid of big dogs or afraid of Rottweilers. You get that, people who love one breed, but they have a problem with another. Jack showed dogs of other breeds too, you know. Susan told me that most handlers don't make a living from one breed."

Something flickered in his eyes. "What?" I asked. "You know something about that, don't you? What?"

"It's an active investigation, Ms. Brennan."

"Oh, so I tell you everything, and you clam up? There's no law that says I have to share, you know."

"There are a lot of other dog people I can talk to for background."

"But I'm the only one who saw him, who now has heard him, and who has a slashed neck to show for it."

"You're something else, Ms. Brennan. You know that?"

I didn't tell him what he was, just met his pale blue gaze steadily.

"Okay." He gave an exaggerated sigh. "He didn't make a living off the dogs. His grandparents set up a trust for him. Income only, he couldn't get at the principal, but the income isn't too shabby. Between the trust and what he made from the dogs, he lived pretty well. We wondered about that as soon as we interviewed another handler. Evidently they usually own their own kennel and live there. They have assistants and kennel help and do a lot of work with the dogs every day."

"He rented space in a kennel," I said.

"Yeah, and that means he didn't make anything for a dog that was just staying with him. He didn't do the work of keeping it and didn't get the money either."

"He did work with his dogs, though."

"Sure, but it's not the same."

We sat thoughtfully for a while, eating the coffee cake and drinking coffee in a fairly companionable silence.

"Well," he said finally, "I guess we'll go over the interview reports and look for any sign of clients or business associates who might be afraid of Rottweilers. Maybe talk to some of them again and ask specifically. In the meantime, do you have a boyfriend you could move in with or someone else?"

"Excuse me? Did a 'boyfriend' or any man, for that matter, save me at Jack's place, or last night? Exactly what is a 'boyfriend' supposed to do to keep me safe, lock me in his closet?"

"Okay, so you don't have a boyfriend." He grinned at me. "You still need to keep yourself safe."

"I'll do that, thank you," I said, standing up to let him know he was leaving. "After all, preventing my murder isn't your job. You can investigate afterwards— if he kills me in the county."

He stood too, but didn't move immediately. The humor was gone from his face.

"I'm serious, Ms. Brennan. He's going to try again, and the dogs won't protect you when he decides to switch to a gun. You need to go visit family or friends for a while—out of town, or better yet out of state. I'll have deputies drive by here as often as they can, but we can't really protect you. You need to be sensible."

"I'll be fine," I said.

We parted this time the same way we parted after our first encounter—very unhappy with each other.

8

MY MEETING WITH THE PROSPECTIVE client was a disappointment. The head of the small company would have hired me, I thought, but his office manager couldn't get over the fact I was a one-woman operation and had neither partners nor employees, just a friend in the same business who covered for me now and then.

Her concern zeroed in on the worst feature of my way of doing business. There was no way to assure them that emergencies with two clients at once never presented a problem, especially since the last frantic scramble was fresh in my mind.

She wanted my cheaper hourly rate, but she also wanted the guarantee of availability only a company with higher rates would provide. I left them to make their decision and wasn't optimistic about which way they'd jump.

The meeting had been in the Denver Tech Center, where the last of summer's flowers still bloomed in sculpted beds. Maples along the curving streets were starting to show fall colors, and the day was gorgeous, with just a few puffy white clouds floating across an intense blue sky. The ever-changing Rocky Mountains were a deep blue-black, their small summer snowcaps gleaming.

The temperature was still several degrees below the predicted seventy-eight, so that even in the high-necked white knit blouse I would not normally have worn on such a day, I felt comfortable, in fact gloriously alive.

My navy pantsuit had also been a good choice—the trousers were loose enough that they slid easily over the gauze bandages protecting my knees. All in all, one less client was of no concern whatsoever.

Back in my car, which still had a gaping hole where one window used to be, I decided to stop at Susan's on the way home and try to talk her into a restaurant lunch. In the middle of the week and the middle of the day even on I-25 traffic was light. I saved the toll by using Lincoln Avenue instead of E-470 to get back to Parker and then to Susan's. Calling her would only get me her recorder, even if she was home.

Like mine, Susan's house was in one of the older areas of Parker on one of the five-acre lots that were standard at the time the houses were built. The house was a rambling, pale yellow ranch with white trim.

The garage attached to the house had chainlink kennel runs off of one side, and a second, detached garage housed vehicles. The dogs spent very little time in the kennels, of course, and when Susan answered her door, four black and tan companions greeted me too.

"Come on in," she said. "You're in perfect time for lunch. Just tuna fish, but I've got some of those scrumptious filled tarts for dessert. Do you want white or wheat?"

So much for my yen for a restaurant meal.

"Are you sure? I was going to take you out to lunch, not mooch off you."

"If you'd been a few minutes earlier, I'd be delighted, but I've already mixed the tuna. White or wheat?"

"Wheat," I said with resignation. No one who advises stopping to smell the roses—or in my case, to admire petunias—ever mentions that the time lost may mean tuna fish for lunch.

Susan's kitchen was all light wood and white tile. The design included a built-in eating area that let us chat companionably as she prepared our sandwiches. I sat on a comfortably padded chair, petted the dogs, and let myself relax. Where we ate and what we ate weren't important. I'd come to Susan for help.

My questions were going to have to wait a while though. As Susan set out our plates and poured us both tall glasses of iced tea, she started telling me about the latest misadventures of her youngest son. Wesley had actually gotten a job again.

"He never should have taken the position in the first place," Susan said. "I told him he should hold out for something better and I'd help him with this month's bills, but of course he doesn't want help, he wants to be responsible."

I had just taken a mouthful of iced tea, and I swallowed quickly for fear hearing Wesley's name and the word "responsible" in the same sentence would start me choking.

Thank goodness Susan was too full of indignation over Wesley's unfair treatment to pay attention to my reaction. After all the similar stories I'd heard over the years, and after meeting Wesley himself a few times, I knew the problem was that Wesley thought his mere presence at any work site ought to be more than enough for any employer. He resented anyone who actually expected him to work. This time the job had lasted a whole month, but Wesley was now back in his usual state of unemployment. His mother had to be the only person in the world who didn't suspect he preferred it that way.

Listening to the story, I kept my mouth full of sandwich to help me make no comments at all except an occasional sympathetic murmur. As always, I wondered what it was about motherhood that could turn a strong, intelligent woman into a total fool.

We had finished the sandwiches and Susan was opening the bakery box containing the tarts by the time she stopped trying to convince both herself and me that Wesley was really a wonderful son. I ate three of the little tarts, telling myself that anyone who kept her mouth firmly shut on the subject of Wesley McKinnough deserved them.

When Susan finally wound down, I told her about the attack the night before.

"My God, Dianne, I've been wondering about that blouse in this weather. Let me see."

There was no way not to show her and no real reason not to, but I felt a strange reluctance. With eyes closed so I didn't have to see her face, I pulled the neck of my blouse away from my throat and lifted my chin. After a few seconds, I let go of the cloth and opened my eyes. Susan was silent, shock all over her face.

While she recovered, I told her about Lieutenant Forrester's visit that morning and our conversation.

"He's right," she said. "You have to get away. You can stay here."

"No, I can't," I said reasonably. "It's not just me. It's me and three dogs and a cat. And how long would it take for somebody to find me here?"

"We could manage until they catch him, and it's more . . . civilized here than where you are. There are more people around, my husband . . . ."

"You were all alone when I got here today. The sheriff's people aren't going to catch him. They haven't a clue. Unless maybe they catch him when he comes after me again."

"Don't say that! Maybe you should move."

"Susan."

"All right, I know you can't. There has to be something we can do."

"There is something we can do. We can figure out who it is."

Susan looked totally nonplused. "How can we do that if the police can't?"

"Because whoever murdered Jack is someone who knew him through dogs, and we, especially you, know dogs and dog people. You know all about the part of Jack's life that had to do with showing dogs. You're going to point me in the right direction, and I'm going to do the legwork."

"You are not. And I'm not helping you get yourself killed."

"Yes, I am, with or without your help, so you're going to help me so that I *don't* get myself killed. Now, why would someone want to murder Jack?"

"They wouldn't. There are people who didn't like him, and people get passionate about their dogs, but no one would kill someone over winning or losing at a dog show."

"The show world is a small version of the larger world. Surely there are all the usual twisted relationships—greed, passion—the same things that make people kill each other everywhere. Think."

"What if you find him? What if you start doing your 'legwork' and you walk right into him? Have you considered that?"

"Yes. I'm taking the dogs when I can and I'm taking my gun all the time," I said, pointing to where my purse sat on the counter.

Susan stared at the leather pouch as if a cobra had just stuck its head out of the opening. "You have a *gun*?"

"Yes, I have a gun. It was my first Christmas present from John. He even taught me how to use it."

"You yourself have always said Butch was the only good thing that you got out of your marriage." Susan's disapproval was so strong the kitchen was chilly with it.

"Well, I was wrong then. He left me a Rottweiler and a .38, and right now I'm grateful for both."

"And do you have a permit to be carrying it around like some gunslinger?"

"I doubt there were any gunslingers who carried their Colt .45s in purses," I pointed out. "But, no, I don't have a carry permit. I'm going to apply for one tomorrow. If Lieutenant Forrester isn't afraid I might shoot him the next time we have words, maybe he'll help. If not, you know what they say, 'Better to be judged by twelve than carried by six.'"

In the end, Susan stuck to her own guns. She simply refused to admit she knew of anyone who could have killed Jack Sheffield. We did, however, make a list of people who had known Jack and who might have information that would lead to his killer. First thing the next morning, I would take my car in for a new window. Then I'd take the time to apply for the carry permit. After that I was going start visiting the people on the list. Maybe one of them knew something that Susan didn't.

9

BEFORE SETTING OUT THE NEXT morning, I spent some time with each of the dogs. Millie was doing better on leash and learning basic commands, but believed "Stay" meant "Stay Until You Feel Like Moving," and we were working on it. Sophie enjoyed simply going through the commands to prove she knew them better than any other dog I brought to the house ever would, but our experience in the King Sooper's parking lot had left me determined to work on her recall until she would fly back to me no matter what she was chasing.

I had so far been unable to find any way to train Robo at all and had given up weeks before. He had reacted to all my attempts by simply staring off into space as if unable to see or hear me.

So I just brushed him for a while with Sophie's favorite brush and then gave him a bit of a massage. He was as unmoved by my touch as by my voice, which made spending time with him hard, but I felt that I was paying a debt of honor. At least he looked like a dog someone cared about.

I did my sincere best to explain to the dogs that the day was going to be too hot for them to stay in the car while I did all the visiting on my schedule. Millie settled happily enough in her crate with a chewie, Robo wandered off before I finished talking, but Sophie made it clear I would probably return to find her dead of a broken heart.

Leaving them home always made me feel guilty. This time my own fear made it worse. I patted my purse to be sure the gun was still tucked inside and set out.

My first stop was an auto glass shop. Replacing the broken window went quickly once the repairman got around to my car.

My trip to the sheriff's office in Castle Rock didn't produce such a happy result. As I rather suspected, by the time I got a concealed weapon carry permit, Jack Sheffield's murderer would have time for several more attacks. Since I hadn't been recently discharged from the military, wasn't a retired law enforcement officer, and couldn't prove I'd completed a handgun training class in the last ten years, I needed to take a training class and have that proof before I could even start the process.

The idea of asking Lieutenant Forrester about exceptions to the requirement flickered through my mind for a scant second before I rejected it. The carry permit would just have to wait until I could make time to take the required class.

The first name on the list Susan and I had come up with was Carl Warmstead. Maybe he wasn't a suspect, but he had to be the best source of information about Jack Sheffield and his life. If anyone had any insight into what made Jack tick, it ought to be the man he'd lived with for years.

With the morning's chores out of the way, I called Carl from the Village Inn in Castle Rock where I stopped for a quick lunch. He agreed to see me before I could even give him a reason, but to my dismay, he was working at home and not in the impersonal office I expected.

Parking in front of the house that still seemed like Jack's made me feel slightly sick and very nervous. At least I didn't have to summon the courage to walk around the back. I rang the bell at the front and followed Carl into the living room that, without the sheriff's men all over it, looked even more beautiful than I remembered. The pale gray carpet and walls were accented by pastels of peach and green.

Carl was as handsome as Susan had described, a tall, slim, blond man with sky blue eyes and impeccable manners. He got me seated on a comfortable chair upholstered in soft peach and made sure I was neither hungry nor thirsty before lowering himself to the matching loveseat.

"Finding Jack must have been awful," he said, fussing with the crease in his slacks, "but I don't see how I can help you deal with it."

"That's not why I'm here," I said, and then gave him the minimal explanation I'd rehearsed.

He stared at my neck. Once again I'd hidden the cut as much as possible under the high neck of a knit blouse, and I didn't offer to show him the wound.

"You can't seriously think you're going to find a murderer the police haven't found yet," he said.

"He's going to find me again if I don't," I pointed out.

"I'll tell you anything I can," he said, "but I just don't believe I know anything that will help."

"Okay, first of all do you really feel sure Jack wanted a dog to make you leave the house and not for protection?"

"Absolutely. The only reason we were still together is that we hadn't figured out how to divide our property. That's one of the problems when there's no way to divorce your partner." He gave a wry grin.

"I know a lot of people who don't think divorce courts are a great way to go either," I told him. "Did you have much to divide except the house?"

"The house, everything in it, cars, a piece of mountain land, investments . . . ."

"Oy."

"Yes, indeed, oy. At first we discussed it pretty reasonably, but then . . . he started trying to seduce every guy he met. Even though we were through, it seemed . . . like a deliberate insult, you know? We started fighting then worse than when we were actually breaking up."

Carl looked around the room, obviously liking what he saw. "This house is my home, and I've got every bit as much invested in it as Jack did. Bringing in a dog was his way of making me move out, and he was right that once I was physically out he would have had an edge for getting the property divided in a way favorable to him. He always liked an edge."

I was so busy thinking about the apology I owed Susan over Jack's intentions with Robo that I would have missed the last part of what he said, except for the bitterness in his voice as he said it.

"Always? What kind of an edge? An edge on who?"

"On anyone, everyone. He was competitive and winning mattered to him. He didn't do anything illegal, never really broke any rules, but he'd, oh . . . for instance, there was this one woman who showed her own dogs. Terrific dogs, and she had a bitch that was consistently beating the bitch Jack was showing. He found out this woman was sensitive about her weight, so while they were waiting to go in the ring he'd get close to her and talk to someone else and tell a fat joke. So she stopped winning so consistently. Once at a really big show, he talked to her directly and said how he liked the suit she'd worn at the last show so much—it made her look thinner. You know, as if what she had on that day didn't. He thought it was funny, said it really made a difference. He won the class."

"You're not making him sound like a nice guy."

"He was okay most of the time, more than that, generous even, but when his competitive instincts got going—well, look out."

"So he started feeling competitive with you about the property division?"

Carl looked thoughtful for a moment, then nodded. "Yes. That's a good way to put it."

He couldn't really tell me any more. I asked him to look at Susan's list of people who knew Jack to see if he could add any names.

He reviewed the list and then surprised me by saying, "This looks pretty good to me. You not only have everyone I know who had problems with him in the last year or two, but you've even got them pretty much listed with the angriest first."

So it seemed that after denying anyone had reason to be angry with Jack, Susan had given me the names I'd asked for.

I thanked Carl and left, thinking over what I'd learned as I drove west toward my next appointment. Maybe Carl didn't think Jack's competitive behavior defined him, but in the world of show dogs it would. Competition is what dog shows are all about.

10

BEAR CREEK KENNELS, WHERE JACK kept his show dogs until his falling out with the owners, was southwest of Denver. I sailed across town on C-470 in less than twenty minutes. Even on days when traffic or construction made for slower going, Jack had probably considered the drive reasonable, and he didn't have to keep office hours. He could have avoided rush hour traffic easily.

Susan and Carl both agreed that Jack's parting with the kennel's owner, Dorrie Stander, had been ugly. In our phone call, Dorrie had been sympathetic to my situation and more than willing to see me so long as I arrived before the kennel closed at six.

The kennel buildings were surrounded with a chain-link fence that would have done a maximum security prison proud. Evidently during business hours the fence had no security purpose because the gates across the driveway were wide open. No dogs or dog runs were in sight, and I heard no barking. I parked in a paved, tree-lined lot in front of a large white building with bright green trim. Narrow strips of grass and low shrubs set off the entrance.

The reception room was clean and cheery with pale yellow walls and beige tile floors. Somewhat to my surprise, the scent was of floor wax, not dogs. The receptionist looked up from her paperwork, took my name, then picked up her phone.

I sat down in one of the blue plastic chairs along the wall and smiled at the older woman already waiting there holding an adorable long-haired dachshund in her arms. The woman smiled back shyly, but the little dog grinned without reserve, looking at me with bright, curious eyes.

In no time at all, a man wearing a blue jacket with the kennel logo on it came through a swinging door, letting the faint sound of barking from somewhere deep in the building slip through with him. His friendly smile was bright in his round, coffee-colored face, and he obviously knew who he was looking for.

"Hey, Mrs. Aitkin. Hey, Dumpling," he said, scooping up the little dog and talking to her nose to nose. "Are you ready for a vacation with your pals?"

The woman got to her feet and gave him a bulging tote bag. "Her toys and her mat and her vitamins are there, and so are all the usual instructions, just in case you have someone new on staff," she said.

"No problem. We're all old hands," said this paragon of customer relations. "She's going to have another great time here with us, and we'll have her bathed and groomed and looking her beautiful best to go home next week."

The kennel man carried the little dog back through the swinging door, holding her on his shoulder and talking softly to her as he went. The woman stared after Dumpling for a moment before leaving too.

The next time the door swung open, the thin, intense-looking woman who came through it headed straight for me. Dorrie Stander had on the same blue jacket as her kennel help. From the look of her, she also did the same work they did and just as much of it. Her black hair was pulled straight back in a pony-tail and her makeup was minimal, with only traces left of the morning's lipstick. The hand she extended for shaking had short, unvarnished nails and calloused palms.

"Come on back to my office," she said immediately after introducing herself and putting us on a first-name basis.

She led the way through the swinging door into a hallway, then to the first office on the right, which was more businesslike than homey, with the same flooring and painted walls as the reception area and a beige metal desk and cabinets.

Only some distinctive pencil sketches on the wall behind the desk gave the room any personality. If the soft-eyed spaniels frolicking in the sketches were Dorrie's own dogs, her choice of livelihood involved her heart, not just her pocketbook.

Once I had eased my sore body onto the hard wooden seat of her visitor's chair, Dorrie leaned back in the desk chair as if to convince me how relaxed she was. The nervous way her fingers played with a pencil she had taken from the desktop betrayed her.

"I didn't kill Jack Sheffield. I probably had more reason than most, but since I didn't kill him a year ago when he screwed us to save his own sorry butt, I wouldn't have bothered now when the whole thing is history. The police talked to us right after Jack was killed, and they must have been satisfied. They went away and didn't come back."

"Us?"

"Me and my husband. We run this place together."

"Were you here that morning?"

"Yeah, we both were. The cops talked to us and to some of the staff and they seemed satisfied with that. Like I said, they didn't come back."

"I know you didn't kill him," I said, even as I wondered about her husband. "It was definitely a man I saw leaving his house that morning, but if I don't figure out who it was before he finds me again . . . ."

"You said he attacked you."

"He only missed doing to me what he did to Jack by a bit," I said. "That's why I'm wearing this blouse when it's still like summer."

Dorrie threw the pencil back on the desktop and leaned forward, staring intently. "I see some of the cut, by your ear. You need a bodyguard, not help from me."

"I can't afford that, and I can't afford to just pack up and leave town, so I need to figure out who it is and let the cops take it from there."

"The cops ought to protect you. They ought to find him."

"Maybe so, but they haven't found him, and they can't protect me."

"I'll tell you anything about Jack you want to know. Probably there are lots of people who felt like me. I wouldn't throw him a rope if he was drowning, but to actually kill him . . . nobody I know would kill him like that."

"You said what he did to you might make someone want to kill him. Tell me about that. I never really knew him when he was alive, and I need to find out about him now," I said.

"Yeah, well, Jack boarded his dogs here for years. I mean that. He didn't get his customers to board here. *He* boarded their dogs here, and he paid me, and then he billed them more than he paid as part of his whole bill to them for training and showing. I guess you could say I got what I deserved in the end. I knew what he was doing, knew he was sharp enough to cut himself, but he paid on time and his dogs were steady income, so I figured it didn't matter, but of course it did matter, and it caught up with me in the end." She paused then and picked up the pencil again, obviously angry at herself as much as Jack.

I encouraged her to continue. "So what happened?"

"He let a dog out, a really valuable bitch his best client had imported from Germany. The idea was to show her here, advertise a lot, and then breed her to another import and get big bucks for the puppies. He said a lot of Americans think the German dogs are better, but they don't import them as much any more because they have tails. I guess you know about that."

I nodded. "I don't show or breed, but I'm on a couple of Rottweiler email lists, so I know docking tails has been illegal in Europe for a while now. Even so, the pro-German people make a pretty good case for the quality of their dogs. They have a breed warden system over there, and dogs have to meet standards to be bred. In this country as long as both parents have papers it doesn't matter if they're cross-eyed cripples, AKC will register the puppies."

"Yeah, well, I learned more about that kind of crap than I ever wanted to know," she said.

"The bitch they imported must have had a tail," I said. "Was she so good they thought she could win at AKC shows with it? I guess a few dogs do."

"They amputated the tail," she said.

Shocked, I sat back in my chair too quickly and winced at the pain. Dorrie and I just looked at each other for a moment. Finally I found my voice. "Jack didn't try to talk them out of it?"

"I guess not. It was Jack who picked her up from the airport, and he took her straight to the vet. He brought her here then and expected us to deal with it. Long trip in the belly of a plane, strange place, trained in a different language, hurting like hell. The son of a bitch! I should have kicked him out then. If only I'd kicked him out then."

Like all docked breeds, Rottweiler puppies have their tails cut when they are mere days old and the tail is a soft bit of cartilage. Amputation on an adult dog with a thick tail is quite another thing.

In spite of deep division and disagreement in the breed over the European versus American rules on docking, breed associations are trying hard to write rules that will keep people from doing exactly what Jack's client had done, obviously with limited success.

"But you didn't kick him out," I said quietly.

"No. That poor damn dog. Maybe I deserved what I got. Jack sure deserved what he got, even if it took a while to catch up with him. After Maida—that was her name, Maida—was healed up enough, he started working with her. He'd come after hours to work with his dogs. That was part of our deal, that he wasn't underfoot too much during business hours.

"So he came one night and she got loose and got out on the road and was hit by a car, and Jack said he'd never been here and our kennel help must have been careless. The client sued us, and Jack testified against us. That's how I know all about tails and imports, I heard all about it in court."

"They won," I said.

"They won, and they won big bucks. No puppy mill bitch ever produced the way they claimed Maida would have. Every puppy was going to be a certain Westminster winner, and they had people there saying how they'd have paid the earth for a puppy."

"Why are you so sure it was Jack who let her loose? Couldn't it have been one of your people here late that took her out?"

"No! For starters my people *work* here. They don't sneak back after hours to mess with a dog by themselves. Anyway, one of the neighbors across the street saw Jack that night. Saw him try to catch the dog, and when he couldn't, saw him give up and drive away. He just drove away, the bastard! The neighbor called Animal Control, but by the time they got here, she'd been hit. Animal Control got her to a vet."

"She didn't die?"

"Not then, but she had to have three or four surgeries. It cost thousands, and she had to be spayed. Supposedly she was going to get all kinds of therapy for years. I heard later that she died in the end. A blood clot or something.

I was silent for a moment, sickened at the unnecessary suffering and death of a dog I'd never known. Finally I got myself back to the subject. "If a neighbor saw what Jack did, why didn't you win in court?"

"The neighbor didn't get a license number or anything. He just said he saw a guy trying to catch her and the guy could have been Jack and the car could have been Jack's car. Some other client said he was at her house that night. It didn't matter how many locks we had or how many gates. There was Jack sitting there looking all preppy and his clients in their Gucci and Armani. It was easier to believe some low-wage kennel help did something stupid, and if not, what the hell, we were insured, right?"

I thought of how the kennel worker had eased Dumpling's owner's mind and crooned to the little dog as he carried her away with her bag of goodies from home, and suddenly was almost as angry as Dorrie. Still, I felt compelled to ask, "You *were* insured, weren't you?"

"Sure. Insured with a big deductible. And the company dropped us like a hot potato as soon as the jury found against us. We had a hell of a time finding other insurance, and we're still paying through the nose for a crummy policy."

We discussed her dealings with Jack for a while longer, but other than what she had already told me, which certainly confirmed and intensified the impression of Jack Sheffield I'd gotten from Carl Warmstead, Dorrie didn't reveal anything significant.

"Come on," Dorrie said. "I'll show you our kennel setup, and you tell me if one of our people left a gate open and let the dog out by accident."

Curious, I followed her through the building, past several rooms with workmanlike setups for grooming, all of which had dogs standing on grooming tables being worked on. Big and small, wet, dry and fluffy.

The grooming business was flourishing. The sight made me grateful I'd stumbled into a breed that was if not quite as much of a dog grooming dream as a Boxer or Doberman, darn close.

At first the kennels themselves seemed ordinary. We walked down an inside corridor with dogs in chainlink kennels on one side. Like most kennel setups, the runs went through the wall to the outside, and there was a sliding door in the wall which could be lowered to keep each dog in or out as necessary for cleaning.

Dorrie took me through a door to the outside and I saw the layout of the kennel area as a whole and was impressed. We were in an open courtyard with long lines of kennel runs on three sides. The center of the courtyard was lawn edged with a wooden fence that kept the three small dogs playing there with a young kennel worker from seeing or getting near the kenneled dogs around them.

"Oh, that's great!" I exclaimed. "Do they all get some play time out here every day?"

"No," Dorrie said. "Some owners want it and some don't. To be safe, most dogs have to go out alone, but those three live together. It costs extra because it's labor intensive."

Maybe so, but how nice for those dogs who got the extra. Somehow I had faith that Dumpling was going to be out romping on the grass every day during her stay.

"The thing is," Dorrie said, "if one of us took a dog out, this is where we'd take it. And if we left a kennel gate open inside, the dog would still be inside, raising hell up and down the line of kennels, but inside. If we left the gate to a kennel run open on this end, same thing, but the dog would be out here. To let a dog loose on the road, you have to take it out of its kennel and then take it through doors to get out of the building. You'd pretty much have to do it on purpose."

"Can you go directly out that way?" I asked, pointing to a door in the wall that was the fourth side of the courtyard.

"Yes, the fire department made us put that in for an emergency exit. You can't get in here that way without a key, but you can get out. We've got a fence and another gate out there so there can't be any accidents." She walked over and opened the door so I could see the fence and gate.

Looking over the setup I didn't see any way a dog could escape to the road accidentally.

"Did Jack train his dogs here?" I asked.

"Sometimes, but it starts the kenneled dogs barking, particularly after hours when nothing else is going on. He'd go out to the parking lot in front most of the time."

"Is there lighting out there at night?"

"You bet," Dorrie said. "We always leave it pretty well lit, and there are extra lights Jack could turn on."

"What about the gates to the road?"

"They're to keep people out when nobody's here, not to keep anything in. Anybody who came in would open them and leave them open."

"Keys?"

"He had keys, he had to, but so did some of my senior staff. And me. And my husband."

"So they didn't really point a finger at anyone specific, just said it had to be someone from the kennel?"

"She was kenneled here, it was our responsibility, we should have kept it from happening."

No wonder Dorrie was bitter.

Behind me I heard an angry male voice, "What the hell are you doing? I told you not to talk to anyone about that bastard or that damn lawsuit!"

I turned to see a large, dark-haired man with a hard face set in angry lines striding toward us. Dorrie acted as if she hadn't heard him.

"That's my husband, Lee," she said.

Better Dorrie than me. He ignored me completely and cursed her, Jack Sheffield, Maida, and Maida's owner, Myron Feltzer. Dorrie might be bitter about what Jack had done to her, but her husband was still violently angry. The girl who had been playing with the little dogs quietly gathered them up and disappeared into the far kennel corridor.

How often did the kennel workers witness a scene like this, I wondered. For that matter, how often were they subjected to Lee Stander's temper? I abandoned any thought of any of my dogs ever staying at Bear Creek Kennels and felt sad for Dorrie.

There didn't seem to be the slightest chance that Stander would calm down enough to answer any question of mine on any subject, and definitely not on the subject of Jack Sheffield. Rather than risk making things worse for Dorrie, who stood as if turned to stone, I mouthed a thank you to her and made my escape.

As I drove back toward the highway I decided to do some research on colored contact lenses. Lee Stander had the dark brown eyes one would expect in a man with his olive complexion, but he was the right height and build to be the man I was looking for. He certainly exuded the kind of violence I expected from the man who had killed Jack and attacked me, and the way he had ignored me . . . . For Dorrie's sake I half hoped he was the one. She'd be better off without the jerk.

11

SHADOWS WERE LENGTHENING, BUT THE sun was still a comforting distance above the mountains when I got home. A message from Susan on my voice mail gave early warning that she was so eager to hear about my day she was going to drop by in hopes that I would be home and ready to chat.

I might have enough time to satisfy my curiosity about contact lenses on the Internet before she arrived if I hurried. Apologizing to the dogs for leaving them home alone all day, I let them out into the yard, and raced upstairs to my office in the spare bedroom to start my search.

Half an hour later, I let Susan in through the front door and the dogs in through the back. The dogs bounded into the kitchen in a herd, but at least they were willing to wait politely for attention. Susan was not.

"So?" she said.

"So I have a salmon fillet ready for the oven that will make dinner for both of us. Salad first, rice with, is that okay?"

"I'm not inviting myself to dinner. I want to hear how your visits went."

"I'll tell you over dinner. Call home and tell your husband you're keeping me company. He'll have to fend for himself."

Susan called while I finished the salads and poured iced tea. As soon as she hung up, I started telling her all about my day.

"So you didn't get the carry permit," she said with a frown.

"No, but I started the process," I assured her. To my relief, she let the subject drop and didn't force me to tell her what stood between me and the permit.

"Do you really think Lee Stander could be the one?" Susan asked.

"He's still angry enough about that lawsuit and Jack, and he seemed to be—I don't know how to describe it—bottled up fury. I can picture him hitting her, and I don't have to stretch to picture him attacking me, but it's hard to believe he's married to her and they have the kennel as a business and he'd be that afraid of the dogs."

"You're putting too much into that. Most people would be afraid of the dogs running at them like that."

"In the parking lot, yes, but he was afraid of Robo that day at Jack's, and Robo was just standing there looking at him."

"Mm." Susan didn't sound convinced. "What about his eyes?"

"They're brown, but I just did some research on colored contact lenses on the Internet. Carl's eyes made me think of it—they're too blue to be real. I found a site where you can pick the color of your own eyes from a list and then choose the color you want, and an image comes up that shows what different brands of lenses would make your eyes look like. And what's more interesting is, at least on this site, most of the lenses that make dark eyes light give them kind of an unnatural look. Some of the blue lenses were downright eerie looking."

"So that's it!" Susan said excitedly. "Lee Stander covered himself all up with black clothes and only his eyes showed and then he changed the color of his eyes and nothing was recognizable."

"Well, it's a possibility. Except I always thought the mask and all that black clothing was to keep from leaving any trace evidence, not for a disguise. He must have known Carl Warmstead wasn't home. If someone did stop by to visit that morning, he could expect that they'd come to the front and ring the doorbell."

"But even if he took off the ski mask when he left the house, he had all those black clothes on. Anyone who saw him dressed like that in August would remember," Susan said doubtfully.

"He was coming out the back door when I saw him. I think he planned on killing Jack, pulling off all that black clothing in the yard and slipping right on to the jogging paths in shorts and a T-shirt. A big fanny pack would hold all the black stuff—and the knife. Changing your eye color seems extreme. No one could identify a person from their eyes. If someone were that careful . . . . Stander didn't seem careful, he seemed— explosive."

"Have you told anyone about the contact lenses?"

"No, not yet." Explaining to Lieutenant Forrester that I had been out investigating on my own was not something to look forward to. "I'm going to talk to the others on the list first. Jack really was a rotten person, you know. Maybe everyone on the list will turn out to have been violently angry at him."

"He wasn't all bad," Susan said, "and you may believe Standers' version of events, but remember a jury didn't. What if someone from the kennels did let the dog out? Maybe Dorrie Stander doesn't even know it and doesn't want to believe it could happen. Jack wasn't evil."

"Do you think what he did with Maida's tail was good?" I said.

"Of course, not," she said sharply. "I think it's despicable, just like you do, but what if taking too strong a stand against docking the tail just lost him the Feltzers as clients? What could he have done?"

"Oh, I don't know, told them to take their business elsewhere, stood on principle, done the right thing, something like that."

Susan gave me a hard look.

"You're being naive. He would have lost them anyway, and they would have gone to someone with less scruples and the dog would have been worse off, not better."

"You're assuming Jack had scruples. Tell me about a scruple he had."

Susan was quiet for a long moment, then sighed.

"All right, I can't. He was charming and fun to be around and he helped me in minor ways from time. He'd lend me equipment, carry things for me, things like that, but I can't say I ever saw him stand on principle. I can't say that about a lot of people I know casually."

"People who knew him pretty well describe a first-class manipulator, ethically challenged to say the least."

"That doesn't mean he deserved to have his throat cut."

"No, but it may mean more than one person hated him enough to do it."

We discussed the people on the list I'd seen and the ones I was going to see the next day and what to do about it right through dinner and were having coffee when the dogs ran to the door to let me know someone was arriving.

The doorbell rang a minute later. The deputy on the doorstep was checking to see if the strange car in my driveway was a sign of trouble. Susan was pleased to see that Lieutenant Forrester was keeping his promise to have his deputies drive by as often as possible. Yet after she left, as I double checked my door and window locks, I wondered if Jack Sheffield's murderer was going to leave his car in sight in my driveway if he came calling.

12

MY APPOINTMENT THE NEXT DAY with Harry Jameson, Jack Sheffield's main competitor in the area, was for late morning at his kennel. There are only so many dog owners who can and will pay a professional handler to keep, care for, train, and show a dog, and Harry and Jack had been long-time rivals for the same customers. I didn't know Harry but had seen him at shows. My recollection was of a hatchet-faced man with thinning brown hair, thick through the chest and maybe not quite tall enough to be the killer.

After her morning training session, Millie once again had to settle in her crate with a chew toy, but even though the fall day was going to be too warm to leave dogs in the car, Sophie, in paroxysms of joy, and Robo, in calm indifference, were coming with me. Harry lived closer to Colorado Springs than to Denver. After a quick stop at my computer to print Mapquest's directions, I headed for I-25 and turned south.

The drive to Colorado Springs is one of my favorites. The highway runs past vast tracts of undeveloped land, some of it state owned and protected. At first the land beside the highway is rugged. Rocky hills dotted with scrub brush poke out of grasslands cut with ravines. The looming flat-topped formation from which the town of Castle Rock takes its name is just one of the more distinctive of these geographical features. For a while, snow-capped Pikes Peak seems to be straight ahead.

Further south the land gentles, and open shortgrass prairie rolls away from the road. That morning the mountains to the west were a deep blue-black, clearly outlined in the early autumn sky. For a little while, I gave myself over to the wild beauty and pushed away thoughts of the threat behind me and the interview ahead of me.

After more than ninety minutes of such simple pleasure, I exited the highway and began driving east. The area became more and more rural, and Harry's house turned out to be a pretty older home with natural wood siding. I drove slowly up the long driveway, trying to mentally prepare for anything that might be waiting.

Harry, a plump blonde woman, and two girls about ten and twelve who favored their mother, were doing fall cleanup work in the flower beds bordering a small patch of green lawn. Two Rotties stopped supervising the gardening long enough to run to the waist-high chainlink fence between the yard and the driveway and give several deep barks to warn me to behave myself and to let Sophie and Robo know who ruled the territory.

West of the house and perhaps a hundred feet behind it dogs in chainlink runs zoomed back and forth, barking with excitement. The runs had shade cloth covering their tops for six or more feet close to the building. In spite of the distance, I could see that not all the dogs were Rottweilers. Harry worked with several other breeds.

After a few words to his wife, Harry left his family and dogs in the yard and came out to meet me. "You're not planning on leaving those dogs in the car, are you?" he said critically, looking at Sophie and Robo through the car windows.

"No. I was half afraid to make such a long drive without them, and I figured you wouldn't mind them around. I'll keep them leashed."

"All right," Harry said. "In fact, let them stretch their legs if you want. We'll talk in my office."

I jumped at the chance to bring the dogs along, but wasn't willing to let them loose to really "stretch" their legs. Robo, I knew, couldn't be bothered running over to the house dogs or the kenneled dogs and starting a barkfest, but Sophie would be happy to urge every dog on the place to greater vocal heights. I leashed both dogs and followed Harry along the worn path back to the kennel.

The room Harry ushered me into was strictly utilitarian and not an office in any way. The floor was bare concrete. Everything necessary to groom and care for a dog of any breed was positioned conveniently close to the raised bathtub, extra large grooming table, and powerful dryer. When clients visited Harry at home, hospitality must be provided in the house, not here, where the only furniture was a tattered stuffed chair, and the scent of wet dog lingered in the air.

Harry leaned against the tub with his arms crossed and his face still set in a scowl. Maybe he cared enough about dogs to make sure mine weren't waiting in a hot car, but he plainly wanted me gone and gone quickly. I was still stiff and sore enough that the chair looked good but too stubborn to sit if he wouldn't. I propped myself against the grooming table, imitated his position, and looked straight in his unfriendly eyes, whose dark blue color no longer seemed crucial.

"As I told you over the phone, I'm trying to find out enough about Jack to have some idea who killed him because whoever it is has gotten it into his head I can identify him, and he attacked me the other night."

"Jack was killed weeks ago. Why would you think someone trying to steal your purse now has anything to do with it?"

"He wasn't trying to steal my purse. My purse was sitting right there in the grocery cart and he never tried to take it. He tried to drag *me* into a van."

"Oh, come on. Admit it. You had your fifteen minutes of fame, and you liked it and you're looking for more. Maybe I don't blame you, but that doesn't mean I have to spill my guts while you play amateur detective."

Harry had been uncooperative over the phone, agreeing to see me only when I wouldn't take no for an answer, but he hadn't actually been rude. Evidently since then he had decided he really didn't want to talk to me. Too bad for him.

"Does this look like something I was *looking* for?" I said, pulling the turtleneck of my knit top away from my neck and raising my head so he could see under my chin. After a few seconds, I let go of the collar and forced my chin down from unnaturally high to merely a belligerent tilt.

"He tried to kill me, and the only reason he failed was my dogs went right through a car window and came running. I know it was Jack's killer, and the sheriff's investigators agree." At my tone, Sophie stopped exploring the room and returned to my side. Robo stayed where he was by the door.

We stared at each other for another few moments before Harry sighed, his expression softening slightly.

"All right, you're not crazy, and I owe you an apology. I'm sorry for jumping to conclusions. But why are you sure it's the same guy? Why would it be, what, more than a month later?"

"He probably crawled out from under his rock again because I helped Susan McKinnough in the rescue booth at the specialty show, and a lot of people wanted to hear about the day I found Jack's body. I think he heard a second-hand version of what I said with embellishments added about how I could identify him. I didn't start *playing* amateur detective until *after* he attacked me."

Harry ignored my sarcasm. "You don't go to many shows, do you?"

"Usually just the big shows at the Stockyard Complex in February."

"Maybe he was at the specialty and seeing you was a shock."

"Maybe, but I didn't recognize him and couldn't recognize him, and he seems to have believed that until about the time of the show."

The scowl finally disappeared entirely from Harry's face, and he relaxed. "I have an empty kennel run. Your dogs will be okay there. Come on up to the house and we'll talk."

As we walked the dogs toward the kennel run, I turned and asked as causally as I could, "Do you remember where you were the morning Jack was killed?"

Harry laughed out loud at me. "I was puttering around here like always in the middle of the week. You think I killed him because he beat me out for Best of Breed the weekend before that?"

"Did he?"

"No, as a matter of fact. We both got beat by an owner-handler."

Was it realizing I really had a reason to be asking him questions that made him cooperative all of a sudden, I wondered, or was it hearing from my own mouth that I couldn't identify the killer?

Harry opened the gate, and I led Sophie and Robo inside. Sophie was obviously unhappy over being treated like an ordinary dog. Robo just as obviously didn't care.

As I walked with Harry back to his house, I tried to decide if he was a possibility as the killer. In a blue work shirt and jeans, his barrel chest was noticeable and didn't fit into my memory of the killer, but would I have noticed such a detail under the loose-fitting black clothes the killer wore? Harry was also slightly too short, I thought, but he had on worn leather shoes with an ordinary sole today. Would running shoes with thick, cushioned soles give him enough extra height?

As we entered the yard, its two guardians came over to check me out. They were beautiful dogs. I was no expert, but they looked as nice as anything I'd seen in the show ring at the specialty show. The male was an older boy with flecks of white on his face and a gray chin, but the female looked in her prime. "Are these your own dogs?" I asked.

"They're family pets," he said in a dismissive tone, then introduced me to his wife, Lannie, and daughters, Terry and René.

After a few quiet words to his wife, Harry led me around the house to a backyard even prettier than the front. Shade alternated with sun. Lush grass was laced with paths of brick pavers, and the gardens were bright with the yellows and oranges of late-blooming marigolds and mums. Harry and I sat at a glass-topped wrought iron table in the shade of ash trees that had not yet begun to give up their summer green for fall gold. He got right to the point.

"I probably can't tell you the kind of thing you want to know about Jack. He and I bumped into each other at almost every dog show, but I can't remember ever talking to him about anything but dogs. We were competitors, not friends."

"I heard he could be a . . . ," I hesitated trying to choose my words carefully, "keen competitor."

"Sure he could. So can I. It's that kind of business. You win enough and your customers are happy and stay with you. You lose enough, and you have no customers and you're out of business."

"So you don't think he carried it too far, tricked people in order to get an edge on them?" I asked.

"I heard things, but I never saw it. For all I know people tell stories like that about me. Jack was good with a dog, and he was good to his dogs, a good all around handler. Dogs liked him. We helped each other out a little now and then, not a lot, but he'd lend me a piece of equipment, or take a dog in the ring if I was short handed and he didn't have a dog for the class, that kind of thing."

Either Harry was dissembling or there was a side to Jack Sheffield no one but Harry and Susan had ever noticed. Before I could shape my next question, the screen door at the back of the house opened.

Harry's wife pushed through, carrying a tray with a pitcher of lemonade and three glasses on it. She had buttoned a loose-fitting white blouse over the halter top she'd worn for gardening and run a comb through her long blonde hair.

We made small talk about the gardens and the weather while Lannie set out the glasses and poured. She had the slightest of accents, Scandinavian maybe, more a matter of word patterns than pronunciation. Lannie pulled out a chair and sat at the table with us, and I brought the subject back to Jack.

"Your husband is the first person I've talked to other than Susan McKinnough who has anything nice to say about Jack Sheffield," I told Lannie.

"And who else have you talked to?" she asked.

"Well, I suppose you have a point there," I admitted. "So far I've talked to Carl Warmstead, and they were breaking up, and then to Dorrie Stander." I saw the blank looks on both their faces and added. "Dorrie owns Bear Creek Kennels. You know about the law-suit, don't you?"

"We know about the suit," Harry said, "but if I heard the kennel owner's name it didn't stick in my mind. I never met the boyfriend either. Isn't he allergic?

"Yes. Supposedly that's why Jack never had a dog of his own and kept his show dogs in the Standers' kennel instead of having a set up like this."

I looked toward the kennels. Robo was almost invisible, lying in the shade. Sophie sat at the fence facing us, and I thought I could feel the power of her indignant stare. Stifling the pangs of guilt she was so good at provoking, I turned back to Harry and Lannie.

"And supposedly, because they were going their separate ways, Jack could finally have a house dog and was adopting a rescue, but Carl says Jack was bringing a dog in to push him out faster—faster and maybe without his full share of their assets."

Harry took a swallow of his drink. "Divorces can be messy," he said in a way that made me think this marriage wasn't his first, "but Susan McKinnough was willing to adopt a dog to Jack, right?"

"Yes, she was, but do you believe Jack was adopting a rescue because he just wanted a dog?" I asked. "Your dogs are so beautiful. They look like retired show dogs. Don't professionals like you have clients wanting you to take dogs all the time?"

Harry didn't answer right away, and his wife jumped in. "Yes, we do, but you have too narrow an idea of what is rescuing," she said. "See our Bear over there? Yes, he was a good show dog, a great show dog even. So this grand dog goes home to his rich owner . . . ."

"Lannie." Harry's voice carried a warning, but his wife ignored him.

"Don't you, 'Lannie,' me. His owner used to take out big ads and walk around the shows with everyone knowing who he was and congratulating him. Then time passes, Bear is retired, and dog shows bore Mr. Big Winner, and all of a sudden we get a call, can we keep the dog, he's going to Europe. And you should have *seen* the dog that came back to us. Fat and dirty and smelly, his coat all rough, and his nails so long it must have hurt to walk."

She glared at me as if I had a part in this disgrace.

Harry touched her hand, then took up the story. "Here we were trying to figure out a way not to let him have the dog back, and if we'd only known, he was trying to figure out a way not to take the dog back."

"So what happened?" I asked, drawn in by the story.

"He came back from Europe and kept calling and saying he'd get the dog soon but never showed up. After months of that I told him the girls had gotten fond of the dog and asked him if he'd let them have Bear and we'd forget the board bills. I don't know what we'd have done if he hadn't agreed, but he did, and I could hear the relief in his voice. So is Bear a retired show dog, or is he a rescue?"

"I guess he's both," I said slowly. "But isn't he valuable as a stud dog if he won that much?"

"Only a few dogs ever become popular enough to earn much in stud fees, and Bear never did. Of course, his owner never worked at it. I know he ignored inquiries when the dog was still winning. We don't want to get into that end of the business either."

"What about the bitch?" I asked.

Harry and his wife exchanged a glance. "Tell her," she said. "She should know all rescue dogs don't come from shelters. Jack is dead and we have the papers. They can't do anything to him or to us. So tell her Maida's story."

Maida! When Lannie said the name, the bitch's head came up, and I looked again at her pretty face with its dark, almost black, almond-shaped eyes. Her perfectly shaped ears cupped her face closely and gave it a distinctly feminine cast in spite of the breadth of skull and shortness of muzzle. Her rich mahogany markings contrasted perfectly with her coat, which shone in the sunlight like polished onyx.

"I think I know the beginning of her story," I said softly.

"I suppose you do, especially if you talked to the kennel owners," said Harry. "The thing is when the lawsuit was over, her owners found themselves with a dog who was useless by their standards. So they told Jack they wanted her euthanized on the q.t."

I stared first at Harry and then at Lannie, hardly able to believe my ears. "So what stopped Jack from doing what they wanted? He did what they wanted with her tail, didn't he? He drove off and left her to get hit by the car, didn't he?"

"No," said Lannie. "He sat in our kitchen and almost cried. He felt terrible about everything. He was driving around looking for her when she was hit."

"He lied about what happened to save himself and let Standers take the blame, didn't he?"

"Yes, he did," said Lannie solemnly, "and he felt very guilty, and maybe we were wrong too, because we did not tell anyone what Jack admitted to us. The lawsuit was over then and we decided not to do anything. Jack had no insurance and the kennel did, and Myron Feltzer is a powerful man. Jack was afraid of what Mr. Feltzer would do to him if he admitted what happened, not just money but ruining his reputation, making sure he never got more clients."

"And what about the whole thing with her tail?" I asked. "Did he claim he was too afraid of Feltzer to say no to that?"

Harry shook his head at me. "Dianne, you may be horrified by docking an adult dog, and I may think it stinks and hope I'd have the guts to refuse to cooperate with a client over it, but the fact is it happens more often than anyone admits. And it's going to keep happening as long as dogs with tails aren't competitive in AKC. Jack probably wouldn't have imported a tailed dog himself and docked her, but he didn't see it the same way you do either."

From my email lists, I knew that there were AKC judges who refused to even judge a Rottweiler with a tail. Susan, the only dog show competitor I knew well, would never consider docking an adult dog. Of course, she had never imported a dog from Europe, but even tailed rescues were harder to place than docked dogs. Susan took them in and just worked harder to place them.

Lannie picked up Maida's story again. "Jack told Mr. Feltzer he had to have a signed paper permitting him to dispose of the dog. Jack typed the paper himself and gave it to him to sign. That's the word on it, 'dispose.' So there he was. He had the dog and the paper, but he could not take her home because of his friend, and he could not take her to the new kennel where he was keeping his dogs because Mr. Feltzer might find out about her, so he took her to a different kennel. He thought about calling your friend Susan, but he was afraid that Mr. Feltzer might find out he had not 'disposed' of the dog in the way he was supposed to if he did that too. He didn't think a signed piece of paper would protect him."

"So," said Harry, picking up the story, "he was in a bind. Maida was still pretty crippled and a kennel with a cement floor wasn't the place for her, and he knew it, but he didn't know what to do. Then one day he overheard my discreet wife here telling Bear's story to someone at a show."

"People need to know these things," said Lannie. "If more people knew when they do bad things, that everyone would hear about it . . . ."

"If they knew that, then they'd sneak at it better, and we wouldn't have Bear or Maida," said Harry cynically. "Anyway, this time it worked out because after that Jack drove down here, with Maida, of course. He knew it would be a lot harder to say no with her right there."

"And he gave us the paper Mr. Feltzer signed and he gave us a paper from him to us, making her our dog," said Lannie.

"All of which would be spit in the wind if Myron Feltzer really came after her," said Harry. "But it's been quite a while. Feltzer wouldn't want her back. He wouldn't want anyone to know what he did—what he meant to do. But I hear he and his wife tell people she died of post-operative complications, so if she's dead, our live dog can't be her. She's microchipped now, and the chip is registered in our name. It's not something we worry about too much."

"She doesn't look at all crippled," I said.

"She doesn't, does she?" Harry said, grinning at me. "We got one of those big round stock tanks and a heater for it, filled it to the brim, and Lannie and the girls spent hours helping her swim in the thing. She swims like a fish now, and she hasn't limped or shown stiffness for months. Terry wants to get a PAL number for her and try her in obedience."

"Do it," I urged, "but maybe you ought to get that PAL number with a name other than Maida."

I asked a few more questions but the Jamesons insisted they had told me all they knew about Jack Sheffield. We said our goodbyes, and Lannie went back to her garden and her daughters, but Harry walked me back to the kennel to get my dogs.

He laughed at the cool reception an unforgiving Sophie gave me. "The strong-willed ones like that are the best kind," he said. "She's a pretty girl, do you know her background?"

"She was turned over to rescue by people who claimed they didn't know that puppies chew," I said. "They had her papers, but it's average backyard breeding—Susan says there are some well known dogs when you get a couple generations back but that's all. You don't have to stroke me, I know her heart is a champion's but her body isn't quite there."

In my eyes Sophie was simply beautiful. However, I'd seen enough of Susan's show dogs to know that while Sophie didn't have rescue ears, her ears were a tad too long and so was her muzzle. She toed out in front in what dog people call an "east-west" front and probably had several other faults show people could name that I didn't know or care about.

"I'm not stroking," Harry said. "I didn't say she'd set the show ring on fire, I said she's pretty, and she is. Now, the male—all you'd need is a few judges with really liberal attitudes about the importance of eye color. Showing him only at indoor shows might have helped. Eyes can look darker inside, out of the sun. Where's he from?"

Harry listened to Robo's story intently, and to my surprise when I told him about my current total lack of success in getting Robo to do anything but eat and sleep, he didn't offer any advice on training methods.

"Give it time," he said. "Maybe he'll never bounce back, but at least he's safe with you."

The scenery flew by on the way home unnoticed as I mulled over what I'd learned from the Jamesons and tried to fit it in with Carl Warmstead's and Dorrie Stander's views of Jack. Carl had emphasized Jack's greed and manipulation at the end of their relationship, but the two men had lived together for years. There must have been some respect and affection for much of that time. Dorrie was justifiably bitter that Jack had lied and shunted his own liability for letting Maida loose on her, but they had done business together for years before that dreadful night.

Sighing, I recognized the weakness in my own interviews—I had let both Carl and Dorrie tell me only about the ugly ends to their relationships, not about the beginnings or years in the middle.

Did Susan and Harry, who had never known Jack well, actually give me a more realistic portrait of him? Maybe so, but Harry had admitted Jack was highly competitive, and of all the things I'd learned about Jack so far, it seemed most logical that his desire to have an edge on anyone he was dealing with or competing against was what had gotten him killed.

I wondered if Jack ever realized how much remarks such as his would hurt and anger an overweight woman. Add to that the fact that he had used that pain and anger to win over a dog she undoubtedly thought the world of . . . . If Jack Sheffield had gone through life behaving like that, it wasn't hard to accept that he'd finally driven someone to murder.

But Lieutenant Forrester was satisfied that Carl Warmstead was out of town the morning of Jack's murder. And much as seeing Lee Stander hauled off in handcuffs would please me, I couldn't accept that his fury would suddenly turn murderous a year after he and Dorrie lost the lawsuit.

Harry Jameson's initial behavior toward me had been calculating enough that I could envision him planning a successful murder, but now that I knew Harry and his family a little, I liked them, and if Harry had a reason for killing Jack, he'd hidden it from me successfully.

Thickening traffic made me stop daydreaming and pay attention the rest of the way home.

13

THE NEXT DAY WAS A Saturday, and not one of the people still on my interview list was available. Several had not yet returned my calls. They were probably all on a mass trek to a dog show in some remote part of the state. If the fates were giving me any breaks at all, the murderer was also firmly committed to a weekend far away.

After restlessly moving around the house picking things up and putting them down again in the same place, I gave up the pretense of housework. The calendar had turned to October, but the summer-like weather was holding, and the day was too lovely to spend inside. Much to Sophie's disgust, I took Millie outside to further her education.

Millie loved attention, any attention. She didn't merely wag her nub of a tail with joy, but her whole body. The way I trained was the way I had learned years ago in the course from which Butch had finally graduated. So when Millie pulled straight ahead on her leash, I did an about face and walked briskly in the opposite direction, which gave her a pretty hard leash correction and left her to catch up. To teach her the command to sit, I positioned her beside me, pulled up on her collar and pushed down on her fanny while telling her, "sit."

After many sessions, Millie walked on a leash most of the time without pulling and sat on command. She could sit and hold a stay for up to half a minute now, but I was having much less luck teaching her the down command using the method I had used with Butch.

First I had Millie sit at my left side. Then I reached down and put my left hand on her left shoulder. Next I picked up her right front leg with my right hand and used my left hand to push her toward her now theoretically unsupported right side, while saying, "Down," in my best trainer's voice.

Instead of collapsing into a down position, Millie twisted and squirmed and took advantage of how close my face was to kiss me thoroughly. I was the one who ended up on the ground in the down position, with Millie bouncing around me, diving in to wash my face again and again.

When I hid my face in my arms, she started on the back of my neck. Finally, fighting giggles, I conceded defeat and climbed to my feet.

"This time I'm ready for you," I told Millie trying to suppress the laughter and sound stern. "I've brushed up on this, and we're moving on to Plan B."

Once again I put Millie in a sit at my side. This time I stayed upright but put my left foot on the leash and began to pull up using my foot and the leash as a pulley system. Millie resisted the pressure valiantly but in the end had to give in. Of course, she only gave in with the front half of her body; her back end stuck up in the air in a pitiable imitation of a dog's play bow until I gently pushed her hips sideways and forced her all the way down. At that point she rolled on her back, spreading her hind legs in the universal canine plea for mercy.

Ignoring the fact that I now felt about an inch high, I repeated the exercise another dozen times until Millie was going down with very little resistance, although she ended up on her back each time. Calling it quits for the day, I took her face in my hands and told her, "I'm not just pushing you around for no reason. We want the people who adopt you to know you're the best dog they've ever met, don't we?"

Millie gave me a subdued version of her previous exuberant face washing, her long pink tongue licking the air but not reaching my face. She wasn't the first rescue to react this way to my training efforts. Most untrained dogs dislike lying down on command and have to be forced down in the beginning.

Why was this typical bump in the training road with Millie bothering me so much? I was teaching Millie things she needed to know, not abusing her. An image of Robo's face flashed through my mind. I pushed it right out again and concentrated on Millie.

Back in the house, I poured myself a glass of iced tea and sat at the kitchen table to drink it. Sophie sat inches from me, eager to go outside next and practice anything at all.

"You don't feel abused when we train, do you, girl?" I asked her.

I took the twitching of her stubby tail as her agreement that training was a delight and she was more than ready to get at it.

My attention, however, was focused on Robo, who sprawled on a rug in the corner, secure in the knowledge he was safe from any attempts at training. I still brushed and massaged him regularly, but his total lack of response had made me give up trying to teach him anything.

Now I looked at him with renewed interest. The instructor I'd learned dog training basics from had disdained using food lures. Dogs should not be bribed he had declared. They should work because they wanted to. They should work because they knew they had to. Susan had recommended that trainer, and his methods were her own.

Yet because Susan had also recommended that I join several email lists devoted to the Rottweiler, I had been reading messages from owners who referred to my kind of training as "J&P." Depending on how outspoken or perhaps how zealous the email advocate of other methods was, J&P translated as anything from "jerk and praise" to "jerk and puke."

Some of the discussions grew hot enough to send out cybersmoke. Rottweilers needed a firm hand and had to respect their owners cried the J&P advocates. Human beings don't work for free argued the foodies, who believed in training with treats, so why should dogs work for free?

Clicker trainers advocated use of small metal noise-making crickets in plastic boxes *and* food. If you can train a dolphin with our no force methods, they asserted, you can train any animal.

My attitude had always been "if it ain't broke, don't fix it," and what I had learned years ago worked for me. Still, the arguments I'd read had been thought provoking. A little surfing around the net and some reading about the so-called "positive" training methods had made me even more curious. Yet when I tried to discuss what I'd read with Susan, I got nowhere.

"These people who shove food down their dog just to get it to sit are fooling themselves," she said. "What happens the first time they really need the dog to do something and they don't happen to have a pocket full of treats?"

"They say they only use the food to teach and then they slowly fade it away and just use it occasionally."

Susan rolled her eyes. "I've never seen any of them fade anything. They shovel so many treats down those dogs they probably never have to feed them regular meals."

"But everyone uses liver bait when they show dogs in conformation," I pointed out.

"That's absolutely different," Susan said. "You have to maintain an up attitude in a show dog. Every one of them would sit without being bribed."

When I tried to discuss clicker training with Susan, the discussion ended fast.

"Oh, for Heaven's sake, Dianne, surely you have more sense than to be drawn in by that New Age nonsense. You're not going to hang crystals from their collars instead of vaccinating, are you?"

Well, no, I wasn't, but I knew the vets at the nation's top veterinary schools had changed their vaccination protocols and no longer recommended annual vaccinations for common diseases. And I was intrigued by the thought of being able to train a dog without force.

So as I sat in my kitchen that Saturday morning, still feeling vaguely disturbed by my training session with Millie, I looked across the room at Robo and came to a sudden decision. The only thing Robo ever did with enthusiasm was eat. How could waving a little food around in front of his nose hurt?

I scrounged through the refrigerator and came up with some cheddar cheese. As I reduced most of the cheese block into a pile of small cubes, I gave Millie a few pieces as an apology of sorts and Sophie a few with the promise that we'd go work on her recalls soon. Feeling almost guilty, I pocketed the rest of the small bits of cheese, snapped the leash on Robo and led him out to the backyard.

Robo really wasn't bad on a leash; he never pulled. He just lagged behind as much as the leash allowed and looked so depressed he was depressing. I shortened the leash until he had to walk fairly close to my left leg or pull. Then I took some of the cheese out of my pocket and held it so that if Robo's mouth met the cheese, he'd be in perfect heel position.

We marched in a large circle, and as I'd fully expected, Robo ignored the cheese in my hand no matter how much I waved it around in front of his nose. When I stopped, so did he, and since then he was willing to take the tidbits, I gave him a few on general principles. What else was I going to do with all those little pieces of cheddar?

Discouraged, but feeling obliged to give the method a thorough and whole-hearted effort, I stepped off again. Bent at the waist, waving cheese and crooning to the unresponsive dog like a fool, I barely caught the quick flick of Robo's eyes. His gaze slid across my face and away so fast if I'd been mid-blink I would have missed it.

I stopped dead in surprise. Robo never looked into a human face. Looking at me was one of the many things I'd never been able to get him to do. I would hold the sides of his face and talk softly to him, and he'd looked off into space as if I wasn't there.

I popped another bit of cheese into his mouth and started circling again. Nothing. I stopped, fed cheese, circled again, stopped, fed cheese, circled again. Circle after circle. Just when I was about to give up, it happened again. Robo took another quick peek at me as if flirting with the devil.

Susan would definitely have described my reaction as "shoveling" cheese into Robo. With an effort I forced myself not to hug or pet. He'd never given any indication he cared about either of those behaviors from a human one way or the other, but I didn't want to take the chance of doing anything he didn't actively like. I took him back to the house feeling—what? Triumphant? Happy? Successful? All of those things.

Energized, I cut up the rest of the cheese and gave one piece to each of the dogs. "This is a bribe," I informed them. "You each have to promise not to squeal on me to Susan. Deal?" None of the dogs denied the bargain, and they each accepted another payment.

Sophie followed me out to the yard with her usual enthusiasm. The training I'd done with her for years had never dented her exuberant self in the slightest, but the last of the cheese weighed heavily in my pocket. Would giving her a bit of cheese for a particularly good recall ruin all her training? Probably not, and after all, the cheese would just get stale and go to waste if I didn't give it to her.

For her recall practice, I left Sophie in a sit and walked varying distances from her and then called her. She flew to me time after time. I was about ready to call it a day anyway, when Sophie broke her position before I called her and ran to the fence, barking. My stomach dropped. The gun was in my purse in the house. Before I could decide whether to start running myself, a thin dark man appeared at the fence.

"I thought I heard you back here," he called. "Can you leash your dog? I'd like to talk to you."

After a single command, Sophie came to me as if we'd been practicing. I slipped her a last piece of cheese, but didn't leash her. We walked to the fence together. My visitor's khaki slacks and knit shirt looked too casual for a salesman, but it never hurt to be sure.

"If you're selling, I'm not buying," I warned him.

"I'm not selling, I'm Ty Mullin, and you've been leaving messages on my phone for days."

Tyrone Mullin. He had been a good client of Jack's until about a year ago. Now that I had a face to put with the name, I knew there was no chance he was Jack Sheffield's killer, but maybe knowing why he was Jack's *ex*-client would be interesting.

"I expected a call back," I told him, "not a personal visit."

"I don't like being a murder suspect, and I thought the chances of convincing you I didn't kill Jack would be better in person."

He had no idea how right he was about that. If I let him know his ebony skin and almost black eyes put him absolutely out of the suspect category, would I be unable to get any other information out of him?

"What makes you think anyone suspects you of killing Jack?" I asked. "My messages only said I'd like to talk to you about him."

"The canine grapevine is a wonderful and efficient thing," he said, holding his open hand out to Sophie and starting to make friends. "Now what will it take to get you to scratch me off your list? I don't even remember the exact date Jack was killed any more, but I brought my calendar with me in case I definitely was somewhere else."

"Hasn't anyone from the sheriff's office contacted you about that?" I asked.

"Nope. You're the first."

Evidently Lieutenant Forrester didn't agree with me about the murderer coming from the dog show world enough to send deputies out to interview Jack's former clients. Of course, maybe the sheriff's office had some way of knowing in advance there was no way Tyrone Mullin was the man I saw.

"Look, Mr. Mullin, you don't have to worry about it. I know you aren't the man I saw leaving Jack's that morning, but I'd appreciate it if you'd tell me what you can about Jack."

"Oh, so you're willing to spread rumors behind my back, but face to face, all of a sudden you know I'm not the one," he said. "If you know that, how come you kept calling my house?"

If I let him work himself into real anger, I'd never get any information out of him anyway. Better to tell him the truth now, calm him down and hope he'd be willing to talk to me.

"I called because I wanted to talk to you about Jack," I said. "And, yes, I've been thinking any man who had dealings with Jack might have killed him, but when you introduced yourself just now, I knew it couldn't be you. The man I saw had a ski mask on, but I saw his eyes and a bit of skin around them. He was white."

That gave him pause. And I hadn't even mentioned that he was also too short, too skinny, and with as much gray as he had in his hair probably too old.

After a moment the scowl faded from his narrow face, and then he grinned. "Are you telling me for once being black means I'm *not* a suspect? Man, it must be true that if you live long enough everything happens to you. Next time I'm stopped by some cop for DWB I'll remember this."

"DWB?"

"Driving While Black," he told me. "Probably you think we make that up."

"Actually, I don't," I said. "When I was first divorced and driving an old junker I'm pretty sure I got stopped a lot late at night for DWP—Driving While Poor. Maybe I don't blame the cops, but it was kind of scary."

"Damn right it's scary, and I do blame them," he said.

I just nodded. "I've been working with the dogs for a while, and it's about time to go in and get something cold to drink. Can I talk you into having an iced tea or a Coke with me and telling me about Jack?"

"Nah, I need to get home," he said. "I just wanted to make sure no one was out playing detective and making me a murder suspect."

"Please," I said. I told him how little I'd seen the morning of Jack's murder, about helping Susan with the rescue booth at the specialty show, and about the attack in the King Sooper's parking lot only days after the show.

He looked at Sophie in wonder and whistled. "Wow. That's pretty impressive, the dogs saving you like that." He kept staring at Sophie for a moment, then looked up. "Okay, what the hell, I'll tell you what I can, but I don't know anything that will help you."

Sure he did, but as I let him into the yard through the side gate and led the way to the house, I wondered if he'd tell me.

Back in the house, I made small talk while washing dog drool and cheese crumbs off my hands and pouring iced tea for me and a Coke for Tyrone Mullin. When he realized Robo had been in the car with Sophie the night the dogs rescued me from the killer's knife, he looked relieved.

"Truth is, I didn't believe you about the car window when I was just looking at the one dog, but seeing the big male, sure, the two of them could take a car apart."

That was a possibility I didn't even want to contemplate. "Mr. Mullin . . . ."

"Call me Ty. We're all but breaking bread here together, aren't we?" He grinned at me again with a roguish look that made me wonder if he'd showed up at my door planning to charm his way off my suspect list.

"Okay, Ty it is," I said. "How did you come to be a client of Jack's?"

"Well, let's see. Where to start. I worked with a guy who showed his dogs and he kept inviting me to go to a show, kept telling me how much fun it was. My wife and I finally went one weekend, more to shut him up than anything. His dog was pretty enough, I guess, a Bouvier, but while we were at the show, we saw the Rottweilers, and man, that was it for me. I'd seen them before, but street dogs, you know. When I saw those show dogs, well, it was love at first sight as they say."

"How about your wife?"

"It took me a while to talk her around. She started out wanting a little fluffy dog, but once she met some of the Rottweilers, she started to see it my way. The second show we went to, on our own that time, there was this big male—he was such a clown, kind of yodeling at the guy handling him, playing to the crowd."

"Had you had dogs before?" I asked.

"Sure. Well, not really. Both of us grew up around family dogs. Mixes, you know. When we first got married we always lived in apartments, no yard or anything. We never thought about a dog. But there we were, our kids were grown and out on their own, we'd just moved into a house with a nice fenced yard, and we decided we wanted a dog, and a dog we could show. So we were talking to some of the people at that show about it, and Jack heard us."

"And he sent you to a breeder."

"No, lots of people gave us names, but Jack *took* us to a breeder, and he all but picked a puppy for us." He named a breeder I'd heard of but never met. "You know, he acted like, here's the one I'd take, but it's up to you. You know what puppies are like. They were all cute. We'd have taken any one of them. And so that's how we got Max."

"Sounds like Jack did well by you then," I said. "Max was a great show dog. But to be honest, I don't know what puppies are like, at least not little ones. The youngest I've ever had was Sophie, and she was almost five months old when I adopted her."

If I were being *really* honest, I not only didn't know what small puppies were like, all I knew about Max as a show dog was that Susan had gone on and on about him when making up the list of who I should talk to about Jack. Of course there had never been a peep out of her about the far more pertinent fact that Max's owner was not of the same race as the murderer.

"Well, in one way you missed out," Ty said. "Puppies that age are *cute*. In another way you got the best of it, because they can drive you crazy, always into stuff, but Jack helped us there too, told us what to do. And right from the beginning he'd come over maybe once a week or so and work with the puppy and show us how to stack him and things like that."

A stack was a show pose, but if Ty went much further into dog show vernacular, he'd lose me. "So Jack handled Max's show career right from the beginning?" I asked.

"You bet, and he did a damn fine job of it too. Max won his championship at fourteen months old, his first Best of Breed a couple of months later, and his BISS the next year."

Oh, boy, BISS is Best in Specialty Show. He hadn't lost me yet, but if I didn't keep a look of complete understanding pasted on my face I was going to get treated to one of those drawn out explanations of AKC rules and titles that Susan was always giving me. Ty was on a roll.

"You know how many people try all their lives and never get a dog like Max? And here we are, complete novices, and we luck into getting Jack to help us and he picks us out a dog like Max. Do you have any idea how lucky we were?"

I nodded as knowingly as I could and tried to get him to roll in the direction I wanted to go. "So you were happy with Jack and you didn't stop showing Max because you had problems with him?"

"Hell, no! If anybody told you that, they're lying. Max did enough winning. We retired him. He won another Best of Breed last November, and we decided to retire him while he was still on top. Sure my wife got a little upset with Jack that one time, but it was nothing. We talked it over, and she saw that it was nothing, that it was all a mistake. Jack was our man."

Ty was no longer looking at me, but staring at his glass, swirling the ice cubes in the little bit of Coke left at the bottom. Given the feisty nature he'd already shown, if I tried to find out what his wife had gotten upset about, he'd surely dig in and refuse to tell me.

I got up and poured the last of the can of Coke into his glass and refilled my own glass, deciding to leave the disagreement between Jack and Tawana Mullin alone for the moment.

"So with Max retired are you retired from dog shows too?" I asked, sitting at the table across from him again.

He shook his head. "No, we're hooked. We've been talking about getting another puppy and starting over, but with Jack gone, I don't know—we need to think about it some more. My wife has been showing Max in rally and obedience anyway. She started taking him to obedience classes while Jack was still showing him. Jack didn't like it much, but my wife can be—let's just say, once Jack saw that what Tawana was doing wasn't hurting Max, he came around."

I really needed to talk to Tawana Mullin. "It sounds like your wife had some minor disagreements with Jack. What was the little thing that upset her?"

"Nothing. It was just nothing, and if you think you're going to make a big deal of it, you're wrong." He stood up, intent on leaving rather than telling me what I wanted, needed to know.

"Please, Ty. Jack is dead. Nothing can hurt him now, and maybe he'd rather see his murderer caught than have you keep any secrets. I can't help but feel if I can just find out enough about Jack, it will show me who would have wanted to kill him. Can I talk to your wife? Can I call her?"

"No, damn it. He just told this little joke, and she took it wrong. We got it all straightened out. It was nothing."

"Please?" I did an imitation of Sophie's best guilting look.

"I'll tell her what you want. If she's willing to talk to you, she'll call you. Don't you call us again."

With that Ty, who was probably Mr. Mullin to me again, walked out, leaving me to try to figure out how I could have handled the conversation better.

14

AN HOUR LATER, I WAS on the computer, busy signing up for an email list dedicated to positive dog training methods, when the phone rang. I knocked it half off the desk in my hurry to answer. The voice in my ear was not Tawana Mullin's, and Susan picked up on my disappointment immediately.

"I'm obviously not the person you were waiting to hear from," she said. "Have you got a new boyfriend? Who is it, that lawyer?"

"He's married, and no, I don't," I said. "But I am waiting for a call from someone I really want to talk to. Can I call you back later?"

Susan was agreeable, and I went back to the Internet, thinking I'd wait till early evening, then call Susan back. Silly me. Half an hour later she was on my doorstep.

"I had a call from a family that sounds perfect for Millie," she said. "That's what I was going to talk to you about, so since you want your line free, I decided to just pop over and see how she's doing for myself."

Susan only needed a few minutes to run her hands over Millie from head to toe, look in her mouth, handle her feet, offer her a rawhide chew, and take it back. "She was pretty good about all this when I first took her in," she said, "a little touchy about her feet, but basically good. How is she about her nail trimming?"

"Fine. And she's very good at basic commands except for the down. We're working on that. Are you taking her somewhere tonight?"

"Oh, no, I just wanted to see how she's doing. I don't have the written application with references yet."

A light bulb went on in my head. Susan may have had a phone call from someone who sounded likely for Millie, but until she got a written application with references, she never took anyone seriously. The real reason she was in my kitchen was for an update on what was going on, and she didn't want to wait, maybe for hours, until I called her back.

So I told her all about my visit with the Jamesons. Knowing she'd keep the secret, I also told her about Maida. She was as delighted to hear the story as I had been. "Damn Myron. Still, it worked out in the end. Who would have believed it! See. I told you Jack was a nice man."

Jack had been a very human mixture of nice and far from nice, and Susan knew it as well as I did by now, but I didn't argue with her. Instead I told her about Tyrone Mullin's visit and what I hoped to learn from his wife if she called me.

"I'm half afraid he won't even tell her I'd like to talk to her. And if he doesn't, I'm going to have to track her down somewhere where he can't stop me from talking to her, I guess."

Susan nodded her head in agreement. She was about to leave for home when the phone rang. As soon as she realized the caller was Tawana, she sat right back down, listening to my side of the conversation as avidly as I listened to Tawana.

"Ty got home pretty upset," she told me. "It took me quite a while to get him to tell me what happened."

"I was afraid he wouldn't ask you to call me," I said.

"He wasn't going to. I had to pry it out of him, and I waited till he went upstairs to call you so he wouldn't be right here trying to stop me from telling you. He thinks I'm crazy. We had big fights about it when it happened, and finally I figured it was better to just let him think he convinced me I was wrong, but I wasn't. I know what I heard, and I know what he meant."

"What Jack meant?"

"Yeah. It was a threat. He said it all jokey and every-thing, but it was the first time I said I thought we ought to retire Max. We can't afford to send him all over and get him way up in the national rankings. Jack was always pushing for that, and we can't do it. And so what if we could? He's got all his health clear-ances. He's already got some nice puppies on the ground, and we could breed him as much as we wanted, but we're being picky about the bitches we accept. So I said I wanted to retire him and show him in obedience myself, and maybe try agility, tracking, maybe herding. It looked like fun. Heck, it *is* fun."

She had accomplished what her husband hadn't and lost me entirely with her talk of national rankings, but I had an expert sitting at my kitchen table who could explain anything vaguely dog related to me the minute I hung up. Tawana was going on about her ambitions for Max. I waited for her to pause for breath and broke in.

"So what did he say that you took as a threat?"

"It *was* a threat."

She was even touchier than her husband. "So what did he say that was a threat?"

"I can't remember the words exactly. You see, the thing is . . . . How do you feel about drugs, you know, just a little, 'recreational use' as they say?"

The way I felt was inflexibly anti. If I found out anyone had brought an illegal substance into my house, I'd run them out so fast their head would spin from more than the dope. But Tawana wasn't in my house. Of course, her husband had been, but if he'd had something on him, I'd been blissfully ignorant at the time. My silence gave me away before I decided what to say.

"Yeah, well," Tawana said. "I'm not too keen on it myself, but Ty, you know, he thinks it's no worse than a beer, and so you see, after Max won his first Best of Breed, we were all excited, and we took Jack out to dinner, had a few drinks, and then we came back to the house, and Ty did a line, and we all smoked some, and that was that. We were celebrating, and Jack was celebrating with us, and we never thought any more about it."

"But if Jack did drugs with you, how could he use that to threaten you? He broke the law too."

"Girl, you are an innocent, aren't you? Have you ever heard of confiscation laws?"

"I guess so, but isn't that for dealers?"

"No, it is not. The law says property used in committing a crime can be confiscated. A little pot won't do it, but cocaine will. You can lose your car, you can lose your house. And the cops love doing it. It's all money in their pockets. Maybe white folks living in fancy houses don't have to worry about it, but Ty and I do, and Jack knew it."

"So he said if you didn't try for a national whatever, he'd report you for having cocaine?"

"No, not exactly. He said it like he was joking, but he wasn't. It was like, it would be a shame if you lost your house because you wanted to play games with your dog instead of letting me show him proper."

"But you retired the dog and started showing him in obedience yourself before Jack died anyway. Ty told me that today."

"You're damn right, I did. But not till after Ty and I fought like caged tigers over it for weeks. For a while I thought we'd end up divorced, only we'd never have been able to agree on custody of Max. Our kids are up and out, but they were starting to figure out something was wrong and getting worried about us."

"But if you decided to make peace by pretending Ty was right and Jack was joking, and you really didn't think he was joking, how could you go ahead and retire the dog?"

"Because I got Ty to promise to get rid of everything in the house and not to bring anything else home. Why do you think I can tell you about this? Lord above, we're grandparents now. It was high time for that college kid foolishness to stop anyway. For all I know you'll be calling some cop hotline the minute we hang up, but there's nothing in my house now and never will be again, or my husband will be losing more than custody of the dog."

Next time I was at a dog show, Tawana was going to be on my list of people to meet. Just from our phone conversation I could tell she was my kind of woman.

"Thanks for telling me," I said. "And you might like to know you're not the first person who's told me something along these lines."

"Really?" Tawana said. "Joyce Richerson, right? I figured he'd be making jokey threats to her next."

"No, I haven't talked to her yet. I'm hoping to see her tomorrow. What makes you think he tried something like that on her?"

"Oops, I'm sorry," said Tawana in a happy tone without a trace of remorse. "I shouldn't have said that. Gotta go."

She wasn't going to let the cat another inch out of the bag, and she had already helped me out more than I'd dared hope. We said goodbye with mutual promises to look each other up at the February show, and I turned to report to Susan, who was barely containing her impatience.

"Drugs? Jack was into drugs?" Susan said with disbelief.

"No, he wasn't, not really." I summarized Tawana's side of the phone call for her.

When I was done, we sat in silence for a minute, then I got up and started making coffee to give Susan time to absorb it all.

When she spoke her voice was faint with shock. "I can hardly believe it, but so many people have told you things like this. She thinks he tried a threat like that with Joyce Richerson? Oh, Lord, I hope not. I can't imagine her standing for anyone even trying that. Joyce is a tough, tough woman, very demanding, but

Jack was doing so well for her. She must have been happy with the way he handled her dogs. Anyone would be. In fact I remember Jack telling me it was good timing that the Mullins retired Max because that young dog he's showing for Joyce is top quality, and he couldn't do justice to them both."

"Tawana was talking about getting a national ranking. She said Jack was always pushing them to do that with Max but they couldn't afford it. What's that all about?" I asked her.

Susan was silent so long I was about to ask what was wrong, when she finally spoke. "National rankings are a whole different ball game. If we're talking about national rankings . . . ."

The coffee was done and I set out cups and filled them, then prodded Susan into telling me more. "So does showing for a national ranking take more skill, or what?"

"Not exactly," said Susan, "but it's turned into something close to a chess game these days. The competition is divided by sex, so let's say we're talking about the number one male Rottweiler in the country this year. That's going to be the male Rottweiler that beats the most other dogs over the course of the year. So let's say that there are two shows coming up. First of all you decide on the probable number of Rotties that are going to be shown in each place. Let's say there are going to be fifty Rottweilers at one show and a hundred at the other."

"Then you enter the show where there will be a hundred."

"Maybe. Maybe not. That's where strategy comes in. You look and see who's judging Rottweilers at each show. Maybe your dog has been shown under them before and you know how they like him, maybe you have to ask around about what the judges like."

"So if the judge at the smaller show is the one who likes your dog, you go there," I said.

"Not necessarily. You also want to know what other top dogs might be at each show. What if the judge of the bigger show likes your dog, but he likes some other dog just a little better, and that other dog may be at the bigger show?"

"Okay, I see how it can get complicated," I said. "So you want your handler to be able to help you figure all this out?"

"Yes, but I haven't even begun to list all the factors. If your dog wins Best of Breed, he's given credit for beating every Rottweiler shown that day, but if he wins the Working Group, he's given credit for beating every dog of every one of AKC's Working Group breeds that was there that day, and at an all breed show, maybe the group judge is a different one from the Rottweiler judge. Your dog might be able to win over only fifty Rottweilers, but if he won the group, he might win over hundreds of dogs, and if he won Best in Show . . . ."

"He'd have won over every single dog at the show, maybe more than a thousand dogs at big all breed shows," I finished for her.

"Exactly, so let's also say that you know of another show where the Rottweiler judge loves your dog, and the Working Group judge has said that your dog is the best dog of any breed he's seen in twenty years, and he's also judging Best in Show, but that show is in, oh, let's say, Massachusetts. What do you do then?"

"Wish you were in Massachusetts?" I suggested.

"No. Your handler packs up your dog and the two of them fly to Massachusetts for the big win."

"Wow, I never imagined. Don't dogs get so stressed out they get sick?"

"Sometimes. Ideally you have not only a great conformation dog, but one that loves the hubbub of the show ring and doesn't mind traveling and flying. And you need the same in a handler."

"I see." What I saw was that at every show there should be little dollar signs floating over the dogs, or maybe over their handlers. "So Tawana wasn't kidding when she said they couldn't afford it."

"No, because you also have to consider that if a handler is traveling all over the country for one client, he can't be at the local shows for clients who want their dogs shown there. So the handler is going to want some compensation for the business he's going to lose. And the fact is Max is a nice dog, a very nice dog, and he finished in the top ten last year as it was, but if you're talking about the very top—some years it's a very hard row to hoe. You need the dog, you need the handler, you need the money, and you need more than a bit of luck. Of course, it can also be very worthwhile if you want your dog to become one of the top stud dogs in the country, being bred to only the best bitches, producing stunning puppies everyone wants."

"Not to mention what an ego trip it is," I said.

"There is that," Susan admitted with a smile.

"So does Joyce Richerson have the money and ambition to campaign a dog the way Jack wanted?" I asked.

"Yes, she certainly does," Susan said.

"Is this young dog she has now good enough?"

"Probably."

"And would she have let Jack campaign him?"

Susan hesitated, then said, "No, I don't think so. That's what got me to thinking when you mentioned national rankings. Right after Jack died, she sent the dog to a top California handler who showed the number one dog a couple of years ago, and the number two dog last year. And if Joyce has her heart set on Carter being the number one Rottweiler in the country next year, she'd have sent him there no matter what Jack wanted."

"So it's possible Jack may have tried to get her to let him campaign the dog nationally with one of his little blackmail schemes?"

"Oh, Lord, I hope not," said Susan. "She would have squashed him like a bug."

We stared at each other a moment, struck by the meaning of what she had just said. Then Susan reversed herself.

"I didn't mean that. You just say those kind of things—she'd kill him if—I didn't really mean it. Joyce wouldn't try to have anyone killed, especially not over something like who shows one of her dogs, and Jack can't have known anything about her that would give him any leverage over her. She'd just fire him. For that matter I can't believe whoever did kill him attacked you. Are you sure it wasn't a mugger after money?"

I laughed out loud over her wistful tone. "It really shows how bad things are when you're wishing for a mugger. I'm sorry, Susan, but I'm very sure. My purse was sitting right there."

After Susan left, I admitted to my own wish that my attacker had been a mugger. A mugger or anything at all other than a man who dressed and masked himself for a deliberate and planned murder. How much longer did I have to identify him before he came after me again?

15

DIALING JOYCE RICHERSON'S NUMBER Monday morning, I reflected that the weekend had not been entirely wasted. Unless Tawana Mullin was making things up, Jack Sheffield had graduated from looking for an edge in any situation he saw as competitive to threatening clients to try to keep them in line. Behavior like that had to be the motive for his murder. Surely someone on my list would let slip information that would point me in the direction of the person who had murdered Jack rather than give in to his demands.

Joyce owned the kind of dog that could have fulfilled Jack's national ambitions. Had he tried a spot of blackmail on her? Even if Joyce wouldn't discuss her own relationship with Jack, she must have information that could help me. She should have ideas as to who had hated Jack, who had envied him, who might have wanted him dead.

As these thoughts ran through my mind, the phone rang so many times I expected to hear the sound of the call rolling over to voice mail, but then Joyce herself picked up.

After introducing myself and describing my troubles, I got right to the point, would she be willing to help me with information about her former handler?

"I've been hearing rumors about Jack's death and what you saw from half the dog world," Joyce said. "I'd love to get the straight skinny right from the source. What do you think I can tell you?"

"I'm not sure," I admitted, "but I'm hoping just talking about Jack and the handling he did for you might give me some ideas. Would you mind a visit? I'd love to see all your dogs anyway." If that last didn't get me in her door, she wasn't a real dog person.

"I'd be happy to show you the kennels," Joyce said. "You realize that Carter isn't home right now? With Jack gone, I went ahead and sent him to Joseph Loomis in California. Do you know Joe?"

Thanks to Susan's insider's picture of the upper stratosphere of dog show competition, I did know that Carter was the dog Joyce was planning a national campaign for in the coming year and that Joe Loomis was the California handler she thought could deliver the goods.

"I don't know Joe, but I've certainly heard of him," I said. "I'm sorry to miss Carter, but seeing the dogs you do have at home will be a treat."

As I hung up, I remembered that even though she denied it seconds later, Susan thought Joyce was capable of killing someone who threatened her. Could Joyce have hired a killer to remove a threat to her? If she did hire a killer, would she consider removing a witness to his crime in the same light as removing a potential threat to herself? I took the gun out of the center compartment of my purse and pushed it into a side pocket where it was easier to reach.

The verbal directions Joyce gave me to her home in Morrison were so straightforward I skipped Mapquest, tucked Millie in with her chew toys, loaded Sophie and Robo in the car, and set off.

Fall had finally arrived. The day was heavily overcast, cool enough that the dogs could wait safely in the car even if I spent quite some time with Joyce. As I drove west on C-470, the mountains were ghostly shadows of themselves, barely discernible through low clouds, but my mood was bright. A middle-aged woman could not be Jack's murderer. Visiting her was safe enough, and I was going to find out something that would lead me right to the killer.

Joyce lived in an area of older homes so far apart I guessed they were on twenty or thirty-acre lots. Her property was on a slight rise and the gray house rose even higher, three-stories, with railed wood decks on each level. The garage had doors for four vehicles, and I suspected the pretty, traditional style barn to the south housed dogs, not horses.

Before leaving the dogs in the car with the windows down several inches, I gave them a lecture about the necessary integrity of car windows.

"I am really grateful you broke the window that one time," I told them, "but that kind of thing is for emergencies only, not just a way out of the car if you get bored. You wanted to come. Now you have to wait and not make a fuss."

Robo was so impressed with my speech he turned his back on me and lay down. Sophie stared at me intently with a look of infinite understanding, but I felt a lot less than confident that her expression meant she agreed with me.

Before ringing the front door bell, I looked back at the car. Neither dog was visible. The Toyota looked very small and very old where it sat in front of the closest garage door.

Joyce answered the door herself. She was as attractive as I remembered from seeing her ringside at dog shows in the past, and the silky mauve pantsuit she wore accentuated a taut, well-maintained body. She had, however, reached the age where no magician could completely hide the years. Her blonde-streaked brown hair was perfectly styled in soft curls, but the tightness of the skin over her prominent cheekbones didn't match her neck and cried "facelift." I added ten years to my previous estimate of her age.

She led the way across a marble-tiled foyer and into a large room done in a greenish gray, full of ultra-modern furniture of metal and black leather. The west wall was all glass—windows and French doors. On a clear day the view of the mountains would be breathtaking. Today the gray outside added to the coldness of the room. Joyce motioned me to a chair, seating herself on the couch opposite and leaning forward eagerly.

Before I could ask her anything, she began quizzing me about the day of the murder. She was so keen, she affected me as negatively as Marjorie Cleavinger had. So she got the short version of that day—Jack's body barely glimpsed, little blood, masked killer I couldn't tell a thing about. When she realized she wasn't going to get the kind of graphic detail she hoped for, she finally sat back and relaxed.

"Now, what is it that you want to know from me?" she asked.

"Tell me about Jack," I said. "Who would have wanted to harm him?"

"No one would have wanted to harm Jack. He was a darling man—handsome, charming, and *very* good with the dogs."

Now I leaned toward her. Hoping to impress her with the seriousness of my situation, I tried much the same words I'd used on Ty Mullin.

"Joyce, Jack is dead. Nothing anyone says about him at this point will hurt him, and his killer seems to be convinced I'm a threat. Several people I've talked to have admitted Jack liked to try to use a bit of leverage on people now and then. Did he ever try anything like that on you, say to get you to let him campaign Carter nationally?"

For just a second Joyce's mouth flattened into an annoyed slit, but only for a second, then her friendly, open expression was back.

"I can't imagine what you're talking about. I discussed my plans for Carter with Jack, and he understood I was going to send the dog to Joe Loomis to campaign next year. Jack may have wished I'd let him keep the dog, but he accepted my decision. Anyone who told you it affected my working relationship with Jack, or that Jack wasn't going to continue showing the rest of my dogs is just plain wrong. If Jack hadn't been killed, he would have had Carter for the rest of this year. Have you been talking to Harry Jameson?"

"I've talked to Harry," I admitted, "but we never talked about Carter, and he wasn't the one who explained the ins and outs of campaigning a dog nationally to me."

"Well, if Harry thinks he'd have gotten my dogs back because Jack wouldn't accept my decision about Carter he is absolutely wrong, and he isn't going to get them back with Jack gone either. Harry's been just plain rude to me since we parted ways, and I'd stop showing dogs before I'd do any business with him again."

"So Harry used to handle your dogs? Before Jack? What happened?"

"Yes, I used Harry years ago, before I knew better. He did a nice enough job with the dogs, when he was available, but there were times when he simply insisted he had to keep a weekend clear for some event or other his children were involved in. I feel if a man is going to be a *professional* handler, he ought to be showing dogs and not attending some kindergarten graduation."

How often had Harry done that, I wondered. Maybe only once. Once would have been enough.

I leaned back against the slippery leather chair. "So you went to Jack, and he guaranteed he'd be there for every show."

"Something like that." She gave me a small, self-satisfied smile. "Actually Jack heard I was unhappy with Harry's priorities and came to me. He told me he was almost sorry to have won Best of Breed at the show I missed since mine was a much better dog—it was Carter's grandsire I was campaigning back then. Jack pointed out that he was unencumbered by the kind of family commitments Harry had."

If Harry had really been angry to lose this woman's lucrative business, I was going to have to move him up on my suspect list, particularly if Jack had stolen clients from him more recently with similar tactics. Then again maybe Joyce was the only client Jack had ever successfully lured away from Harry, and maybe Harry had been glad to see the back of a woman who gave every indication of deserving Susan's description of "demanding" and maybe a few stronger adjectives.

Before I could start to ask another question, Joyce looked toward the doorway, and her face lit up. A man dressed in tennis whites hesitated there, a racquet dangling from one hand.

"Do come in, darling," she said. "How was your game?" Without pausing to give him a chance to answer, she motioned to me. "This is Dianne Brennan. She helps Susan McKinnough with those poor, sad rescue dogs, and she's the one who found Jack Sheffield's body. Do come in and meet her."

Twice before in my life I'd been introduced to men so handsome my reaction had been uncontrollable—and embarrassing. I was staring but couldn't look away, knew my mouth was half open but couldn't close it, could feel the flush rising up my neck and spreading across my cheeks.

Too young for me, I thought. Not to mention too rich and too good looking. His hair was dark, with a startling streak of pure white in the front that somehow emphasized his youth, as did a golden tan that all but glowed in the dreary room.

Joyce laughed with delight at my reaction, as well she might. He must be her son, I thought, and she had every reason to rank her own production abilities right up there with her champion dogs'.

"It's a good thing I'm not a jealous woman," I heard Joyce say as if from far away. "Half the women who meet Erich react just like you. He's beautiful, isn't he? Dianne, this is Erich Kohler, my husband."

Husband! Her words broke the spell, enabling me to tear my gaze from Erich and look at Joyce. She was still half laughing at my reaction, entertained by it, not slightly insulted.

Husband! I risked another glance at him and found myself back in control of my facial muscles.

Erich had to be used to women making fools of themselves when introduced to him. The look he gave me was knowing.

"I'm pleased to meet you, Ms. Brennan," he said, exhibiting the good manners I was not.

Then he turned to Joyce, "You didn't tell me you expected company. I would have showered at the club before coming home."

"Oh, that's all right," she said. "Dianne called about visiting after you'd left. She would have the most interesting story if she'd tell it." She gave me a hard look that said she knew I was holding out on her. "She saw Jack's killer the day of the murder, but she won't give me any gory details. Now she thinks the killer is after her and she's trying to find him first."

"Isn't that the job of the police?" Erich asked.

He had an accent, more than Lannie Jameson, less than Arnold Schwarzenegger. German, I thought.

"Yes, it should be," I admitted, "but I'm convinced the murder has to do with the dog world, and the sheriff's department doesn't seem to agree. At least they haven't talked to several of the people I've visited. Have they talked to you?"

"No, of course not. There's no reason for the police to talk to us," Joyce said.

"Well, I think they should have," I said with resignation. "You were his best customer. In fact, I have a list of people who were involved with Jack through dogs, and I've been talking to everyone I can reach on the list. Would you look at it for me and see if you know of anyone I should add?"

Where Erich now sat on the couch he was closer to me than Joyce. I pulled the list from my pocket and held it out to him. His hand barely closed on the paper when Joyce reached over and plucked it from him without a word. She barely glanced at the list before handing it back to me.

"It looks complete to me. All you could add would be clients who had him handle a dog only now and then or people who live out of state. You're not spreading your net that wide are you?"

"No, not yet," I said with a sigh.

"To be honest," Joyce said, "I think the police have the right idea. No one in the dog world killed Jack. We may be terribly competitive, but it hasn't reached the point where anyone would kill over wins and losses at dog shows. There was money in Jack's family, you know. I should think that would be the best place to look for murderous feelings."

If she was right, maybe Lieutenant Forrester was arresting someone at that very moment. Somehow I doubted it.

"Now, I know you wanted to see the dogs," Joyce said, getting to her feet. "Let's do that so that your trip won't have been totally in vain." As Erich rose also, she added, "Will you come with us, darling?"

He nodded, and her face lit up the way it had when he first entered the room.

Joyce led the way to the backdoor past other elegantly furnished rooms and a shining, spotless kitchen. As we followed the gravel path toward the barn that indeed housed kennels, she walked by my side, letting Erich tag along behind us.

She chatted away about her breeding program, and I listened with half an ear. She made yearly trips to Germany and visited kennels there to keep an eye on the best of their breeding stock.

"It's a good excuse for a European vacation," Joyce said, "and it gives me an idea of what new blood I want to bring into my lines every now and then. That's how I met Erich, on one of my trips there."

She looked back over her shoulder flirtatiously as she said this, but I kept my eyes on the path ahead.

On the outside the barn might look like an old fashioned home for horses, but on the inside everything was ultra-modern and designed to make caring for the dozen dogs housed there as convenient as possible. Across from the kennels, one room contained a tiled washroom with raised tub. Another room was full of grooming equipment.

"This is a great setup," I said, peering through doorways. "Washing dogs would be fun with equipment like this."

Joyce acknowledged my compliment with a nod and called out, "Gary! Gary, are you here?"

A heavy, graying man emerged from a room in the back. His belly hung over his belt, and his jowls hung over his neck, but even so, he gave an impression of strength.

"Yes, ma'am. I was just doing some paperwork while I waited for you and your guest."

"This is Gary Crawford, my kennel manager," Joyce said. "Gary, this is Dianne Brennan. She helps Susan McKinnough with those poor, sad rescue dogs."

When Joyce had introduced me to her husband with those exact words I'd been too busy staring at him and trying to control my face to register the condescension in her voice. This time I caught it.

So Joyce was one of those breeders who thought rescue dogs had nothing to do with her Rottweiler royalty. Too bad I didn't have a copy of one of the pedigrees sometimes turned in with rescues handy to show her. Royalty usually shows up just a couple of generations behind those poor, sad rescues.

Even so, as Gary pulled one dog after another from its kennel, stacked it in the aisleway, and trotted it up and down for me to admire, I was impressed. Joyce's recitation of each dog's pedigree, wins, and sometimes the successes of offspring didn't hurt either. Two female puppies shared the last run. They were about the same age Sophie was when she first came to me, well beyond infant puppy cuteness yet still endearing in their gangly youthful innocence.

"Are you keeping these two?" I asked.

"Only one," Joyce answered. "I couldn't decide until recently which one was the better show prospect, but now that I know, that one on your left is going to Connecticut next week."

The puppy on the left tipped her head at me and grinned a puppy grin. I wished her a safe and not too frightening trip in the belly of the plane she would travel in. And I wished her an owner who kept her in the house and loved her for more than show wins. She was the reject, and she might be the lucky one, I thought, looking at the puppy on the right with sadness.

As Gary put the puppies back in their run, I returned to the subject of Jack Sheffield. "Did Jack ever say anything to you, maybe in a joking way along the lines that you'd regret it if you didn't let him show Carter?" I asked.

"To the contrary, he tried to influence me by saying if I let him show Carter, I'd never regret it," she said, "and now that he's gone maybe I wish I'd agreed. It would have meant a lot to him."

"Did he ever tell you about anyone else who was upset with him, even if he didn't think they should be?"

"No, he did not," she said. "If a handler wants to stay in business, he does not discuss one client with another."

"Was there another dog like Carter coming along in the area that he hoped to be able to talk the owner into campaigning nationally?"

Erich had been staying quietly in the background, letting Joyce show me the dogs and do the talking, but he spoke up now. "Dogs like Carter do *not* come along every year in an area the size of Colorado. My wife's dogs are outstanding, and no one would expect to find their like at the snap of fingers, and Jack knew this. Now, you must excuse us. We are meeting friends for luncheon, and I must shower. Gary will show you back to your car."

Joyce gave me a small smile as if to say, "Isn't he sooo strong," but I wasn't fooled. She was letting Erich send me on my way because that's what she wanted.

The way she had plucked my list out of his hand without giving him a chance to even look at it told me who was in control of this odd marriage.

I thanked Gary and assured him I didn't need an escort to walk to my car. Joyce might not like my poor, sad rescue dogs setting foot on her property, but I let Sophie and Robo out of the car to walk them around for a few minutes anyway.

To my surprise, Sophie shot out of the car so fast she almost pulled the leash from my hand. She circled around, nose to the ground, intent on interpreting some doggy message left there. When she didn't quit on her own after a few go rounds, I pulled her away and took her to walk on the grassy area beside the driveway, scolding her out loud as we went.

"Yes, other dogs live here, and yes, they have all sorts of testosterone and estrogen to leave in their scent, but they're none of your business, and believe me, you wouldn't trade places with them if you knew how they live."

I had plastic bags in my pocket ready to pick up after the dogs but didn't need to use them. As I loaded the dogs back in the car and set off for home I felt virtuous anyway, even if Gary would have been the only beneficiary. At a guess neither Joyce nor the boy toy even knew how to use a pooper-scooper, but I wondered if he knew how to use a knife, and if his wife would ask him to use one for her, and what his answer to such a request would be.

16

BACK AT HOME, I PUT Millie out in the yard where she could play with Sophie and harass Robo. My plan to call Susan and ask her why she hadn't saved me a lot of embarrassment by warning me about Erich faded away as I played the lone message on my voice mail.

"This is Myron Feltzer," the booming voice said. "If you want to see me, I can give you a few minutes this afternoon at home. Five to five-thirty. I'll expect you unless I hear to the contrary."

Feltzer's voice was curt and rough enough to fit my image of a man who would import an adult dog from Germany and have her tail amputated so she could be shown successfully in this country, a man who would collect large sums for injuries to the dog and then order her destroyed because she was of no further use to him. Myron Feltzer, in fact, sounded like someone I wouldn't mind seeing go to prison for the rest of his life, and if he couldn't be convicted for mutilating and discarding dogs, murder would do.

Since all the cheese was gone, there was nothing in the house I wanted in a sandwich. Balancing an apple on top of a carton of yogurt in one hand and carrying a glass of iced tea in the other, I went upstairs to the computer and ate my quick lunch while getting directions to the Feltzers' on Mapquest.

The trip would be more than a two-hour drive west into the mountains. I always avoided driving unfamiliar roads after dark if I could, and driving unfamiliar mountain roads after dark was even less appealing. Still, I calculated leaving the Feltzers' house by six would have me close to home before full dark. I would be able to tuck myself and the dogs safely away for the night with gun at hand and sheriff's deputies driving by now and then.

Gnawing on the apple core, I stared at the computer screen thoughtfully. The machine couldn't answer the questions swirling through my head for me; it could organize the information I'd gathered so far.

I opened my spreadsheet program and started a new document, listing everyone I'd talked to so far in the first column, titled "Suspects." Carl Warmstead, Dorrie and Lee Stander, Harry and Lannie Jameson, Ty and Tawana Mullin, Joyce Richerson and Erich Kohler. My second column was for "Alibi," and there I put a check mark across from the name of Carl Warmstead.

Next came "Physically Able," and Carl Warmstead, Lee Stander, Harry Jameson, and Erich Kohler were definitely physically able. The next column was for "Lied," and I checked Harry, who hadn't mentioned stolen clients, and Ty, who hadn't mentioned drugs.

Across from Joyce Richerson's name I put a question mark. Maybe she was telling the truth about Jack accepting her decision to send Carter to a different handler. Yet everything I'd learned so far indicated

Jack Sheffield had been determined to find a client to support him in a national campaign and willing to pressure clients to get his way. Yes, Joyce Richerson was a tough woman, but so was Tawana Mullin, and Jack had tried pressure on the Mullins.

I backspaced over my question mark and changed it to a check mark. Joyce's denial wasn't believable. Jack must have tried in some way to get her to allow him to continue showing Carter.

After staring at my chart for a while, I deleted the lines for Carl, Dorrie, Lannie, Ty, and Tawana. Then I reinserted Carl's name. Maybe it wouldn't hurt to see if Lieutenant Forrester would tell me where Carl had been when Jack was killed and whether there was even the slightest chance he could have snuck back to the house and killed the lover who was trying to push him out.

Joyce had mentioned money as a motive. Did Carl now own the entire house outright? Had Jack had a will that left Carl his worldly goods? Who did inherit, and how much was there to inherit?

My next column was "Heard Gossip," and I checked every name but Carl's. Then after a moment, I put a check by his name too. If Lee Stander could have heard an exaggerated version of my encounter with Jack's killer third- or fourth-hand from a customer, Carl could have heard it from a friend who had known both Jack and Carl and had contacts in the dog show world. All it would take was a comment in a friendly phone call.

"Afraid of Dogs" caused another inner debate. Carl's allergies didn't necessarily mean he was afraid of dogs. Then again, if he had avoided dogs all his life . . . . In the end I put a question mark in that column for Carl. Both Lieutenant Forrester and Susan had shrugged off my contention that the killer had to be afraid of dogs. However, I was the one who had seen him run, knife and all, from a totally non-aggressive Robo in Jack's backyard. He had also panicked in the King Sooper's parking lot. I had heard that fear-filled gasp and felt the man freeze behind me. I was the one who was alive because of the frenzied way he had thrown me toward the dogs while trying to slash my throat.

In the same situation an experienced dog man like Harry Jameson or Lee Stander would have used the extra seconds necessary to kill me, then thrown my *body* at the dogs. And whether Erich Kohler had been merely an employee at the German kennel where Joyce had met him or, more likely, a member of the Rott-weiler breeder's family, he would also have known he had time to kill me and still escape the dogs.

The last column was "Motive" and across from Carl's name I typed, "spurned and/or money." For both Lee Stander and Harry Jameson, I typed "revenge," then added, "stop customer loss" to Harry's entry. Harry would be far more likely to kill to stop future ruination of his business than merely for revenge for past losses. For Joyce, motive was "avoid blackmail," and for Erich, "obey rich wife."

My chart made Carl, the only one who supposedly couldn't have killed Jack, the best candidate to have done just that. I called the sheriff's office and asked for Lieutenant Forrester. He wasn't there. I left a message asking him to call me in the morning.

Before saving my spreadsheet, I added a line for Myron Feltzer, then went back downstairs and called the dogs in. Thankfully, Millie hadn't learned any of Sophie's guilt-evoking tricks yet. She settled down quite happily with a large black rubber kong toy with its hollow center stuffed with biscuits and kibble embedded in peanut butter.

Sophie and Robo followed me out to the car and hopped in the back as if they hadn't already spent most of the morning confined there, and I started for Feltzers.

Hours later, as my little car puffed up another long grade, I finally approached the Feltzers' house. No houses were visible on their road. Mailboxes marked openings in the wall of pines where driveways had been hewn out of the forest.

When the Feltzer mailbox appeared, I turned onto the gravel drive and left the car in first gear as it struggled almost straight up. Did these people stay home from the first snow until the spring thaw? Or did they travel on snowmobiles all winter?

The house had been built into the side of the mountain, garage underneath, living space layered on top. Dark brown siding and decks emphasized the lack of light under the trees. Buttoning a light jacket over my sweatshirt didn't add enough warmth in the chilly mountain air. Before I convinced myself that the whole place was too sinister-looking to approach and got back in the warm little box of my car, a cheery female voice called out from over my head.

"Are you Dianne Brennan? Come on up. The only way in is up the stairs."

Reassured by her friendly welcome, I climbed the steep wooden stairs to the deck above. Ginny Feltzer's freckled face was as friendly as her voice. Her curly reddish hair matched the freckles and glowed against the dark gold of a bulky knit sweater. I envied her that thick sweater and the black wool slacks underneath almost more than the trim figure the outfit showed off.

"Come on in," she urged. "You haven't got enough on for this weather, and the wind's starting to pick up. Don't mind the dogs. She loves everyone, and he'll just hang back until he decides you're okay."

She opened the sliding glass door and led me into a living room with oak flooring and wall paneling that was almost as dark as the exterior of the house but far more inviting. Area rugs and plump upholstered furniture in deep red with gold patterns added color and warmth.

The dogs were Rottweilers, of course. After the sterility of Joyce Richerson's house and with my preconceived ideas about Myron Feltzer, I hadn't expected to find dogs underfoot and treated as beloved family members here. The female was heavy in the last stages of pregnancy and put her head in my lap as soon as I sat down. As predicted, the male took up a position near Ginny where he could keep an eye on me.

I rubbed the head in my lap, and the bitch immediately climbed up beside me on the couch.

"Nadia get down," Ginny ordered.

Nadia showed no sign of having heard and made herself comfortable beside me with her head in my lap.

Ginny started toward me. "If you give her any encouragement at all, you'll have an eighty-pound lap dog— more than that now with the puppies. I'll get her off you."

"Don't make her get down," I protested. "She's fine here."

"Okay, if you're sure, but that head can get awfully heavy. Can I get you a cup of coffee or tea? Or a cold drink, but you look like you need warming up."

"That would be great," I said. "Anything hot."

My expectation was that Myron would show up and tell me what I wanted to know while his wife was in the kitchen, but there was still no sign of Myron when Ginny returned. I held the steaming cup she handed me out to one side and leaned over to sip so that the hot coffee couldn't spill on the trusting head in my lap. Maybe it was time to give up on Myron and see what his wife had to say. Ty Mullin's wife had certainly been worth chatting to.

"Did your husband tell you that I'm trying to learn as much as I can about Jack Sheffield and who might have wanted to kill him?" I asked.

"He sure did. And I heard all about how you saw his killer leaving his house that morning." She gave a dramatic little shudder. "I'd have fainted dead away and he could have cut my throat too with me just laying there."

"That's all too close to what happened," I told her. "But I only almost fainted, and I had a dog with me that's almost as impressive as your boy there, and the killer ran."

"But you *saw* him," she said. "You saw him and now you're looking for him everywhere so you can call the cops on him."

I wondered how much time Ginny had spent in the ladies' room during the specialty show. "I saw him, and he seems to have decided I'm a threat to him somehow, but the truth is I couldn't identify him if he walked in this room." And when was her husband going to do exactly that? "That's why I'm trying to learn enough about Jack to figure out who would have wanted to kill him."

"And you think it could be Myron?" she said with amusement.

"Not really, but do you know where he was that morning?"

"At his office," she said. "At least that's where he almost always is on a weekday morning, and I don't remember anything being different then. I can't even remember when it was now, but we saw it on the news when it happened. Does he need an alibi? The police have never talked to us."

"If the police haven't talked to him, he certainly must not need an alibi," I said, thinking evil thoughts about Lieutenant Forrester. "Mostly I'm hoping he might tell me something helpful. You were clients of Jack's for a long time, weren't you?"

"It depends on what you mean by a long time. We started with Jack, let's see, about four years ago."

"Who showed your dogs before that?"

"Harry Jameson."

Harry again. Damn it. I *liked* Harry and his family. "What made you switch handlers?"

"Oh, it's hard to say exactly one thing. Harry's attitude is that if he's the handler, you're paying him for his expertise and you ought to do what he says. And of course Myron feels since he's paying he ought to get what he wants. They just bumped heads once too often over that kind of thing. Myron wanted to show Joe here in Kansas City." She nodded toward the big male at her side. "We were willing to fly Joe and Harry back there, and it wasn't as if there was an important local show to miss that weekend. Well, Harry said he wouldn't do it, that the judge wouldn't like Joe enough for it to be worthwhile. So we were at a local show just before the Kansas City entries closed, and Myron and Harry were arguing about it, loud enough to be heard, you know?"

I nodded. Just from hearing her husband's message on my phone, I could imagine how easy it would be to overhear him in an ordinary conversation much less an argument.

"Afterwards Jack came over and said he couldn't help but hear, and how he didn't believe in not competing just because the judges weren't in your pocket. And the upshot of it all was Jack took Joe to Kansas City, and after that he showed all our dogs for us."

"So how did Joe do at that Kansas City show?" I asked.

"Didn't win, didn't even get a long look for that matter."

We grinned at each other in mutual appreciation of the irony. Harry had been right, but being right had cost him a customer.

Before I could ask another question, furious barking sounded outside. Nadia scrambled up and off the couch and ran with Joe to the glass doors. Both dogs were hackling and giving low growls, ready to take on the strangers outside.

I was right behind them, peering out as best I could with the dogs keeping me from getting to the door.

"I need to get out," I said to Ginny. "I left my dogs in the car. I need to see what's set them off."

Ginny took hold of the dogs' collars and pulled them back. "Go ahead and check, but I bet it was deer.

They're thick all over up here, and it's the right time of day for them now."

Squeezing past the dogs and out onto the deck, I stared down at my car. Sophie and Robo were no longer barking but looking intently into the forest that started only a few feet from where the car was parked in the driveway. As I watched, Robo turned away and lay back down, disappearing from my sight below the windows. Whatever had set them off was gone now, and they were still safely in the car.

I slipped back into the house, shivering after just a minute outside, and accepted another cup of coffee. When I took my former position on the couch, so did Nadia. We were old friends now.

"So you left Harry and went with Jack," I said, trying to get the conversation back on track. "Did Jack ever try to get you to go for a national ranking with Joe?"

"Joe was in the top twenty the first year Jack showed him," Ginny said proudly. "But Jack knew he wasn't ever going to do much better than that. He's a grand boy, and we love him, but he's not competitive at a higher level than that."

Did Myron Feltzer really love his dogs? Or was it his wife who loved them and Myron who took pride in their victories? I looked down at the head in my lap. Nadia had her eyes closed and looked blissful as I fingered one velvety ear. "So are these two all you have now? Or do you have others being shown?"

"We have two good ones out on the circuit right now," boomed a deep voice behind me. "And the sire of those puppies beside you on the couch is going to be the number one dog next year. Pick of the litter will be out there following in his daddy's footsteps."

Hmm. Did that mean the sire of the puppies was Joyce Richerson's Carter? I decided to exercise the better part of valor and not ask.

As Myron Feltzer walked into the room, it shrank. The effect wasn't from his size alone; his bullish attitude and bluster were what changed the room. His head was large for his body, and his features large in his face.

"Has my wife satisfied you with enough gossip, or do you have questions for me?" He didn't wait for an answer but kept right on talking. "We have to leave in a few minutes anyway, so let's be quick about it."

Considering I'd been on time and he had waited until just minutes before his self-imposed deadline to put in an appearance, he wasn't going to get away with that. I ignored the impatient way he stood there with his arms crossed, somehow giving the impression of tapping a foot without moving.

"Yes, I do have questions. Did Jack ever try to get you to let him campaign a dog nationally?"

"Sure he did," Myron said, surprising me. "We had it all planned out. Then the dog was hit by a car, and that was the end of that."

He had to mean Maida. "Are you saying you were going to campaign the bitch you imported from Germany for a national ranking?"

"Not a ranking, number one. She was tops over there and so were both her parents. It took a long time to find one that good that someone would sell."

He sounded resentful of the time it had taken. Did it surprise him people didn't want to sell a dog like Maida? Most people would sell their souls before they'd sell a dog like that.

"Did you ever think that maybe Jack was lying to you about what happened the night Maida was hit by the car? Did you ever consider that maybe the Standers were right and it was Jack himself who let her loose?"

"Of course not," he said. "Jack was at MaryAnn Balma's that night. She had a new litter and wanted his opinion. She said so in court."

"But you fired Jack as your handler right after the lawsuit ended. If you believed him, why did you do that?"

"Because the son of a bitch let it happen. He should have had a padlock on that kennel run. From now on my dogs are with people who have kennels right on their property and see to their dogs themselves every night. None of this paying somebody else for the hard work."

"Do you think Lee Stander was angry enough over the lawsuit and the way it came out to kill Jack?"

He wasn't expecting that question and actually paused a moment to consider it. "No. He was angry— like a volcano ready to erupt—but why would he kill Jack? It was one of his own kennel workers he should have wanted to kill, or his wife for mismanaging the place. Or maybe me for not letting them get away with it. Damned insurance company originally offered me two thousand dollars."

His answer sounded genuine to me. Maybe he really believed Jack's version of events. I was tempted to tell him what Jack had admitted to Harry and Lannie Jameson, but that could lead to his learning what had happened to Maida. Just out of curiosity, I asked him about Maida.

"What happened to the dog you imported? I heard she had several surgeries."

For the first time, his eyes slid away from mine evasively. "Four. Damn vet bills were enormous, and it was all for nothing. She was ruined."

"It was terrible," Ginny added. "After all those operations and all that time at the vet's, we finally thought she was going to be okay, and she was home here with us. Then she wouldn't eat, and Myron took her to the vet again, and she had a blood clot. It got to her lungs, and she died at the hospital."

Ginny looked both sad and sincere in her belief that Maida had died at the vet's. Had Maida really given Myron his excuse by refusing to eat a meal or two, or had he found a way to fake that? How had he kept his wife from learning the truth from the vet? I'd never know and didn't really want to.

I tried another tack. "After you lost Maida, did Jack ever say anything to you about hoping that Joyce Richerson would let him campaign her dog?"

"Sure he did," said Myron. "He said she was talking about sending the dog to Loomis in California—he's done real well for a couple of people these last years—but Jack was convinced he could talk Joyce around. I wasn't so sure. Joyce has strong opinions about her dogs, and she doesn't take advice easily."

"Did you ever get the feeling it was causing trouble between them?" I asked.

"Hell, no. Just the week before Jack died we all had dinner together after a show. Everyone was getting along just fine. Joyce even let the boy husband off his leash that night. She was coming down with something and went to bed early and left him there with us. He told us some stories about growing up in Germany and all. Usually he just keeps to himself. He had enough wine that night to loosen up some. He . . . ."

"He's just embarrassed," Ginny interrupted. "He did what he had to to get to America, but it embarrasses him."

Myron made a sound of disagreement. "You think he's pretty just like all the girls do. Too damn pretty, I say. He didn't want to just get to America. He wanted to get to America and be rich without working for it. Now he's finding out there's no free lunch. Joyce is no fool. She told me she has an ironclad prenup. If he wants to keep living well, he'd better keep her happy."

Joyce's prenuptial arrangements weren't what interested me right then. I tried to get the Feltzers back on the subject. "What would Joyce have done if Jack really pressured her to let him show Carter?"

"Thrown him right out on his ass," Myron stated confidently. "What's more, he knew it. He might have tried to charm her, cajole her, but he'd never have tried pressure. You've met her. Would you try to pressure her into anything she didn't want to do?"

I shook my head in acknowledgment of the truth of his words. Knowing I was running out of time with the Feltzers, I eased Nadia's heavy head up off my lap a bit and slid out from under, then got to my feet.

"Would you look at my list of people who did business with Jack or were associated with him somehow and tell me if you can think of anyone else I should talk to?" I asked.

At his nod, I pulled the paper from my purse and handed it to him. He took his time reading the names, then handed it to Ginny.

"You don't have the vet he dealt with on there," he said, "but I don't see how that matters. There are people he showed a dog for now and then. You could get them from his billing records, I guess, but you've got the people he dealt with every weekend at every show."

"Do you have any idea at all who might have wanted Jack dead enough to kill him?" I asked.

"Harry Jameson, maybe. He probably thinks Jack stole a lot of clients from him. The truth is Harry's an inflexible son of a bitch. He loses customers for himself. No one has to steal them."

I couldn't think of anything else to ask him. "Thanks for your time," I said, buttoning my thin jacket all the way up to my neck.

"You didn't learn anything you didn't already know, did you?" Myron said.

"No, but you confirmed some things others told me, and that's useful too."

Now I was the one lying. Coming out here had been a disappointing waste of time, and I still had a long drive home ahead of me.

Ginny took her time showing me out, chatting away, and trying to get me to accept a warmer jacket on loan.

"Winter would be over before I could get it back to you," I told her. "Don't worry about me. I'll be in the car all the way home."

I got Sophie and Robo out of the car and took them for a brief walk down Feltzers' driveway, hugging myself against the chilly mountain air and cursing my own foolishness in not taking Ginny's jacket.

Sophie kept trying to pull me into the trees to go after whatever had started the dogs barking earlier.

Robo's only interest in the trees was lifting his leg on as many as possible. Sophie finally accepted my sharp, "No," and got down to business herself.

My teeth were chattering by the time the dogs were finished. Returning to the car and starting the heater was a relief. Night seemed to be closing in faster than it would have at a lower altitude. Maybe my annual difficulty in adjusting to fall's shorter days just had me feeling that way.

I put the car in gear and started to back down the steep driveway, surprised by how difficult it was to turn the steering wheel. When the meaning of the way the car was handling came to me, I stopped right there on the hill, yanked on the emergency brake, got out and walked around to the passenger's side.

At the sight of the flat tire on the front wheel, Ginny's coffee rose sour in the back of my throat. So much for my intentions of avoiding driving in the dark on curving mountain roads.

17

THE GARAGE DOOR IN FRONT of my car rumbled open, backup lights flashed on, and a big black SUV in the garage bay started toward my crippled car then immediately jerked to a stop.

Myron and Ginny got out and joined me in their driveway. She clucked and sympathized. A look that might have been annoyance or maybe just impatience flashed across his face, then he turned matter of fact.

"Bad luck," he said. "I suppose your spare is one of those donuts."

"Yes, it is," I told him, "and I've already used it once. I think it said you could drive fifty miles on it, and I went maybe twenty that time."

Myron just grunted in reply and looked at his wife. "Go call Kenny, why don't you. She can drive that far." He turned to me. "Kenny Piesecki runs a garage not too far from here. If we catch him before he leaves for the night, he'll help you out. I'll get the spare on for you, and you can follow us there."

He ignored my protests that I didn't want to make them late and that I could change the tire myself and directed me in maneuvering to an almost flat piece of ground beside the driveway. I got the dogs out of the car so he could reach the tools and spare.

As Myron started jacking up the front end of the car, Ginny returned with the welcome news that she'd reached Kenny and he would wait for me. Even more welcome was the puffy, down-filled jacket she brought with her and wrapped around me.

"It's an old one I never even wore all last winter," she said. "You can bring it back to me at the February show, and if you forget, no harm at all."

The coat was a size too small, tight under the arms and across the shoulders, but I zipped it all the way up, grateful for the warmth. Ginny made small talk about car trouble and the weather as she petted Sophie and Robo, making me feel guilty for the suspicious thoughts about her husband that kept running through my mind.

"I'm so sorry you're going to be late because of me," I said to her. "I hope you aren't going to miss a restaurant reservation."

"Oh, no," she said, all smiles and openness. "We're just going to drop off a present for a friend's daughter for her birthday. Myron is probably happy we're delayed. Tracey's only seven, and if her birthday party is over and her friends and their parents have all left by the time we get there, he won't mind at all."

Myron finished and threw the flat tire and tools back in my car. I followed them to Kenny's garage, half of me determined to accept that flat tires just happen now and then, and half of me arguing that a flat just happening here and now with an almost new tire was too much to believe.

What if, while I sat drinking coffee with Ginny, Sophie and Robo hadn't been barking furiously at a deer, but at Myron sneaking through the trees. What if my tire was flat because Myron had somehow tampered with it?

KENNY PIESECKI'S GARAGE was a dark barn by the side of the road with grease that might date from horse and buggy days sunk deep in every surface. Kenny himself might not have worked on buggies, but he probably had been under the hood of a new Edsel in its day.

He found the problem with my tire in minutes.

"Not good," he said. "See this? You've got a nail right through the sidewall. I can't fix that."

The only reason my spirits didn't fall at his words was that they were already on the floor.

"How could that happen?" I asked him. "If I ran over a nail it wouldn't be in the sidewall, would it?"

"Happens sometimes," he said, shrugging. "What we have to figure is how to get you going again. I don't have this exact tire in stock, and you don't want to run this car with tires that don't match for long."

He looked at me, questioning.

All I cared about was getting back on the road fast. If Myron had driven the nail into my tire, he had to make nice with the birthday girl's family, then drive Ginny home and find an excuse to go out again before he could come after me. Maybe my flat was just one of those things. Even so, getting back on the road and putting as many miles between me and Myron as fast as possible was the only plan I could come up with.

"Put anything you can find that will fit on it," I said. "I'll worry about one that matches tomorrow."

Kenny worked quickly. In half the time my garage back home would take to mount a tire, figure the bill, and run my credit card, he was finished and opening the overhead door, waving me into the dusk of early evening.

He was happy to be done with this favor for the Feltzers, I realized. Eager to get home to his own family and dinner. No more eager than I. At the first stop sign I took the time to pull Ginny's too tight coat off. After that, I trusted to luck that there were no citation-hungry cops hidden along my route and pushed the car as fast as I dared.

Once on the Jarre Canyon Road heading home, I relaxed a little. The pickup ahead set a good pace, and the two cars behind mine made me feel protected. Traveling all the way in the little caravan would have been fine with me, but soon the pickup turned off and one after another the cars behind roared around me, disappearing into the night at a speed I was unwilling to match.

Alone on the road, I tried to take my mind off my nerves by thinking of how I'd fill in the columns after Myron's name on my chart. No alibi. Physically he could be the killer, although he was bulkier than my remembered image. He had lied about Maida if nothing else. His wife had heard the exaggerated version of my story at the specialty show. And he was the first possible suspect other than Carl Warmstead who might have reacted to the dogs the way the killer had.

Myron had dogs of his own and maybe even worked with them, but he didn't work with dogs of all kinds and temperaments day in and day out like the Standers or Harry Jameson. He wouldn't have the experience with Rottweilers that Erich Kohler would have gotten working with them in Germany. The one thing I could not come up with for Myron was a motive.

Then again, maybe I wasn't that keen to find the perfect motive for Myron. He and I would never be friends, but like Tawana Mullin, Ginny seemed to be someone I'd like to get to know better.

I sure didn't want to believe Myron had driven a nail into my tire so that I'd be on the road this late and really, really didn't want to believe he was behind me now, following me with murder on his mind.

My nerves were steadying. I stopped expecting every car coming toward me to cross the center line and come straight at me, although cars coming from behind still had me gripping the steering wheel so tight my hands ached.

He didn't smash into the back of the car. He started to pass in a perfectly normal fashion. The SUV was almost past and I was starting to relax when the big vehicle cut back into my lane right through the front end of my small car.

The impact jerked me in my seat. The airbag exploded. Blinded by the airbag, darkness and terror, I felt the car plunge over the side of the road and leave the ground. The seatbelt and airbag caught my body as I was flung one way then another, the car crashing through trees, caroming off rocks, and rolling . . . and rolling.

When the car came to rest, I was surprised to find myself not only alive but conscious. The car had stopped on its side with the passenger's side up. The air bag and gravity pinned me to the driver's side door.

Movement in the back made me gather my shaken wits. The dogs had also survived the battering fall. Every time they moved the car rocked slightly. The car wasn't on solid ground but hung up on something. Sophie whined.

I shut my eyes for a moment, trying to clear my head, then had to fight the urge to leave them closed and sink into oblivion. Sophie whined again, and I opened my eyes and faced the mess we were in.

"We're going to be all right," I told the dogs in as calm a voice as I could manage. "Just give me a minute, and we'll get out of here. I'll call for help. We're going to be fine."

The headlights on my poor car were still shining downhill into the night. I could see rocks, bushes and ground below. Whatever the car was hung up on couldn't be too high off the ground.

As I oriented myself, fear returned at such strength the metallic taste filled my mouth. Myron Feltzer or someone else, whoever had run me off the road was out there in the darkness, and the Toyota's headlights were twin beacons, telling him where his wounded prey was. I turned off the lights.

Talking to the dogs about calling for help reminded me of the cell phone. Groping everywhere within reach, I felt leather under the seat on the passenger's side, but my purse was stuck in the narrow space. As I yanked and pulled the purse free, the car moved again. Getting out and getting away had to be worth whatever extra pain falling out of the car would bring.

Undoing the seatbelt was easy. In the end, to get free from the airbag I yanked the door handle beneath me. The door opened partway with a groan as crushed metal gave way. Pushing and struggling, I forced the door open wide enough to slither through and drop out onto the stony ground. Calling the dogs as I crawled, I scuttled out from under the car in what felt like slow motion.

Seconds later the dogs were there with me, and I crooned senseless words of reassurance to them and to myself, trying to hold their warm bodies close against the cold of the night. I'd forgotten Ginny's coat and wasn't going back to the car after it.

When Sophie started growling, the sound was unlike any she'd ever made before, reverberating from so deep in her belly it wasn't a growl as I knew it. She pulled away from me and then was gone, and Robo after her.

"Sophie! Robo!" They didn't return, of course. By the time I stopped my futile shouting, the dogs were far enough away there was no sound of their headlong run through the brush. I was alone.

The night was quiet until a car hummed past high on the road above, the driver and any passengers with him secure in their mobile cocoon. The sound had almost faded away when the sharp crack of a gunshot cut through it. A dog screaming almost drowned out the sound of another shot. I struggled halfway to my feet, fell to my hands and knees and vomited, weeping as shot after shot shattered the night. He was emptying a gun at my dogs. The echoes had barely stopped when I heard the distant sound of a slamming car door, followed by the roar of an engine and squeal of tires as the killer took off.

He had to know I might be alive if the dogs were. Once again he was running from the dogs. Did that mean they were still alive? I never made it to my feet.

I found the cell phone and dialed 911. The connection was so bad only garbled sounds sputtered out. Desperately hoping that the outbound transmission was better, I repeated my location as best I knew it several times, then started crawling up the slope toward the road.

18

SHERIFF'S DEPUTIES ARRIVED in time to stop me from going back over the side of the road at the place where the killer's tires had left rubber when he fled. Sophie and Robo had to be down there somewhere. The deputies treated me as if my injuries were all to the head and refused to listen about the dogs.

When the ambulance arrived, the paramedics took over, peppering me with questions about my injuries and ignoring my fear for my dogs. There was little doubt that if I tried to walk away, they would physically restrain me.

My first savior was a lean man wearing a ball cap and plaid flannel shirt who pulled his pickup off the road to see what was going on. He asked one of the deputies if he could help.

"No, sir," the deputy said brusquely. "You need to drive on and go about your business."

Involved in an intense effort to keep myself calm enough to persuade someone to look for Sophie and

Robo or to let me do it, I was only half aware of the man as he got back in his truck and started to drive off. When he stopped again, and went over the side with a flashlight, one of the deputies left me and ran up the road.

"Hey, you," he yelled. "Get back here. You can't do that!"

But he did. He came back up with Sophie in his arms, Robo and an angry deputy trailing behind. He laid Sophie gently on the gurney the paramedics had prepared for me, tipped his hat, walked back to his truck and drove off.

Sophie was unconscious but alive. Seeing her there, with her blood pooling on the cover of the gurney forced the officers to accept I wasn't crazy from head injuries. Even so, Sophie would have died while they debated what to do had it not been for my second savior, who arrived in another cruiser with lights flashing.

She assessed the situation at a glance and started giving orders. "Get the bleeding stopped," said Deputy Carraher to the paramedics. "There's a vet a little way back up the canyon with his office in his house. He takes emergencies. We'll take her there."

"We can't work on a dog," said one of the paramedics. "I don't know anything about dogs."

"Do what you'd do with a person," said Deputy Carraher. "Dogs bleed the same way."

The second paramedic was ignoring his partner's objections and working on Sophie, applying pressure bandages. "She needs blood," he said. "She's lost a lot. Do they do transfusions on dogs?"

"Yes, they do," said Deputy Carraher. "Vets do. Let's get her in the ambulance."

"Look, we can't do that," said the first paramedic. "I'm sorry, but I'm not losing my job over it, and we can't transport a dog."

He had his hands on his hips and was looking belligerent. Carraher didn't waste time on him. "Okay, then I'll take her."

She and the second paramedic carried Sophie to her car and eased her onto the back seat. I climbed in, pulled Sophie's head into my lap and held her. The paramedic ran to the ambulance and came back with a blanket that he tucked around my shoulders. His care started tears slipping down my face.

The officer who had been giving the orders at the scene before Carraher arrived had followed us to the car, objecting. "She has to stay. We need a report, and she needs medical treatment."

"Ms. Brennan isn't going to cooperate a damn with you until we take care of the dogs," Deputy Carraher said. "Believe me, I've seen her in action. I'll get a report from her at the vet's and be back here as soon as I can." She got into the driver's seat and started the engine.

"Robo," I managed to croak.

The deputy got out again, disappeared in the lights, and returned leading Robo by the collar. She put him in the front seat beside her, and we took off, lights flashing. As she drove, she talked to the crackly voice on the radio, asking them to call ahead to the vet.

"Thank you," I said. "I thought you didn't like us— me or the dogs."

"I was having a bad day," she said. "And I never liked these big macho type dogs. I have cats."

"I have a cat too," I said.

"Yeah, well, I have to admit I changed some of my ideas about Rottweilers that day when I saw how that dog behaved at the vet's. Either one of my cats would have left scars on anyone that did that much poking and prodding. How's she doing?"

"She's still breathing, but it's so shallow it's hard to tell."

"We're almost there."

She turned off the highway and flew along a narrow access road with no perceptible reduction in speed, then turned again and was forced to slow down by the washboard surface of the dirt road.

Sophie's body bounced on the seat, and I held her harder to keep her in place. Mercifully, Deputy Carraher slowed again and this time turned into a driveway as steep as the Feltzers'. The house we approached was set into the side of a hill the same way, but the first floor was the vet clinic and ablaze with light.

Between us, Deputy Carraher and I carried Sophie to the door. A thin, elderly man with a shock of white hair and skin pale in the artificial light held the door open for us.

He led the way through the waiting room back to an operating room, where we laid Sophie on a stainless steel table. An equally aged woman dressed in green scrubs was already laying out surgical equipment.

"I'm Dr. Rolland Hunsaker," he said, his stethoscope moving over Sophie. "This is my wife, Hettie. She's been serving as my anesthetist and assistant at surgeries like this for years."

"More years than either of us wants to admit," Hettie said with a smile. "And we've worked on more gunshot dogs together than we'd like to admit either. It's usually hunting dogs during the season. What happened this time?"

Seeing with a glance that I was beyond explaining, Deputy Carraher answered for me. "This was no accident. It was deliberate."

Dr. Hunsaker motioned for silence and listened even more intently through the stethoscope, then looked at me. "She's your dog?"

I nodded.

He asked me the usual questions about Sophie's age, history and health, and I answered as best I could.

His last question was, "How much do you want us to do?"

I recognized veterinarian shorthand for *how much are you willing to pay.*

"I want you to *fix* her. So long as she's not suffering for nothing and there's any hope, I want you do anything you can."

He nodded. "All right. You wait outside. I'll let you know as soon as I can."

I followed Deputy Carraher back to the waiting room and eased my aching body onto one of the hard plastic chairs.

"You surprised me, not arguing about waiting out here," Deputy Carraher said. "I expected you to pitch a fit and want to stay with her."

"I'm so filthy I shouldn't be in an operating room, and if I pass out I don't want them stopping to fuss over me."

"Ah, that sounds more like the Rottweiler lady we all know and dread dealing with," she said. "Now, you know I need to get enough information from you to fill out an accident report. If I go back there without it, I'll be unemployed tomorrow."

"Robo is still in your car."

"I'll go get him. Then will you cooperate?"

She left without waiting for an answer and returned with Robo and the blanket I'd left in the car. I wrapped the blanket around myself with gratitude, wondering if I'd ever feel warm again, then pulled Robo close. Indifferent as he was, his living presence was a comfort of sorts.

I did my best to answer the deputy's questions and told her all about my visit to Feltzers, the flat tire, and Myron Feltzer's black SUV.

"But you can't say for sure it was a black SUV that hit you." she said.

"No. I'm pretty sure it was an SUV—it had that square shape—and it was a dark color, but that's all."

Deputy Carraher sighed. "If only the dogs could talk. They could give us an i.d."

At that moment Mrs. Hunsaker opened the waiting room door. "Oh, good, Rolland said he thought he saw another dog in the car. Your girl needs blood and we don't have any dogs here that we can use as donors. Have you owned Sophie all her life? Has she ever had a transfusion?"

"I adopted her when she was five months old and she's never had a transfusion since," I said, "but I don't know her blood type or his."

"We can get away with transfusing her with un-matched blood once," said Hettie. "It's an advantage dogs have over people, and this is going to be Sophie's time because if she's going to make it she needs blood and she needs it now. Bring that big boy on back here."

I started to get up, but Deputy Carraher put a hand on my arm. "You stay here so we don't have to fuss over you. I'll go with him, and I won't let anyone hurt him."

I sank back down gratefully and forced the horrific images of Sophie out of my mind by considering whether to call Susan and ask her to rescue Millie, home in the crate. Susan would have to drive up to my dark house, take the spare key out of its hiding place, and fumble for the lights. The killer had to know I was still alive. What if he was waiting at the house? Even if her husband or Wesley went with her, I couldn't send them into that potential danger.

Unfair as it was, Millie was going to have to wait. Tomorrow I'd talk to Susan and tell her Millie needed to go to another foster home where she'd be safe.

When the deputy returned with Robo, her face was set in the same hard lines as the first time I'd seen her so many weeks ago, and she didn't sit down again.

"I have to get back," she said. "Is there someone I can call to come get you?"

Now that I knew she used that look to mask emotion, the change in her attitude frightened me.

"What did you find out?" I whispered. "Is she dead?"

"No, she's not," she said sharply. "They don't really know anything yet. They're still assessing."

"Don't do that to me. What did they say?"

She hesitated, scanned my face, then shrugged. "It's pretty bad. Without the blood there'd be no chance at all, with it . . . ." She shrugged again. "The first thing is for her to make it through the surgery, and you should know that soon. I really do have to get back. Are you sure you don't want me to call someone? You need a doctor."

"I'm beat up pretty badly, but everything works, even if it hurts." I tried to smile at her. "I didn't even realize I'd crossed back into Douglas County on the way home. Now I'm glad I did. However this turns out, I'll always be grateful for your help. You go ahead. I'm staying here until I know."

She nodded at me. "Good luck." Then she walked out, and the white room was suddenly colder and much more lonely.

19

TIME CRAWLED. I STARED AT the door Dr. Hunsaker would come back through, part of me fearing the news he would bring, part of me unable to believe that mere bullets could extinguish Sophie's grand spirit.

The sound of tires crunching on gravel outside made me struggle to my feet to look out the window. Who else would be coming here this time of night? The sight of the high, square shape of an SUV made my pulse quicken for a second before the light bars on the roof registered. The sheriff's department had both sedans and SUVs. The driver got out, and I recognized the easy roll of Lieutenant Forrester's walk.

I wrapped the blanket tight around myself and sat back down, wishing he'd just disappear. Tears started seeping out of my eyes and sliding down my face against my will once more. Talking to Deputy Carraher, I'd just ignored the steady drip. Now I desperately wished there was some way to hide my emotional wreckage from the lieutenant.

He hesitated beside me, then dropped my purse on the seat of the chair next to me and walked across the room to where a coffee pot sat, hospitality for clients during office hours, empty and dry now. After rummaging around on the shelves above and in the cupboards below, he disappeared through the door to the back and returned with the pot full of water. Minutes later the rich scent of brewing coffee took some of the coldness out of the room.

By that time I'd blotted my face with the blanket and was dealing with my runny nose by sniffling. The lieutenant returned to the chairs, handed me my purse and sat down beside me.

"You dropped this in the road when you left," he said. "Didn't I see one of those little packets of tissues in there?"

Damn him. What had he been doing going through my purse? He looked so clean and in control. I wanted to smear some of the dirt and blood on my hands down the front of his shirt. Instead I dug the tissues out of my purse and blew.

"How is she?" he asked when I was done.

"I don't know yet. They're operating. At least no one's come out to say she's died."

"That's something." He paused, then went on. "How bad are you hurt?"

"I'm all right," I said. "Bruised and sore and starting to stiffen up, but nothing's broken."

"Looks to me as if that right arm is bothering you."

"Everything is bothering me. The car rolled." I stopped cradling my right arm with my left. In truth the pain in my right shoulder and arm was reaching levels that had me thinking evil thoughts about what kind of pain killers Dr. Hunsaker might have in his drug cabinet and how well secured that cabinet might be.

"Want to tell me about it?" the lieutenant asked.

"No."

He accepted that and settled back in his chair. When the coffee was done, he got up, went and filled two of the styrofoam cups piled there ready. I watched him mix two packets of sugar into one cup.

When he returned and sat down, that was the one he handed me. I drink coffee without sugar, but the sweetness spread a warmth inside me that was almost as good as brandy. I took several sips then cradled the hot cup in both hands.

Little by little, his presence stopped feeling like an intrusion. When he got up with his own empty cup and gestured at mine and said, "More?" I nodded.

Then I found my voice, "Yes, please. No sugar this time."

When he sat down with the refilled cups, he said, "Looks like it wasn't Feltzer," then stopped for a swallow of coffee.

If distracting me from my focus on the door was his purpose, he'd succeeded. I looked straight at him for the first time. "How do you know?"

"Deputies paid them a visit. He wasn't too cooperative, but his wife was. They didn't leave the friends' house until close to the time you were hit. The friends confirm that. His wife says he didn't go out again after they got home, and there isn't a mark on his SUV or hers—she has a twin to his. It's dark too, dark green."

"Oh." I drank more coffee, thinking it over. "In one way I'm sorry it isn't him so that it would be all over now. In another way, I'm glad it isn't him. I like Ginny, and it would be awful for her if her husband was a murderer."

"Are you ready to tell me about it now?" he asked.

"I already told Deputy Carraher everything."

"Tell me too. It will help pass the time."

I glanced at the unmoving door to the back of the clinic, decided he was right, and began to talk.

"But I never saw him," I finished. "I can't even identify the car. It was big and long, one of the bigger SUVs, I think, and it was dark colored, but that's all I can say."

"A Humvee?"

I thought about that. "No, different windows, bigger. Not a bigger SUV, bigger windows."

"Chevy Suburban?"

"Like that, but I don't know that it was a Chevy."

"So he pushed you off the road, then he stopped to see how well he'd done. I bet he never even considered an airbag in an older toy car like that."

"It wasn't a toy car! It was only six years old, and it was all-wheel drive! The new ones have smaller windows and are all scrunched up, so I can't even get one like it, and I can't . . . ." I stopped there, unwilling to let the lieutenant know how big a hole replacing the car was going to tear in my finances.

He ignored my outburst. "So he figured you and the dogs were dead or dying, and at his mercy, and he started down the slope. Then the dogs came at him. He shot at the dogs and hit the female, but he missed the male."

"It's my fault," I said. "I all but hung targets around their necks."

"You sure shouldn't have been running all over the place knowing he might take another try at you, but I wouldn't go so far as to say . . . ."

"When the dogs heard him and ran toward him, I yelled their names. It was stupid. I've even been practicing with Sophie. 'Sophie, come.' We've practiced and practiced, and maybe she wouldn't have come back, but I didn't even have the sense to give the command. I just screamed their names, and so I told him they were loose and running at him."

"Look, Ms. Brennan. If you'd sat in the car and waited for help, you and the dogs would be dead now. You're alive. They're alive. Don't be beating yourself up over how you could have done it better. You did well enough."

I shook my head and drank more coffee.

"How many shots did you hear?" he asked. "Six?"

The memory was a dark place in my mind I didn't want to visit. Deputy Carraher hadn't forced me to go back there, but I knew the lieutenant would, and that the information might help.

"More," I said. "First there were two shots, spaced, as if he was aiming. And he was—Sophie's scream was right on top of the sound of the second shot. But then it was wild, just blam, blam, blam. There were at least six shots then, so . . . ."

"So at least eight total, maybe more," he said thoughtfully. "The dogs must have been right on top of him. I wonder if they took him down, or if he was bitten."

I hadn't even thought about that. "One of Sophie's wounds is right in the center of her chest. So she had to be on top of him, or close. Robo was following her, and he's been shot before. That's how he came to Susan—to our rescue—he'd been shot and left for dead. He might know to back off as soon as he heard the first shot, and I think he was following Sophie, not going after anyone himself. Sophie took that night in the parking lot as personally as I did."

The lieutenant asked me several more questions, but I couldn't tell him anything else about the attack. He excused himself and went back out to his car. What would he be passing on that Deputy Carraher hadn't already reported? That the gun was an automatic, I decided, and that my attacker might have been bitten. I hoped he had. I hoped his right arm was missing and he had already bled to death.

When the lieutenant came back in, he picked up where he'd left off. "So he shot one dog and emptied the gun at the other without hitting him, then ran."

"Exactly. With Robo loose and unhurt, he didn't have the nerve to come after me. Even with a gun in his hand, he was afraid to be out there with Robo."

"If you're sure he's afraid of dogs, why are you out and about playing detective with all these dog people? They're the ones who wouldn't be afraid of the dogs."

"How do you know what I'm doing?" I asked suspiciously.

"Jefferson County passed on a complaint to us," he said.

Lee Stander. "So why weren't you on my doorstep forbidding me to talk to anybody?"

"It's a free country. I'd stop you if I could because you're putting yourself in danger, but you aren't interfering with us. Our investigation is going in other directions."

What other directions, I wondered, but the lieutenant was repeating his previous question. "Why are you
so sure dog people are involved?"

"Because I don't believe it's a coincidence that the
killer never bothered me until after I went to the
specialty show and all the gossip that I could identify
him started flying around. He attacked me in the
parking lot of my grocery store a couple days after the
show. And Jack Sheffield was a dog handler. His life
was in the dog world. It makes sense that his killer
comes from that world too. There are people in the dog
world who wouldn't have the experience or know-how
to stay calm in the face of two big dogs charging at
them. You agreed with me the last time we talked."

"Yeah, I did, but parts of Sheffield's life had nothing
to do with dogs. The boyfriend, for instance. So it's
also possible that someone outside the dog world
found out about you. Dog people have to talk to
regular people sometimes. So word got around, and
then you'd have someone whose interest in you was
triggered by the gossip at the show, and he'd be a
regular person who's scared spitless by the dogs. You
have to stop driving all over like this and start protecting yourself."

"How? I can't just abandon everything and go into
hiding. I've already got the friend who backs me up
with my clients taking all my calls. I can't stop my
whole life in its tracks."

"Yes, you can, and if that's what it takes to stay
alive, you should. I'll talk to the sheriff and see what
we can do, but you'll have to cooperate."

"You were right when you told me he'd switch to a
gun and then the dogs couldn't stop him," I admitted,

"and I know you're right about this, but it's so hard to just let him win. Especially after this. If I could get my sights on him, I'd . . . ."

My voice tapered off as the reality of what I was saying and who I was saying it to hit me. So did the fact that when I'd looked in my purse for the tissues, my cell phone was there, but not the gun, which explained why the lieutenant had been in my purse. He'd confiscated the pistol.

Of course, he knew exactly what I was thinking about. "Speaking of your sights, Ms. Brennan, do you have a carry permit for that nice little .38?"

"Not yet. In case you haven't noticed since this all started I haven't had time to take the class that's required. I suppose I'm in trouble over that."

"It did occur to me that you'd be safe in a jail cell. But your friend Owen Turner would be getting you out so fast it wouldn't do much good. It would be legal in your car—if it was unloaded and secured properly."

A fat lot of good it would do me unloaded. Then again it hadn't helped tonight fully loaded. The details of what was going to happen to me over carrying the gun without the permit didn't seem to matter that much either, so I changed the subject.

"You never investigated any of Jack's clients or other handlers or anyone like that at all, did you?" I asked.

"We talked to some of them. That lawsuit he was involved in seemed a good source of motive, but then we found more likely suspects in other parts of his life."

"Carl Warmstead? That's part of what I called you about earlier—to ask if you were really sure he was out of town and couldn't have snuck back."

"Warmstead was in New York. It was a business trip, and he had breakfast with half a dozen people out there. Even with the time difference, he couldn't have done it even if he had a private jet at his disposal."

"Oh." I could hear the disappointment in my own voice. "He really seemed the most likely person."

"Spouses, lovers, and family, that's where we look first and hardest," he said.

"What about the trust you told me about?" I said slowly, thinking about it for the first time. "That's got to benefit someone in his family now, right? Does the income go to someone else in the family, or does the principal go to someone?"

A small smile played around the lieutenant's lips. "If you ever apply for a job as an investigator and want a reference, let me know. Of course I'd have to mention you aren't much for rules. You know I can't discuss our investigation with you."

"Fine," I said. "We won't discuss it." I went back to staring at the door. The problem with that was that talking to the lieutenant had distracted me from my fear and made the waiting easier.

So after another mop up with the tissues, I let my curiosity get the better of me. "Okay, let's say someone in Jack's family killed him because they get the trust money. If that person has nothing to do with dogs, what would make him decide I was dangerous all of a sudden?"

After a long enough hesitation to tell me he had no good explanation, the lieutenant admitted just that. "We can't find that any of them know about you. Are you sure you haven't been involved in anything else that threatened someone?"

I looked at him with disbelief. "Oh, sure, after never having anything to do with criminals for my whole life, I see someone minutes after he's killed Jack and then in a totally unrelated coincidence have someone else trying to kill me. Tell me you believe that."

"I don't believe it. That's the problem. The best suspects we have don't seem to have any connection to dogs or to you. The people you want to focus on don't have any motive."

Now it was my turn for a small smile. I focused back on the door. We sat and drank coffee for a while.

The lieutenant shifted in his seat once or twice, sighed and gave in. "Are you telling me you found a motive for killing Sheffield among those dog people you talked to?"

I just nodded slightly and kept staring at the door.

"All right, Ms. Brennan. I suppose if you focused your energies in the right direction you'd find out everything I can tell you anyway."

He got up and refilled our coffee cups a last time, turning off the pot. When I tasted the bitter dregs in my cup, I made a face and put the cup on an empty chair next to me, but he drank without expression.

After a few swallows, he started talking. "Sheffield's grandparents set up the trusts, one for Sheffield and one for each of his two brothers. The parents are wealthy in their own right, divorced, and out of the picture so far as we can tell. But the brothers are interesting. They each had a trust too, and they each had twice as much as Sheffield, and they got their money outright when they turned thirty."

"But you said Jack's trust was income only for his lifetime. Why would his brothers get control of their money at thirty, and why was Jack's trust smaller than theirs? Did they think he was a spendthrift?" Before the lieutenant could answer, the reason why Jack might have been treated differently than his brothers occurred to me. "They did it that way because Jack was a homosexual, didn't they? It was a way to punish him."

"Maybe," said the lieutenant. "The grandparents are gone, so who knows. His brothers don't seem to be grief-stricken. Sheffield's trust ended with his death, and now they get everything. Outright. Divided equally between them."

"But they already got their own," I said. "Do they need Jack's money now? They each get only half of his trust, and his was smaller than theirs to start with. Is it enough for them to murder their brother over?"

"One of them has already run through everything he had. He's close to bankruptcy now. The other is doing better, but he's a spender. At a guess he'll be happier with the extra money than with a live brother he didn't think much of."

"I do see why you like them as suspects. Family feuds, greed, and money. Even so, I did find . . . ."

The door opened.

Dr. Hunsaker looked even paler than before, exhausted and drained. He gave me a reassuring smile that let my heart return from my mouth halfway down my throat, pulled one of the chairs out from the wall, placed it to face me, and sat down.

"That's a very strong and tough girl you have there, Ms. Brennan. She's made it through the surgery. We'll keep her resting as quietly as possible for the next several days. I've done everything I can and it's pretty much up to her now. Very few dogs would have made it this far. She was shot twice. One wound was minor, and the other almost fatal. There are also a lot of other injuries. I presume that those are from the automobile accident."

I stared at the vet, unable to accept what he was saying. A lot of other injuries. In my mind I saw the shadows of the dogs by me in the darkness after we got out of the car. Had Sophie already been injured then?

Beside me, Lieutenant Forrester was explaining to the vet. "She was run off the Jarre Canyon Road, and the car rolled. The dogs were in the back."

"That explains it then," said Dr. Hunsaker. "Sophie has a broken tibia and broken ribs that aren't from the bullet, but a bullet is what almost killed her. It entered her right side, went through a lung and lodged near her heart. Another bullet—which undoubtedly actually hit her first—hit her sternum at an angle, traveled along the bone and stopped in the axillary region."

As he spoke, Dr. Hunsaker demonstrated the path of the bullet, moving his hand from the center of his own breastbone, across his chest to his left armpit, then waited until I nodded my understanding before he went on.

"That wound wouldn't be life-threatening on its own, but the other did a lot of damage, and she lost too much blood. Without the transfusion from your male, she wouldn't have had a chance. I took as much from him as I dared considering his size. Before you leave, I want to give you some supplements you should give him, and he should stay quiet for the next couple of days too."

When Dr. Hunsaker finished speaking, I asked, "Can I see her?"

Lieutenant Forrester spoke over me, "I need those bullets."

The vet stood up, "Of course," he said. To the lieutenant, "I have the bullets," and to me, "You can see her. The anesthetic hasn't worn off, and we'll keep her sedated when it does, so she won't respond to you."

"Would you look at Robo, too?" I asked. "The way they ran off after the accident I never thought of them being hurt, but of course they were. I had a seatbelt and air bag. All they had was the foam rubber pad and rug that was on the floor of the car in the back."

Sitting in one place for so long had let all my abused muscles stiffen so much I didn't object when the lieutenant helped me up. Once on my feet, I could limp and shuffle well enough.

We followed Dr. Hunsaker to his recovery room, where Sophie was lying on the floor on blankets. She looked small and vulnerable, with large shaved areas, rows of stitches, and an i.v. dripping. Her left hind leg was enclosed in a cast.

"The break was clean," said the vet. "It will heal fine with the cast."

"I understand." I got down on the floor beside Sophie and ran my hands over her, needing to feel the warmth of her, needing the reassurance of the steady rhythm of her breathing.

Robo had some bruising and swelling, but the vet didn't find anything he considered worrisome.

"He outweighs her by quite a lot. When they were thrown around, she would have gotten the worst of it.

If the swelling doesn't go down, or if he gets more stiff instead of less in the next day or so, take him to your regular vet. Don't give him aspirin. Just in case there's any internal bleeding, we don't want to make it worse. I'll give you a safe analgesic along with the supplements. If I'd realized he was hurt too, I might not have taken blood from him, but then—well, it's just as well we did things the way we did."

I wanted to stay with Sophie. Lieutenant Forrester wanted to take me to a hospital. We argued of course. He reminded me of Millie and Bella, waiting at home, and used them to get me to agree to leave. I reminded him of Millie and Bella, waiting at home, and used them to refuse to go to a hospital and insist if he wanted to help, he take me straight home.

So in the end I had to kiss Sophie goodbye and promise her that I'd be back the next day to see her and that she was going to be fine and no one was ever going to hurt her again.

After I shut Robo in the back of the lieutenant's car and settled myself in the passenger's seat, I turned my face to the window so the he couldn't see the tears that were sliding down my face again.

20

THE CAR WAS WARM AND the seat so much softer than the plastic waiting room chair at the vet's . . . . I fell asleep with the crackle of the police radio as background and didn't wake until the car stopped and the lieutenant shut off the engine.

We weren't in my driveway. Bright lights illuminated every corner of the parking area and made reading the signs on the high porte-cochère of the building in front of us easy. Emergency. Parker Adventist Hospital. Lieutenant Forrester didn't even have the grace to look apologetic.

"Come on, Ms. Brennan, let's get you checked out."

"You *liar*. You said you'd take me home."

"I will take you home. Right now I'm serving and protecting. The sooner you get in there and let the doctors make sure you're okay, the sooner you get home."

I didn't move, too tired and sore to be as angry as I wanted to be, but angry enough to start marshaling my resources for a fight.

The lieutenant got out, walked around and opened the door on my side. "If you want me to arrest you for carrying a concealed weapon without a permit, I'll do it. Then you're an injured prisoner in custody, and you get treated that way. It will cause a whole lot more problems in the end, but you're going in there, and you're seeing a doctor."

Knowing he was right didn't make the prospect of waiting for hours for a doctor to see me any more attractive. Hours when I could be home, washing off the dirt and blood, soaking away some of the stiffness in a tub of hot water. I said nothing when the lieutenant told the receptionist that I'd been in an automobile accident and needed to see a doctor. She handed me a clipboard with several forms attached.

With a sigh, I retreated to one of the chairs in the waiting area and began to print my life's history on the forms, surprised at how shaky my letters looked and how hard it was to make my hand form them.

The lieutenant sat next to me. "I'll do that for you if you want," he offered.

His pale blue gaze showed concern and maybe something more that I wasn't in any condition to face. I looked down at the sheaf of forms again, thinking about what some of the questions asked a woman about her medical history.

"No, thank you," I said. "Why don't you go home. This is going to take the rest of the night. I'll call a friend to come get me when they're done with me."

"You already have a friend here to take you home when you're done," he said, still looking at me in that disconcerting way. Then he straightened in the chair and looked away. "Anyway, your dog is in my car."

How could I have forgotten Robo? "You could drop him off at my house," I said tentatively. "And maybe you'd be willing to let Millie out while you're there?"

"This won't take as long as you think," he said. "There's no long line like in the city hospitals. Back at the vet's you were about to tell me what you found out about those dog people that gives any of them a motive to kill Sheffield. By the time you tell me all about it, the doctor will be ready to see you, then I'll take you home. I said I would."

"You said you would take me *straight* home."

"So we'll call it even for the way you hid the dog the day Sheffield was killed. Come on, we had a deal."

Oh, well, talking would keep me awake, and if I fell asleep in the chair I *would* need surgery soon. I finished the forms, handed them in, and began telling the lieutenant what I'd found out about Jack Sheffield.

He listened intently, asking only a few questions as I told him about the people I'd seen and what Susan had told me about their dog-show-centric world. When I was finished he asked me who else I planned to talk to.

"I'd like to talk to Jack's assistant, but she's moved and so far no one seems to have her new address or phone number. And then there's the people who own the kennel Jack moved his dogs to after the blow up with Standers over Maida, and there's a woman named MaryAnn Balma who testified in the lawsuit that Jack was at her house the night Maida was hit by the car."

A woman in scrubs walked into the room looking as if she was ready for another customer. I stopped talking until she settled on a young couple on the other side of the room.

Glancing at the lieutenant, I finished telling him about MaryAnn Balma. "So she committed perjury for Jack, and I'd like to know why. What could he have had on her? He showed her dogs for her, but she's not a competitor like Feltzer. She raises a litter every year or two, keeps a puppy for herself, and has—had—Jack show it to its championship. That's all, and she never really turned her dogs over to Jack. Her dogs live at home. She'd bring a dog to a show and give the leash to Jack right there by the ring. After the show, her dog would go home with her that day, win or lose."

"You know that for a fact?" he asked.

"I know it from Susan, and she's very much one of those people. Even when she doesn't have a dog of her own to show, she often goes to shows just to watch. There are always dogs there related to her own."

"Who shows Susan's dogs?" asked the lieutenant.

"She shows her own. She liked Jack, maybe more than anyone else I've talked to, and maybe that's why. He never handled a dog for her and never would have, so there was no reason for him to try to get information to use against her. He'd never have been able to psyche her out the way he did some of the newer owner-handlers. Susan was probably already showing her own dogs when Jack was in kindergarten."

The lieutenant shook his head. "The fact he was putting that kind of pressure on people means we'd better look at some of them again, but you haven't really come up with anyone he was a real threat to at the time of his death. We already looked hard at Warmstead. Among other things, they owned a lot of property jointly, including the house, and now Warmstead owns it all. But unless he hired someone, he's out of it, and we can't find any evidence that this was a hired killing. In fact, the way it was done mitigates against a professional."

"You mean a professional killer doesn't use a knife?" I asked.

"Not usually," he said. "And the way Sheffield was torn up, it looked personal—a lot of rage there. A gun is surer, easier, and a lot less messy. If this isn't personal I'll be surprised."

That left Joyce Richerson out. She would have had to hire a professional. Unless, of course, she asked her husband to kill Jack for her. Were there marriages where one morning as the wife buttered her toast, she said, "Oh, by the way, dear, there's someone I'd like you to kill for me. Would you mind?"

And what exactly could Jack Sheffield or anyone else try to use for leverage on a woman like Joyce Richerson, who not only didn't care what anyone thought of her marriage to a man young enough to be her son, or even with a bit of precocity, her grandson, but took pleasure from the stunned reaction of people like me? That thought boggled my mind.

As the lieutenant and I sat there, trying to make motive mountains out of motive molehills, the woman in scrubs returned, and this time she was looking for me.

I forced my board-like muscles to move once again. The knowledge that Lieutenant Forrester was watching enabled me to get to my feet without groaning, but no force of will would let me walk away for the mandatory poking and prodding without a limp.

When the doctors were finally done with me, I limped back out to the waiting area, where Lieutenant Forrester sat reading what was now yesterday's newspaper. When he looked up, I didn't wait for him to gloat.

"Not a word. Not one damn word, or you'll be arresting me for assault right here, and you'll be the assaultee."

His lips twitched, but he controlled the rest of his face. "Broken collarbone?"

"Those of us in the know refer to it as the clavicle," I said sarcastically. "The radiologist claims he sees a crack on the x-rays. It hardly feels worse than any of the rest of me, and since you're still here, will you *please* keep your word now and take me home?"

The lieutenant escorted me back to the car. The night was chilly, clear, and quiet, and our footsteps echoed as we walked across the pavement.

Stretched out flat on the back seat, Robo barely raised his head when I got in the car. As the lieutenant shut the door after me and walked around to the driver's side, I sympathized with Robo.

"You look like you feel about the way I do right now, boyo. We'll be home soon if our driver doesn't have any more surprises planned."

The doctor's examination had turned my dull aches and stiffness into fierce pain, and what was going on in my right arm and shoulder was now close to unbearable. The bright blue vinyl sling seemed to be making things worse not better. I couldn't wait to get home and take the wretched thing off. Not only was the pain worse, I felt far too vulnerable.

"Did they give you anything for pain?" the lieutenant asked.

"A prescription," I said. "Don't even think about stopping somewhere to fill it—I'm not taking anything that might drug me. There's Advil at home."

He didn't argue. When he pulled into my driveway, he shut off the engine. "I'm going to help you inside, and then I'm going to look through the house and look around outside. You can call me names, you can call the sheriff's office and complain, but that's what I'm going to do."

Perceptive as he was, he must know how relieved I was not to have to go into the house alone. "Thank you," I whispered, avoiding looking at him.

Millie was so hysterically glad to see me and get out of her crate, I thought she wouldn't make it out to the yard without her bladder giving way after all her long hours of waiting, but make it she did.

Robo followed her without any noticeable stiffness, but when I fed the dogs, for the first time since I'd had him, he didn't finish his food. I felt him over gently. None of the swelling Dr. Hunsaker had pointed out seemed worse. His gums didn't look pale, but would I be able to detect that in the artificial light of the kitchen?

The lieutenant had finished looking through the house while I was feeding the dogs and Bella, then gone outside to check the yard. As he came back in, he said, "Everything looks okay. I checked all the locks, so if you lock up behind me now, you don't have to check again. Promise me you'll get a few hours sleep and then move in with friends for a while."

"I promise. And thank you for bringing me home and for checking. I was going to ask you to do that and wasn't sure how after being such a pain about everything. I'm sorry."

"You're entitled. Most people would be raving or babbling after the kind of day you've had. And here, take this upstairs with you when you go to bed." He laid my pistol on the kitchen table.

"I thought you confiscated that," I said.

"Why would I do that? It's yours, and it's legal for you to have it in your house, which is where it is. Good night, Ms. Brennan."

"Good night, lieutenant." I followed him to the front door and locked it behind him.

The couch in the living room beckoned. Crashing there would be so easy. What drove me up the stairs was the bottle of Advil in the medicine cabinet and the thought of standing under the hot shower, not just to wash the blood and dirt off, but to massage my sore muscles.

Half an hour later I bundled myself in a terry cloth robe and reluctantly put the sling back on. Taking it off to shower had proved the doctor's point beyond my stubborn desire to deny the need for it. Still miserable, and tired to the point of nausea, but feeling a little better for being clean, I remembered the gun sitting on the kitchen table. I didn't want to go down the stairs for it, much less struggle back up. Maybe I'd just go down and sleep on the couch after all.

In the kitchen I picked up the gun and started for the couch when the sound of an engine coughing to life in the driveway made my heart jump. Clutching the gun, I limped to the front window as fast possible and peered out.

As my eyes adjusted to the darkness, I made out the distinctive shape of Lieutenant Forrester's SUV. Why was he still there? Why had he been sitting there with the engine off? And why was he there now with the engine running? The answer I came up with made me unlock the door, yank it open, march out to the car, and rap on the window.

When the window was down enough that I could see his face, I said, "How long are you planning on sitting out here, polluting the air so that you can run the heater?"

He turned the car off. "If the noise is too loud in the house, I won't start it again. It's not that cold."

That wasn't my point at all, and he knew it. "I suppose you think this is serving and protecting."

"Yes, Ms. Brennan, it is."

"How much protection are you going to be if he breaks in the back of the house?"

"I figure the dogs will bark, or I'll hear you shoot him."

"Well, if you want to protect me, I think you ought to do it right and come inside. You can sleep on the couch."

"I don't think that's such a good idea."

"Why? Are you married?" He wore no ring, not that I'd noticed.

"My wife died five years ago."

"I'm sorry." After a pause to consider my words, I went on. "In that case, there's no reason for you to sit out here. Come inside, it's warm, and you can protect better."

"No, ma'am. The department wouldn't approve any more than a wife. I'm all right here, and I have faith you and the dogs can hold him off long enough for me to get in the house."

"You can tell the department you were interviewing me. I'll leave the kitchen light on if it will help."

"Are you asking me to lie to the Sheriff?"

"You don't seem to be a stranger to the practice of deceit."

"Touché," he said, smiling slightly, "but I'll stay here."

"Fine," I said. As I turned away, he turned the engine over long enough to raise the window, then turned it off again immediately. But I didn't go back to the house. I walked around the front of the car, opened the passenger's door, and eased myself into the seat. "I'll just stay here with you. Start it up again and turn the heater on high, please."

He didn't reach for the key. We sat in silence for a moment or two. "Scared?" he said.

"Yes!"

"All right." He sighed in resignation. "The couch."

"Thank you." I knew my voice trembled with relief, but I didn't care.

He protested when I pulled the couch out into a bed, but Millie was delighted. She hopped right up and curled up in a small ball in a corner.

"I'll take her upstairs with me."

"Leave her. At least she's not a bed hog."

I didn't tell him that Millie's technique was to start in a humble curl and slowly stretch until most of the bed was hers.

21

WHEN I WOKE MUCH LATER that day, bright sunlight streaming through the bedroom windows told me the morning was half gone. Bella was a small, comforting warmth at my left side; pretty much every other part of me hurt. I lay there, quietly assessing the damage, unwilling to move and intensify every pain. Then I thought of my overnight guest and of Sophie, gave the cat a warning pat, forced myself up, and headed for the bathroom and more pills.

Halfway down the stairs breakfast scents of coffee, eggs, and toast reminded me how long it had been since I'd eaten. Lieutenant Forrester was sitting at the kitchen table with the morning paper spread out in front of him. He looked slightly more rumpled than usual but still far too neat for someone who'd slept on a pull-out couch bed. At least beard shadow spoiled any look of regulation orderliness.

Millie sat on one side of him, a ladylike puddle of drool at her feet. Robo sat on his other side, not too close, but close enough not to miss out if the lieutenant felt like sharing.

"Good morning." In my own ears, my voice sounded ordinary, giving away nothing of the tremendous relief the sight of him brought.

"Good morning." He gave me an assessing look.

To avoid his gaze and any questions about how I felt, I picked up my purse and started digging through it. "Didn't Dr. Hunsaker give me a card with his number on it last night?"

"Here." The card he held out was one of his own with a number scrawled on the back. "I called about eight, and they said she's stable. Sit down and have a cup of coffee, why don't you, and then you can call and get details while I fix you some breakfast."

"I need to feed the dogs—if they're not full of toast."

"I gave them some of the kibble you fed them last night a while ago," he said, ignoring the subject of toast.

"Did Robo eat his? What about the supplements Dr. Hunsaker gave him?"

"I mixed the powder in his food, and he ate it and licked the dish. He motored around the yard pretty well too. How about you?"

"I'll be okay as soon as the Advil kicks in."

Bella was the only one who hadn't sold out. She wound around my legs while I spooned Fancy Feast into her dish.

Dr. Hunsaker's office confirmed that Sophie was stable, but that was all they really could tell me. If she didn't take a turn for the worse, if infection didn't set in—if, if, if—she might live to come home. I listened to my voice mail messages, and of course heard from Susan several times, eager as always, to know what I'd learned.

"You ought to call her," said the lieutenant as he refilled my coffee cup. "The phone rang every ten or fifteen minutes starting at seven. She's worried."

There was no phone in my bedroom by design, but the kitchen phone must have been like an alarm clock for the lieutenant. Then again, how did he know the caller was "she" and why hadn't the phone rung since I'd been up?

"You answered the phone and talked to Susan."

"She'll be here to pick you up about two. You can stay with her until you figure out what to do."

I didn't even want to contemplate the flak I was going to get from Susan over this. "Thank you so much for arranging my life for me, lieutenant. Aren't you supposed to be at your office?"

He put a small bowl with cut up pieces of an orange and a plate with buttered toast and scrambled eggs in front of me and topped up my coffee cup. "You're welcome, Ms. Brennan. And technically I'm off today, so where I have breakfast is up to me."

"Don't you think since you've slept with my dog, you could drop that Ms. Brennan business and call me Dianne?" I said, taking a bite of toast.

"The department frowns on getting too friendly with persons involved in active investigations."

"You can't keep being so formal when you've been my house guest—sort of. How about 'Dianne' when no one else with a badge is around?"

"All right, Dianne. And my first name is Brian, not lieutenant."

"It's a deal," I said. "So what does being 'technically' off today mean?

"I usually go in anyway, and I will today—later. After you're out of here. Susan says you need to bring crates for the dogs. Those metal cages over there are what you call crates, right? How do they fit in a car?"

"They fold flat like suitcases."

"Good. I'll help you get that stuff ready to go." He sat back down and folded up the paper. "It won't be too long, you know. He's escalating and that means he's going to do something stupid and we'll catch him. We just need to keep you safe until then."

Looking into his serious face, I was again struck by his eyes—pale blue and a very natural pale blue at that. "Have you thought about contact lenses?" I told him what I'd found on the Internet about colored lenses. "Could you find out if any of the people who dealt with Jack wear contacts?"

"We can ask and hope they'll feel obliged to answer, but we can't get medical information without a warrant and sometimes not even then any more."

I'd been thinking of the contacts as cosmetic, part of a disguise, but he was right, of course.

The thin ring of a cell phone sounded, and as Brian answered, I took my dishes to the washer and brought the coffee pot back to refill both our cups. The caller wanted Brian to do something, and he was resisting.

"I'm off today, and I'm coming in later anyway. If you need it now, get McNabb to do it," he said.

The scowl on his face deepened. What he was hearing wasn't making him happy. I found a pen in my purse and wrote in the margin of the newspaper. "Go. S here soon. Will stay locked in."

Brian turned his frown on me, but said what the other end of the phone wanted to hear. "All right. I'll be there in an hour or so . . . . No, I'm not home. None of your business . . . ."

As he folded the cell phone away, I couldn't help but say, "Is that any way to talk to a superior officer?"

"He's not superior. He's a pain in the . . . never mind. You'll leave with Susan and stay with her until we can come up with something better, right? You're giving me your word."

"Yes," I said, meaning it. "Last night was just too much. For a while there I felt like . . . ." I stopped and swallowed hard, unwilling to admit how close I'd come to falling to pieces. "I can't take any more battering right now, but staying with Susan isn't a real solution. I'm not going to bring this kind of violence on her and her family."

"Today and tonight. Then we'll figure something else out," he said.

"Figure out a way to lure him into a trap. Maybe you could use a mannequin as bait. Paint it black and blue and no one will know it isn't me."

"If there aren't any smart remarks coming out of its mouth, no one will be fooled," he said, heading for the front door.

I stood in the doorway and watched him walk toward the car. As he opened the door, I called out. "Thank you. For everything. Thank you."

When he was gone I went inside and locked the front door, then checked every door and window twice.

The problem was Susan didn't show up by two. In fact she didn't even call to explain her lateness until almost three, sounding breathless and harried.

"I'm so sorry. I was almost out the driveway when Wesley drove up. I'm sorry to make you wait, but it's a good thing he caught me. That ex-wife of his dumped the children on him without warning again this morning, and he has an important appointment this afternoon."

Since Wesley's ex-wife was employed, and Wesley never was, her expectation that he would help out with his own children when her childcare arrangements failed seemed reasonable to me. Not only that, Wesley had never had an important appointment in his life. Even so, the inescapable fact was that today I was as guilty of using Susan as he was, and he was her son.

"I'll call for a rental car. Don't worry about it."

"No, no. I'm on my way now. I just have to get the children strapped in, and we'll be on the road. The lieutenant told me what happened and that you shouldn't drive. I'll be there in a little while and you can tell me all about it then."

Either Brian hadn't told Susan very much, or the children really had her flustered. It wasn't like her not to even ask about Sophie. I sat down to wait. Much more than a little while later, I heard a car in the drive and hurried to the door, then stared, wanting to disbelieve my eyes.

Susan wasn't in the familiar maroon van she always drove, but in an ancient Chevy sedan trailing a haze of bluish exhaust behind it. I started out the door and met her halfway up the walk. She was as appalled at the sight of me as I was at the sight of the car. Her grandchildren were strapped in child seats in the back. If there was room in that car for two big dogs, crates, Bella in her carrier, and me, I didn't see it.

"Where's your van?" I asked, realizing the answer even as the words left my mouth.

"I *told* you on the phone. Wesley needed it for his appointment. We'll have to make two trips, but don't worry, it won't take long. The lieutenant told me you weren't hurt, but you are. Is your arm broken? What *happened*?"

Maybe she had told me about the car on the phone. Wesley's name often made me stop listening to the details of his current tale of woe. Right then Susan's granddaughter spoke up. "Grandma, I need to go potty. Right now."

"Me too," echoed the little boy. "And I'm *hungry*."

"Bring them in," I said, getting over my initial frustration with the whole situation. "You're right. Once we get started it won't take long to get us all tucked in at your place."

"Your lieutenant seemed to think it was very important you leave here as soon as possible," said Susan, looking doubtful. Then she gave me a thoughtful look more like herself. "And what did you say he was doing here so early in the morning?"

"I didn't. Bring the kids in and we'll feed them, and I'll tell you all about it."

Neither Millie nor Robo was child approved by Susan's standards. They went out in the yard, and the children came in with us. As I made peanut butter and jelly sandwiches and poured milk, I told Susan what had happened to me on the way home from Feltzers' the night before.

"I can't believe you talked to Brian Forrester and he didn't tell you any of this," I said.

"Brian? Are you on a first name basis with him now? Did you find out if he's married?"

"Susan."

"He told me you were attacked again and you were in a car accident, but he said you weren't badly hurt. He said he talked you into staying with me until they catch the killer. He didn't mention your arm, or Sophie. What was he doing here . . . ."

"He came to the accident scene and then to the vet clinic, and he brought me home. He was serving and protecting. His words. We didn't get back here until the middle of the night, and he was going to sit out in his car in front of the house till morning. I talked him into spending the night on the couch."

"Is he married?"

"Susan."

"It never hurts to ask. Is he attractive?"

Was he? Sort of. Probably. "Not really," I said to Susan. Then I started to tell her about my visits with Joyce Richerson and Myron Feltzer to distract her. I never got further than my first mention of how barren and dogless Joyce Richerson's house was.

"It was just a day when they were doing heavy cleaning or something then," said Susan with assurance. "Joyce always has several dogs in the house. Her older dogs are house dogs, and she rotates the others so they all get house time."

"There was no sign of anything special going on. The house was absolutely sterile. No dog dishes, no dog beds, not a single dog hair. And the puppies were out in the kennel."

"I don't believe it." Susan said almost angrily. Then more softly, "I don't want to believe it. I sent people to her who were looking for a puppy when that last litter was born. I'd *never* send anyone to look at a litter that was kennel-raised."

She pulled out her cell phone and started scrolling through her phonebook entries.

"What are you doing?" I asked.

"Calling Cassie Rayborne. She's Joyce's best friend and she'll know the truth of what's going on."

Which was to say Susan didn't believe me. I got busy putting the sandwich stuff away to keep from saying anything.

The children had finished their sandwiches and were starting to whine. I hobbled upstairs as fast as I could, got paper out of my printer and brought it down with pens and pencils of every color I could find.

They settled back down, covering the paper with scribbles and crumbs. The look on Susan's face told me she wasn't happy with the way her conversation was going.

As soon as Susan snapped her phone shut, I said, "I'm right, aren't I?"

"Heaven help us, yes, you are," said Susan unhappily. "It's the husband. He can't stand anything less than antiseptic cleanliness. And Joyce was so besotted she banished the dogs to the kennel before he even set foot in the house. Cassie says she thinks the real reason is he doesn't like dogs."

"How can that be?" I asked. "She met him in Germany when she was looking at dogs. How could she meet someone who doesn't like dogs at a German kennel?"

"She didn't meet him at a breeder's," Susan said. "She doesn't spend all her time in Europe visiting breeders, you know. I think she met him at a ski resort. I remember that for a long time Cassie called him Joyce's ski bunny."

"So Erich could be who I'm looking for," I said, feeling my pulse quicken.

"Cassie said he didn't like dogs, not that he's afraid of them. A ski bunny gigolo can't be a murderer."

Her primly disapproving tone made me smile. After considering a moment, Susan continued, her expression telling me she had learned something else that upset her.

"Cassie also says he hardly ever comes to shows with Joyce, but he was at the big show at the end of July, and a group of them went to dinner together."

The end of July was less than two weeks before Jack was killed. Susan was toying with a colored pencil, looking unwilling to continue.

"Come on, Susan," I urged. "This is important."

"It's gossip. Cassie's more than a little jealous of Joyce, and she was all too pleased to tell tales. Lord spare us from friends like that." She made a face, got to her feet and ruffled the children's hair. "You stay here and color while Ms. Brennan and I put her things in the car." She picked up one of the crates I had folded and waiting.

"You leave the other crate for me and bring something lighter. We'll load the car and then put the children in."

Cassie's gossip must be the kind that couldn't be retold with young ears listening. I hoisted the other crate with my good arm and followed her outside.

Susan said nothing more about Erich until after we'd managed to maneuver the crates most of the way into the trunk of Wesley's car.

"Heaven knows how much of this is true, so take it with a grain of salt," she warned me. "I wouldn't even repeat it except . . . ." She paused and rummaged in the trunk for a minute, coming up with a length of dirty but strong cord.

"Except this will prove to you Erich isn't the kind who would murder anyone, much less Jack. Here hold this closed."

Obediently I held the trunk lid down over the crates while Susan tied it closed.

"There," she said, brushing her hands off. "That will hold fine from here to my place. Anyway, as I said before, according to Cassie, Erich hardly ever goes to shows, which I guess is true, since I only met him once. And she says, whenever he does go, Joyce hardly ever lets him out of her sight."

She headed back to the house and picked up my laptop computer and the small suitcase I'd packed, and took them to the car while I rounded up Bella and got her into her carrier. By the time I managed to get all my struggling cat's legs through the door to her carrier at the same time, Susan was back. She carried Bella's food and other supplies to the car, and I followed with my unhappy cat.

Back outside, Susan continued with Cassie's story. "So at this dinner, Joyce got sick and went back to the motel but Erich stayed. Stayed, had a few drinks, and got pretty sociable."

Myron Feltzer had mentioned something like this I remembered. Rather than say anything that would distract Susan, I waited until I had Bella's carrier wedged securely in place on the floor of the front side passenger's seat.

When I had finished and Susan was still silent, I prompted, "So what did Erich say?"

Susan was fussing over putting the cat food, cat sand and litter box on the floor of the back seat, obviously reluctant to go on.

"It wasn't anything he said, it was what he did."

"Okay, so what did he *do*?"

"Jack was there too. He got friendly with Jack. Very friendly with Jack. What she was implying . . . ." Susan stopped, unable to put it into words.

I had no such inhibitions. "Cassie thinks Erich slept with Jack."

"It's just gossip. Malicious gossip. But it certainly shows that Erich didn't hate Jack or anything."

I said nothing, remembering something Brian had said about looking first and hardest at spouses and lovers. Gossip or no, finding out more about Erich Kohler suddenly seemed important.

"For Heavens sake, Dianne, why is something that sordid making you smile? Susan asked.

"Because what you're saying doesn't mean Erich didn't kill Jack. It means he has the best motive I've found so far. Just what I saw of Joyce the other day tells me she'd divorce him in a second if she knew he was fooling around. Divorce him and make sure he had to go back to wherever he came from. And that means Harry Jameson *didn't* have the best motive, and I'm glad because I like Harry."

"And you're going to tell your lieutenant this tabloid-like gossip, aren't you? Susan said, unhappiness all over her face.

"I'm sorry, Susan, but yes, I am. It's not evidence but maybe if he looks, he can find evidence. Just think about it. What if Erich wanted the dogs out of the house not because he doesn't like them but because he's afraid of them. Most of us don't like what we're afraid of."

"Anyone would be afraid of the dogs in the situations you were in," Susan said.

I didn't argue. There was no use trying to convince her now. Doubly determined to get Susan on the road as fast as possible, I hustled her back to the house to get the children.

Susan wanted me to leave Millie and Robo and take the few things that fit in the car back to her house in the first trip.

"You know that's not a good idea," I told her. "Whoever the killer is, I'm not leaving the dogs alone here for him to find if he comes looking for me. Millie can go with you on this trip and Robo and I will go with you on the next trip."

My words started Susan on a new worry. "You know you hear all the time about criminals who vandalize people's homes. It would be a shame if when he found you were gone he got in and smashed your mother's dishes."

"He's not a vandal, he's a murderer," I pointed out, giving each of the children a cookie and starting them out the door.

Susan wasn't giving up on saving the kind of things that mattered to her. "He's a criminal, and if he's frustrated because he can't get to you, who knows what he'll do. We'll have room on the second trip. Wesley will probably be waiting at the house with my van when I get back."

No, he wouldn't. He'd show up late with a few beers under his belt. In fact he'd be so late that the children's mother would have come by to get them, aggravated by the need and ready to take it out on Susan.

While Susan was strapping the children into their safety seats, I went to get Millie. She was going to have to ride in the front passenger's seat tied in place with a harness.

I led Millie out to the car and waited for Susan to finish. Millie dove for a piece of cookie one of the children had dropped then started casting around looking for more. Casting around. The same way Sophie had cast around in the driveway at Joyce Richerson's, except that when Susan was ready and I chirped to Millie to get in the car, she gave up her scenting easily and hopped into the car without a backward glance.

I remembered Sophie's intensity, how unwilling she had been to come away from the scent. That led to a reassessment of the way she had tried to pull me into the trees near my car in Feltzers' driveway. My own words came back to me as I remembered telling Brian Forrester that Sophie had taken the attack on me personally.

I stood frozen as certainty hit me. Erich Kohler had killed Jack Sheffield. Sophie had known since the night in the King Sooper's parking lot, and she had tried her best to tell me Erich was the one.

As if from a distance, I heard Susan talking to me. "You really need to come this trip. You can squeeze in the back with the children. I'll ask Wesley to spend the night after he takes the children back to their mother. With both Wesley and his father home tonight, you'll be perfectly safe."

Her words brought me out of my reverie. To be killed by Erich Kohler or saved by Wesley McKinnough? The thought of having to make such a choice started me laughing, and Susan looked at me with narrowed eyes.

"I'm sorry," I said, forcing myself to stop. "My nerves are getting the best of me." I walked over to her and gave her a quick one-armed hug. "I know this is a pain for you, and I know we'll be safe. Thanks for doing this."

Susan's eyes widened with surprise. Neither one of us was usually demonstrative.

"Please come with us. We'll be back for Robo in no time at all."

For once I got to use her own words against her. "Susan, you're worried about a killer smashing dishes. He doesn't have to get close to Robo now that he's using a gun. I'm not leaving him alone here."

"And how are you going to keep yourself safe until I get back for you?"

"I'll lock myself in, and I'll keep the gun in my hand the whole time you're gone."

She argued a bit longer, but her heart wasn't in it. In the end, she started off in a cloud of blue smoke. Watching her go, I thought that staying home alone with Robo was bound to be safer than riding with her in Wesley's rattletrap.

Back in the house, safely locked in, I called the sheriff's office and asked for Lieutenant Forrester. A bored female voice informed me he wouldn't be available until the next day.

"I know it's his day off," I said, "but someone from the department called him this morning and got him to do something. I have to talk to him."

"Do you want to leave a message?" said the voice.

"Yes! Have him call Dianne Brennan. It's important."

I sat there, fiddling with the papers the children had scribbled on, going over it all in my mind. Could I convince Brian I was right? Could I make him see how it all fit? And if I could convince him, could he find evidence to justify an arrest?

Deputy Carraher had said if only dogs could talk. In her own way, Sophie had talked, but I hadn't listened, and she was the one almost fatally hurt.

Thinking of her, I called Dr. Hunsaker's office again. Sophie was hanging on, no change. I told Hettie I wouldn't be able to visit her today after all. Tomorrow, I told her, hoping I could keep that promise.

Too restless to sit, I thought of Susan's worries about my things and decided it wouldn't hurt to put away my favorite pictures. Sitting still just made me stiffer and moving around seemed to make things better. My mother's dishes would have to take their chances. I rarely used them anyway. Once I brought the pictures down from the bedroom, I couldn't decide what to do with them. After considering hiding places for a while, I took them down to the basement and put them behind the clothes dryer. I felt foolish, but it was something to do.

After several trips up and down the stairs with little things, my bruised body had had enough. Calling the sheriff's office again got me nowhere. The same bored voice tried to put me off in the same way. She wouldn't give me the number of Brian's cell phone. This time I wouldn't be put off. Didn't he have voice mail?

He did. I left a long message, hoping it made enough sense he'd at least consider it. When the phone finally rang, I pounced, but it was Susan, not Brian, and she was apologizing again.

"It's just a little thing," she said. "I've heard Wesley talk about it and when the car stalls like this it always starts up after a while. It's vapor lock or something. We'll be going again in nothing flat, and I know he'll have my van back so I can use it for the second trip. I just wanted you to know why I'll be a little longer than we thought."

I reassured her. "Everything's fine here. It was days between the parking lot attack and last night. He won't be back this soon anyway. Maybe I'll go over to one of the neighbors. I'll leave a note on the door if I do."

Putting down the phone, I felt icy fingers of fear racing up my spine. Brian had said the killer was escalating. Erich had undoubtedly interpreted the way I'd gaped at him when Joyce introduced him as some sort of recognition. In my ignorance I'd provoked escalation.

The brightness was already gone from the day and darkness wasn't that far away. The neighbors to the east were friends, but they were out of town. To the south was a couple who hated the dogs. The Wilders had gone out of their way to let me know they were waiting for an excuse to file a complaint. Showing up on their doorstep with Robo didn't seem like a good plan.

Erich would have to break into the house to come after me. He was afraid of the dogs and couldn't be sure I only had one with me. So what was he likely to do? Set up an ambush outside and wait. Sitting at the kitchen table, I watched the start of a glorious orange red sunset, and I imagined Susan coming to get me with her grandchildren strapped in the car.

She didn't answer her cell phone. It was probably sitting in the car while she watched some repairman work under the hood. Anxiety built inside me as I sat there, staring at my watch and pressing redial every three minutes. At last she answered.

"Dianne! The nicest man stopped to help us. The car's running again now. I'll be home in minutes and back for you right away."

I didn't want to argue with her, so I put as much cheer in my voice as I could muster and lied. "You don't have to come back for me after all. Lieutenant Forrester's here, and he's going to drive me over. After we have dinner that is."

"Dinner," said Susan, the matchmaker in her taking the bait as I knew she would. "Oh, that's wonderful. At least I think it is. Did you find out if he's married?"

"No, he's not," I said. "I'll see you later."

Knowing Susan wasn't going to drive into a trap set for me was a relief. Now all I had to do was sit tight and dial 911 at the first sign of trouble.

22

AS THE SUN SET LOWER and lower, I sat in the darkening kitchen with one hand on the cell phone and the other on the gun, straining to hear any slight sound outside. But human ears are limited.

It was Robo who heard him, Robo who rose from his bed in the corner and moved toward the sliding glass door. The same kind of deep growl that Sophie had used the night before rolled up from his belly.

My quiet, indifferent dog turned to an avenging fury before my eyes. His lips curled back so far that even in the shadowy room the white of exposed canines gleamed. His hackles rose until the ridge of erect hair bristled over his shoulders and halfway down his back. He crossed the room with a slow, stalking gait.

The meaning of Robo's incredible behavior finally sliced through my amazement. I dialed 911 and began talking the second the operator answered.

"This is Dianne Brennan." I gave my address. "Someone has tried to kill me twice and he's outside my house right now. His name is Erich Kohler.

Lieutenant Brian Forrester at the sheriff's department knows about it. I need help and I need it as fast as possible."

She wanted details. She wanted to keep me on the line. I dropped the squawking phone and picked up the .38. If Erich was in the backyard with either a handgun or a rifle, Robo and I needed to move to the front of the house away from the glass door.

I hesitated. Some dogs will lash out at anyone who touches them when they are aggressively aroused. If Robo was one of those, trying to get a leash on him and make him come with me might provoke a bite. He was silhouetted against the glass, a clear target for anyone outside.

To hell with it. I grabbed his collar, snapped on the leash, and pulled him toward the living room. He ignored me except to resist my efforts to make him follow. Holding the gun in my right hand, hampered by pain and the sling, I'd never have been able to pull Robo out of the kitchen except that his feet slid on the linoleum and gave him no purchase. Once in the living room, he stopped fighting me, but between nerve-grating growls, he focused intently on something only he could hear.

Was Robo right that the danger was at the back of the house? And if so, what could I do? The house was a trap now, but would running into the night be better? I tried to think of a hiding place away from the house. There was nothing closer than the neighbors, and how could I force Robo to be quiet enough to hide? I was still standing there, dithering, when the glass of the kitchen door exploded inward. Seconds later something clattered across the floor.

The stench of gasoline and whoosh of ignition pre-
ceded the ball of flame that engulfed the kitchen by
less than a heartbeat. Picturing what would have
happened had I still been sitting at the kitchen table
froze me in place until Robo jerked at the leash in my
hand. He paid no attention to the flames roaring in the
kitchen and now focused on the front door as single-
mindedly as he had on the back just minutes ago.

Waiting to see if Robo was right this time would be
suicidal. I yanked on his leash with all my strength,
pulling him to the stairs. He fought me again but this
time terror gave me strength.

I yanked and yelled, and when his feet were on the
stairs, he stopped resisting and bounded ahead. A
front window exploded inward as we reached the top.
I didn't look back.

The windows off the bedroom that served as my
office were over a small overhang on the west side of
the house. Too small to be considered a porch roof, the
overhang merely gave the first floor of the house shade
from the afternoon sun in the summer.

I had no idea how much weight the flimsy structure
would bear, but breaking my neck in a fall had to be
better than burning. I prayed Erich was watching the
front door, thinking if I was alive to try to escape the
flames, the front door or ground floor windows were
the only way out.

The loose-fitting door to the office was a poor barrier
against the rising, swirling smoke. Tendrils curled into
the air from under the door and around the frame. I
pulled the screen off one of the casement windows.

The opening wasn't very wide, and the bar that was
supposed to detach and allow the window to swing

wider stuck fast. Forgetting everything I'd ever learned about gun safety, I used the butt of the pistol to beat at the bar until it fell away.

Somehow I had to find the strength to boost the uncooperative Robo up and force him to squeeze through the opening. I needn't have worried. As soon as I turned from the opening toward Robo, he jumped up, front paws on the sill, back legs scrambling. I got under his back end and lifted, taking a beating from his hind legs as he launched himself out the window.

By the time I got off the floor, he was at the edge of the overhang, crouched on his back end, his front legs dancing at the edge as he worked himself up to jump off the roof.

"No!" I yelled, wasting my breath, knowing he wouldn't listen. "Wait for me."

Finding a way to get out the window myself was more difficult than getting Robo out. The sling hampered every effort. Pulling it off and throwing it on the floor, I dragged my desk chair to the window, coughing now, as more and more smoke filled the room.

After dropping the gun out, I followed it, wiggling through the opening head first. The drop sent waves of pain through my shoulder and collarbone. Fighting a swirling dizziness that I was afraid meant I would pass out, I sat still, sucking in great gulps of clean air, then watched helplessly as Robo stopped playing at it, lowered his front end over the side as far as he could, and let gravity take over.

By the time I crawled to the edge, there was no sign of him. I said a small prayer of gratitude that his trailing leash hadn't caught on the roof and then another asking for help in reaching the ground safely myself. I tried to find a way to hang from the edge and drop down, but was afraid my one good arm wouldn't hold my weight.

The shingles beneath me began to tremble. Cracks and groans of wood splitting and tearing away from the house filled the air. The prospect of falling to the ground amidst old wood, roofing, and nails gave me courage.

I tucked the gun into the waistband of my jeans, lay down along the edge, then eased my weight over the side, hanging by my left arm and leg. When my full weight hit my hand and arm alone, I could only hold on for a split second, then dropped to the ground. This time the jolt did cause me to lose consciousness—for seconds only I hoped. When I came to, the pain in my arm and shoulder had gone from storm to hurricane. I bit my lip and waited for the worst to pass.

I was alone there, huddled against the foundation wall. The blackness around me felt empty. Crawling to my feet finally, I straightened, then took hold of the waistband of my jeans with my right hand to stabilize that shoulder. The acute pain from the fall had subsided a little, and things didn't seem too much worse than they had been. Pulling the gun back out, I moved off into the darkness, wondering how to find Robo without giving myself away.

Shifting orange light from the flames gave familiar shapes a strange and sinister look. At first, the only sounds in the night were from my dying house. I didn't want to hear gunshots as Robo was gunned down the same way Sophie had been, but why was I hearing nothing? Robo had seemed crazed to get to the killer. Was he really hunting Erich in the darkness, or had he just run into the night to get away from the noise and fire?

I moved around the house in the shadows step by step, stopping to listen intently every few feet. In the front yard, the first hint of sound reached me. Another step and another. Was that Robo's growl vibrating through the night? Two more steps, three. The sound was clearer now, rising and falling in menacing waves. One careful step at a time, I moved toward the sound until I could see them in the flickering light.

Erich Kohler lay on his belly in my front garden, his arms thrown out in front of him, his head turned to one side. Robo pinned him there, his front feet on Erich's back, his bared teeth inches from Erich's face. I almost felt sorry for the pretty boy. Almost.

Erich didn't move as I walked closer. The way his eyes were screwed shut told me he wasn't unconscious from injury or fear. He was hiding from the sight of the enraged dog.

"So," I said. "We meet again, Erich. This time you seem to be at a disadvantage."

"Get him off me! Get him off me!"

There was hysteria in his voice. If he panicked and started flailing, Robo might do something that would cause a lot of trouble later on. Erich's state of mind was of absolutely no concern to me, but I didn't want some bureaucrat trying to have Robo declared vicious for his canine version of serving and protecting.

Erich was lying across the shotgun that had blasted a hole through the double glass of my kitchen door. Grabbing the stock, I pulled it out from under him. He started to move, but froze and whimpered as Robo snapped the air millimeters from his cheek. I backed away until shadows hid me, then pushed the shotgun down under some ornamental bushes.

Much as touching him repelled me, I went back again and searched Erich carefully, reaching around Robo, pushing under Erich's body. The knife was in a leather sheath on his belt. As I pulled it away and threw it into the night, I wondered if a lab would be able to find traces of Jack's blood on it—or mine.

"Where's the pistol?" I demanded.

"I did not bring a pistol. Get him off me. Just get him off me!"

"If you don't tell me where the pistol is, he can stand on you till he takes root. Now where is it?"

He was barely coherent, his accent much thicker than it had been at Joyce's the day before.

"I do not know. He came at me out of the night. From behind. From behind me, he came. I dropped the guns when I fell. I do not know where the pistol is. Get him off me. I cannot breathe. Get him off."

Scuffing my feet around in the groundcover of the garden, first I came across an empty backpack, damp and reeking of gasoline. Then I found the handgun. I fumbled around until I found the safety, flicked it on, and tucked the automatic into my waistband.

Having relieved Erich of what I fervently hoped was his entire arsenal, I took hold of the end of the leash that was still trailing from Robo's collar.

"I'm going to pull him off you now," I said. "I don't know what he'll do when I pull on the leash, so don't move. If you move at all and the dog doesn't rip your face off, I'll shoot you. Understand?"

"Yes," he said faintly. "Get him off me. I will not move. Get him off me!"

From as far away as possible, keeping my own weapon pointed at Erich, I gave a little tug on the leash to see how Robo would react. To my surprise, he stepped off Erich and came to me without hesitation. Maybe he was relieved to have me finally doing my share.

"You're the best boy anyone ever had," I whispered to Robo, rubbing him behind the ears.

Raising and hardening my voice, I said, "You can sit up now, but you'd better do it slowly, or I'll let him at you again."

Erich opened his eyes but didn't move. At first what I was seeing seemed to be an effect of the flames leaping and twisting behind him, then it hit me, and I drew in a sharp breath. The dark brown eyes of yesterday were gone. Instead, Erich stared at me with the same disturbing colorless eyes I'd seen in our first encounter.

My contact lens theory had been close, but backwards, I realized. He didn't use contact lenses to change the color of ordinary eyes. He used contact lenses to disguise extraordinary eyes. My amazement changed to caution. There was calculation in those eyes as they shifted from my face, to the gun, to Robo.

"You might get away in the dark before I could shoot you, but you won't outrun the dog," I said, "and if you try to take off, I'll let him go."

He sat up then, moving as carefully as I could want. "I should have killed you the first time I saw you."

"You didn't have the guts to kill me that day. You were as much afraid of the dog then as you are now. What I don't understand is why you ever came after me later. You had to know I didn't see enough to identify you. No matter what anyone said, you and I both knew I didn't see anything that would let me recognize you."

"You described my eyes. If my wife heard what you said, she would wonder. Better she never heard."

"Maybe so, but I also said over and over again that what I thought I saw couldn't be real, that it was only because I was scared out of my mind. No one thought my description was real, not even me. I've thought about it a lot. You know what I think?" He didn't look particularly interested in what I thought, but I told him anyway. "I think you enjoyed killing Jack. And you were happy to have an excuse to do it again."

As I spoke the words, I realized their truth. "You despicable son of a bitch," I hissed. "That's why you didn't just stab me in the parking lot. You wanted to get me in that van so you could take your time. I should have left the dog on you till the cops get here. Even after you had to let me go that night, you knew I was no threat to you. You didn't try again for days because you weren't in any hurry. It wasn't until you saw me in your own house, staring at you like an idiot, that all of a sudden you were in a big rush to kill me."

"You saw something then. You were not sure yet or you would have started telling things to my wife, but you saw something. I saw it in your face."

"No, you didn't. I didn't recognize you. You still would have been safe if you'd just left me alone. I stared at you because I was shocked that Joyce married a boy less than half her age. That's all it was."

"I am not a boy. I take very good care of her."

"Do you? Was sleeping with Jack Sheffield part of your good care? I bet Joyce wouldn't think so."

Fury contorted his face, and his accent thickened. "He got me drunk. I am not a homosexual. He got me drunk, and then he tried to blackmail me."

"No one who saw you that night thought you were drunk. They said you had a few drinks and it loosened you up. Whatever you are, Joyce already knows it. She calls you beautiful. Not handsome, *beautiful*."

He glared at me, hate radiating from the colorless eyes. I had both Robo's leash and the gun in my left hand. If Robo pulled at all, he'd pull the gun with him.

Not wanting Erich to know that my right arm was all but useless, I backed up, never taking my eyes off him, and pushed the handhold loop of Robo's leash over the top of a fence post.

Moving closer to Erich again, I said, "It's a leather leash and only an inch wide. If you run and he lunges, he'll break it."

He didn't believe me. He sat up straighter, and it occurred to me that running wasn't his only option.

I tried to rekindle his fear. "The dogs know who you are and what you did, you know. When I was leaving your house, Sophie started circling over your scent in the driveway, but I wasn't smart enough to understand. I thought she was excited over the scent of Joyce's dogs."

"Dogs." He spit on the ground. "Dogs, dogs, dogs. Big ugly dogs. I told her I wanted to marry her, but she would have to get rid of the dogs. So we married in Europe and came here and there they are in kennels. That has to be enough, she says. She will not get rid of them. I was good to her and she gave me nothing."

Nothing except easy and legal entry into a country others die to get to any way they can, I thought. Nothing except a life of leisure and luxury he was willing to kill to keep. I didn't waste my breath pointing that out to him.

What I said was, "So Jack wanted you to get Joyce to let him campaign her dog nationally, and you couldn't do it."

He spit out a stream of German that sounded vicious even though I couldn't understand a word, then finally switched back to English. "He thought I could make her do what he wanted, let him fly all over the country with the dog. He wouldn't listen! She would never do what I say, and he would have ruined everything."

In the distance I could hear sirens now, louder and louder as they sped closer. I saw his muscles tense, his weight shift slightly. "I *will* shoot you if you get up, you know," I told him. "If you think I won't, think again. You blew away any inhibitions I had when you shot Sophie."

"I'm glad I killed your dog. It screamed and fell down, and I shot it again."

He started to lunge at me then. He really did. That's the only reason I shot him just as the first sheriff's deputies roared onto the scene.

23

"PUT THE GUN DOWN, LADY! Put it down!"

The first deputies to arrive were strangers, uniformed strangers with their own guns drawn, hard faces, and edgy body language. I put first my revolver and then Erich's automatic on the ground and stepped away from them, holding my hands out in front of me.

"I'm Dianne Brennan, and I'm the one who called 911. That's Erich Kohler," I said, pointing. "He firebombed my house and tried to kill me."

The deputies treated Erich and me as equally suspect, one concentrating on each of us. Erich demanded attention, called me a liar, made excuses, pointed out that he was unarmed and wounded. He had merely come to my house intending to talk to me he said, and I had set a vicious dog on him and shot him.

The wailing sirens of more emergency vehicles grew steadily louder. The first fire truck turned into the driveway then rolled right into the front garden and parked there. In minutes a powerful jet of water hit the flames. Too late, I thought with aching regret. The firemen might keep the fire from destroying any more of the trees around the house, but the house was already beyond saving.

An ambulance arrived in the next wave. The paramedics barely gave me a glance before directing all their attention to Erich. At least once they started working on him, he shut up.

The deputy keeping watch on me listened impassively when I told him about the rest of Erich's arsenal—the shotgun and knife out in the darkness where I'd thrown them.

"It all started with Jack Sheffield's murder this summer," I said. "Lieutenant Forrester knows all about it."

"So you're the one," muttered the deputy.

What exactly did he mean by that? Before I could ask, a familiar face showed up. The handsome, familiar face of Deputy Horton, who had been kind on that other awful day when I found Jack Sheffield's body. He exchanged a few words with my stone-faced custodian then turned to me.

"Are you hurt?" he asked, looking at the way I was cradling my right arm with my left.

"My collarbone was broken when he ran me off the road last night, and I threw away the sling when I crawled through a window to get out of the house. A second-story window," I said, hoping for sympathy.

No sympathy was forthcoming. He just said, "Come with me. You can sit down in my car, warm up, and tell me what happened. The paramedics will look at you soon."

Sitting down sounded good, so did warm. Now that I wasn't moving and flooded with adrenaline, the chilly air of the fall night was biting through my jeans and sweatshirt, and every ache and pain was back full force.

"Okay, I just need to get Robo. He's in the way tied to the fence there."

"Leave him. He'll be fine. I need to talk to you." His young face was set in the same hard lines as the other deputy's.

Robo was lying quietly by the fence. I wanted him with me, but it was true that he would be safe where he was for a while. Horton led the way to one of the squad cars and opened a back door. The sight of the door with no inside handle changed my mind about cooperating.

"Arrest me and force me in there if you have to," I said, "but I won't get in unless you let me go get my dog."

He looked uncertain for a moment. Neither of us found out what he would have done.

"You're not getting in at all," said Brian Forrester as he walked around the back of the car. "We'll get the dog, then you're coming with me."

"Lieutenant . . . ." Horton didn't like it at all.

"I'm here unofficially, off duty, and in my own vehicle. Ms. Brennan is hurt. She's refusing treatment by paramedics and accepting a ride with me." His voice dropped low and challenging. "Is that going to be a problem?"

"No, sir, Lieutenant," said Horton, all but saluting.

Brian and I walked across the yard to Robo in silence. All around us, emergency workers did their jobs. Firemen had reduced the flames from the house by more than half and soaked the nearby trees.

The paramedics loaded Erich into the ambulance, slammed the doors behind him, and drove off, lights flashing and sirens blaring. Deputies searched the yard. Flashes cut through the night as investigators photographed everything.

Yet somehow, the sensation of all eyes on us was so strong everyone seemed frozen in place.

We reached Robo, and I whispered a few words of reassurance to him as I unhooked his leash from the fence, then turned to Brian. Tension was in every line of his body, his eyes narrow and mouth tight.

"What's going on?" I asked. "Why did you say you're here unofficially?"

He shook his head. "Later. Did you really shoot Kohler?"

"Only after he firebombed the house and . . . ."

He cut me off. "Did you give anyone a statement?"

"No, Erich was demanding attention, and of course he's wounded, so everyone did pay attention to him. Deputy Horton was the first one who wanted to hear my story, and he wanted me to get in the car first. That's when you showed up."

"Good." He took the leash from me. "We need to get out of here. If anyone stops us, your collarbone is broken. It hurts like hell, and you think you may be going to pass out, and you want me to take you to the hospital."

His attitude was both confusing and frightening. Did I trust him enough to just do what he wanted without an explanation? Yes, I realized. And the pain in my shoulder was reaching new heights.

Not only that, the death throes of my house were too terrible to watch, and I wasn't going to get into the cage of the backseat of an official car voluntarily, with or without Robo.

"Okay," I said. "I'm with you. They took my gun, but if you let me have yours, I'll shoot anyone who gets in our way."

"That not funny," he said through his teeth.

Sure it was. If not, why was I choking back laughter? Or was that sobs?

No one tried to stop us as he led the way to a dark blue Jeep Cherokee. Once Robo was settled in the back and I was in the passenger seat, Brian wasted no time getting us out of there. As he turned off the dirt road onto pavement, I saw him glance in his rearview mirror almost as if he expected to be followed.

"What's going on?" I asked him again.

"I'm officially off the Sheffield case, under orders to take some time off, and most especially and emphatically under orders to stay away from you. Everyone back there knows it. Hell the firefighters and paramedics probably know it."

"But why?"

"Because the deputy who did the drive bys on your house last night reported seeing my car, or actually as he pointed out, the county's car, in your driveway—at 3 a.m., at 5 a.m., and at 7 a.m. Oh, and his report mentioned that the lights in the house were all out. And to make sure the report didn't just get filed away, he told everyone he met about it this morning."

"The bastard! Isn't there supposed to a thin blue line or something? Is that only for city cops?"

In the light from the instrument panel, his face was shadowy, but I could see him finally relax, see the slight smile.

"If it had been anyone but Yates, he would have talked to me first, but he and I . . . see the world differently. The thin blue line probably fades away here and there in the city too."

"So that's why you didn't answer my phone calls."

"Afraid so. After spending the afternoon yes-sirring and no-sirring most of the department brass, I just stomped out of there and didn't even think about messages until almost hour ago. Of course, I thought you were safe at Susan's." His tone was more resigned than accusatory.

I told him then about Susan showing up late in Wesley's wreck of a car. About her grandchildren.

"What a screwed up mess," he said. "Not much else could have gone wrong."

"Sure it could," I pointed out. "Robo could have ignored whatever he heard in the yard, and he and I would be crispy critters right now."

Brian gave another quick glance in the rearview mirror. The road behind us was still empty.

"Are you expecting someone to chase us down and make me get in Horton's car after all?" I asked.

"No, not really, but they'll be wanting to get a statement from you as soon as possible. Which is why I wanted to get you out of there and talk to you first. Before you give any statement, you talk to Turner. Go over everything with him and do what he says."

Surprise kept me from saying anything.

"I'm serious. You need to talk to Owen Turner or another lawyer right away," he repeated. "If anyone wants to talk to you before you see him, have Susan handle it for you, tell them you've taken a sleeping pill or a tranquilizer or something."

"*I* need a lawyer? You think *I'm* the criminal here?" I asked, ready to argue.

"No, damn it, I don't. You're the victim, and the worst part of my job is watching what happens to people like you who get dragged into the system by scum like Kohler. Victims, witnesses, relatives, neighbors. Look at you. You've got broken bones, cuts and bruises all over. Your car's totaled, one of your dogs was shot, your house and everything in it is gone. And, yes, there are some prosecutors who don't think citizens should have guns, much less ever use them. So they'll add to your misery while they chew over whether to charge you or not."

My indignation turned to fear. "And will they?"

"Not in the end," he said. "Probably not. No jury would convict you, and they'll realize that, but having Turner's help will make it a sure thing and get you out from under the threat a whole lot faster."

"Okay," I said. "I'll leave a message for him tonight and talk to him before I give any statement."

We were at the intersection of Pine Lane and Parker Road now. A right turn would take us to the hospital, a left to Susan's. The right turn indicator was flashing.

"I don't want to go to the hospital again," I said. "Please. Nothing's really worse than it was. If a pain killer and rest don't fix things by morning, I'll go to my own doctor."

Wordlessly, he flipped the turn indicator to the left, but we only barely started south on Parker Road before he again signaled a right turn, pulling into the parking lot beside Walgreen's.

"You look like the sooner you get something for the pain, the better," he said. "Stay here. I'll go in. Advil?"

I nodded, then watched him walk into the store. He should have looked unofficial, dressed in jeans, with a sheepskin coat hanging open over a corduroy shirt, but something in the set of his shoulders and confidence of his walk made me wonder if he was ever really off duty.

I leaned back and closed my eyes, but scenes of smoke and fire immediately filled my mind. So I got out, opened the back door, and started a gentle examination of Robo. He rolled an eye at me but didn't move until I tugged his collar and made him sit up so I could get to his other side.

"Is he all right?" Brian said, walking up behind me.

"So far as I can tell, but I don't think jumping out of second-story windows and taking down murderers is exactly what Dr. Hunsaker had in mind when he said he should take it easy for a couple of days."

"That's how you got out?"

"It was the worst part."

He made a sympathetic sound, then said. "Come on, get back in. I've got some stuff for you."

He not only had Advil, he had a bottle of water to wash the pills down. And an arm sling that looked every bit as sturdy as the one the hospital had given me the night before.

"They had it in with knee braces and some other stuff," he said, helping me adjust the neck straps. Warm hands brushed my neck. I fought the urge to just lean into him and hide from the world.

"How's that?" he asked, finishing with the straps.

"Fine," I said. "I'm really sorry you're in trouble with the department over me. It will be worse after tonight, won't it. Will they suspend you?"

"Nah, more of the same. Maybe more time off, but I've got a lot of leave time built up anyway."

"That's not right. They shouldn't do that to you because of me."

"It is right. Getting personally involved with a witness is unprofessional. I jeopardized the investigation and maybe the conviction. If Kohler's attorney finds out about it, he'll claim we conspired to frame his poor, innocent client because he doesn't like dogs and you're obsessed with them. After tonight you and I are going to be strangers until Kohler's convicted and locked away."

He closed my door, walked around and got behind the wheel in a way that told me he wanted to change the subject, but I wasn't ready to let it go.

"Did you tell them I forced you to come in the house and that you slept on the couch with Millie?"

"I did not." There was a lot of male ego in those three words. I knew better than to say more.

He turned to face me. "Look, I should have called a female deputy to stay with you last night. And if I had, you wouldn't have been alone there for Kohler to take another crack at. I've been breaking rules over you since that first interview."

I thought back. "All that happened then was that I made you mad."

"You did. You got to me good, and I let it show. Believe it or not, I don't usually lose my temper like that in an interview—even with a smart mouth like you. Like I said before, it's a part of the job I don't like. Right at the beginning people like you have no idea what it's going to cost them, getting caught up in the system. So there you were, you actually knew a judge well enough to call him for help, and instead of trying to help yourself, you were putting all your effort into keeping the dog away from us. I wanted to wring your neck. I wanted to . . . ."

He stopped himself, deciding not to tell me exactly how much mayhem he'd wanted to inflict, then went on. "Of course, it probably made a difference that you weren't a hairy truck driver or a seventy-year-old grandmother."

With any luck at all, the shadows concealed the self-satisfied smile his words put on my face. I didn't want him to start the car, take me to Susan's, and disappear from my life for who knew how long.

"It will take years before the trial is over and he's convicted."

"Months," he said. "It won't be that bad. I'm hungry. How about you?"

At the thought of food, my stomach contracted sharply, letting me know the sandwich and couple of cookies I'd had with Susan and her grandchildren had been too little too long ago. And of course getting food meant putting off the drive to Susan's.

"Yes, I'm hungry, but I can't walk in anyplace looking like this."

"Drive through," he said, starting the car.

I ordered a double cheeseburger, large order of fries, and chocolate shake. This was a major comfort food kind of night. But something else niggled at me.

"You haven't asked what happened," I said.

Brian's eyes met mine in the semi-darkness. "No, I haven't."

"I can't tell you?"

He was silent so long I expected him to say no, but in the end, he crumbled his hamburger wrapper into one of the bags, crunched the bag and said, "Oh, go ahead, I've got nothing to take notes with, and I've got a lousy memory. So do you because by tomorrow you're going to forget we ever had this conversation."

So I told him about it—all of it, the sounds and the smells, and the fear—and felt a vast relief in the telling. When I was done, I asked him, "So am I a criminal too? It felt right. It still feels right."

"As far as I'm concerned, if you'd shot him between the eyes with the dog holding him down for you, you'd deserve a medal, but my opinion doesn't count. You talk to Turner before anybody else."

"I will. I promise." I leaned back in my seat and relaxed, feeling better than I had since that morning. It had to be the ibuprofen kicking in, starting to ease the pain. What else could it be?

24

THE SIGHT OF THE BURNED out wreck of my house sometimes brought tears, sometimes rage, sometimes the
fog of depression. On a cold morning in late January,
for the first time since the fire, a sharp stab of joy ran
through me as home came into sight.

I parked Susan's farm truck in the driveway and sat
for a moment, admiring the clean new world created
by the previous night's storm. Three inches of fresh
snow blanketed the land, obliterating the gouges and
ruts left by fire trucks months before. Even the skele-
ton of the house looked less tragic against a background of intense blue sky, bright sun, and glittering
white carpet.

An early morning phone call from the contractor,
assuring me that demolition would start on schedule
next week had a lot to do with my upbeat mood. His
call was only the latest piece of good news in a series
that had started with another phone call—from Owen
Turner, letting me know that the county attorney
had decided not to prosecute me for shooting Erich

Kohler. And that decision had been a turning point. After that, the many demands for interviews from sheriff's officers, prosecutors, defense attorneys, investigators, and reporters dwindled, then stopped.

Sophie and Robo had no appreciation for scenery through a windshield. They wanted out, out to stretch their legs in a yard bigger than a postage stamp, out where the wind carried a slight tang of Canada and far northern places and no trace of exhaust.

I positioned a knit band over my ears, zipped my parka all the way up, and let the dogs out of the truck and into the yard. They destroyed the pristine surface at a dead run, zigzagging back and forth, chasing each other, stopping only to catch their breath that plumed in the air around them and to taste the snow, plowing their muzzles through it, then taking off again.

Robo rolled, leaving a Rottweiler angel in the snow. I threw loosely packed snowballs at them, laughing at the look on Sophie's face when she caught one and it dissolved in her mouth.

Seeing Sophie strong again, running without a limp even in frigid air and wet snow, made me think back to the day after the fire. When I told Susan that Owen Turner was in court all day and couldn't see me until the next morning and that I needed to avoid giving any official statement until after talking to him, her solution had been simple.

"Then let's go get Sophie," she said. "When you called they said she was better this morning, right? If we're on the road and not here, no one can corner you to ask questions you don't want to answer. The emergency vet right here in Parker has around the clock staffing and intensive care. If that's what she still needs, Dr. Hunsaker will be happy to transfer her and get a good night's sleep."

"Maybe we could just visit her, Maybe she shouldn't be moved yet." And how could she be moved safely anyway?

Susan acted as if she hadn't heard me. "Before we start to the vet's we can stop at Motor Vehicle and get you a new driver's license. And at the bank for temporary checks. Have you called your insurance company yet?"

"Yes, I called them, but I'm not so sure about moving Sophie. They only said she was a little better. She's not out of danger yet."

Susan didn't debate degrees of improvement with me. She called the emergency vet and extracted a promise to consult with Dr. Hunsaker immediately. By the time we finished another cup of coffee, the vet was on the phone again. My vague objections and fussing worries gradually faded as I talked to both Dr. Hunsaker and the emergency vet. The vets weren't just going along with Susan, they genuinely agreed that Sophie would be better off in a critical care ward.

So Susan turned her van into a well padded, cozy canine ambulance, and we transported Sophie, drawn and weak, to the local hospital. That was only the first of the many kindnesses Susan and her family showed me in the following weeks. Even Wesley tried so hard to help I vowed to listen in the future to Susan's endless Wesley stories with a more open mind. Backsliding on that vow was a constant problem, but I tried.

A silver SUV slowed in the road and turned into the driveway, its engine so quiet the only sound was of snow crunching under tires. Sophie came to my side, and together we studied the approaching vehicle. Recognizing first the Lexus symbol on the shining hood, then the tall, angular man in the driver's seat, I relaxed but only a little.

Time spent with Owen Turner meant attorney's fees. Yet now that the county attorney had made his decision, wasn't all that supposed to stop? And why was Owen tracking me down here instead of calling and setting up an appointment at his office?

As he pulled up beside Susan's truck and parked, two heads popped up in the backseat. Narrow, elegant heads that I knew would match narrow, elegant bodies. Greyhounds.

Slipping through the gate, I left Sophie and Robo in the yard and walked over to the car.

"Good morning," Owen said as he stepped out into the snow. Somehow, dressed in boots, parka, and a woolen hat, he looked more like a lawyer than ever. "Susan told me you were here and that bringing Barry and Misha along would be okay."

He studied me for a moment, sun flashing off the gold rims of his glasses, then added, "You can stop looking so worried. My schedule was turned upside down today when a hearing was continued, so I'm taking the morning off. This is strictly a social call."

His words let me give him a genuine smile of greeting, but the little cautionary voice inside me didn't turn off completely. Somehow I suspected that when a criminal attorney had a court hearing canceled, he usually headed straight back to his office and tackled other work. Owen had never struck me as whimsical enough to just load his dogs in the car one morning and visit a client whose problems he had solved weeks ago.

Seemingly unaware of my skepticism, Owen introduced me to Barry and Misha. Neither greyhound was gray. Barry was fawn with a bit of white on his chest. Misha had stripes and patches of dark hair swirling over his fawn coat—brindle. We introduced the greyhounds to Sophie and Robo first through the fence.

When that went well, I held the gate and Owen led his dogs into the yard. After a few moments of polite doggy sniffing, the greyhounds took off along the fence line. Recognizing almost instantly they couldn't begin to keep up with the racing dogs, Sophie and Robo gave up the chase and went back to their own games.

"Thank you for letting them have this," Owen said. "We take them to Chatfield Reservoir and dog parks as much as possible, but it's hard in the winter. This is a treat for them."

"It's my pleasure," I said, watching in awe as the dogs' long strides carried them to the far end of the five acres at amazing speed. "Misha and Barry. Would someone in your house be a Barishnikov fan?"

Owen gave his familiar small controlled smile. "My wife. Not many pick up on it." He pulled his hat down as far as he could, turned up his collar, and hunched against the cold. "So how are your canine hero and heroine doing?"

"Fine," I said. "They're both themselves again. The only problem is that means Robo's back in his shell. I keep trying to lure him out again, but so far no luck."

The cold was beginning to get to me too, just standing there as we were. In the tangled mess Erich Kohler had made of my life, only one thread seemed to be the kind a lawyer might think he could knit neatly into place. Wanting him to admit the real purpose of his visit, I tried teasing it out of him. "So are you working for Joyce Richerson now? Is that why you're here?"

To my surprise, for the first time since I'd known him, Owen's response was not controlled. "Of course not!" he said sharply. "You're my client! It wouldn't be ethical for me to represent her."

"Owen, I'm sorry. I was joking. I didn't realize that, and after all, I'm really an ex-client now."

"That's irrelevant," he said, calm again. "To represent someone else involved in the Kohler case, there would be . . . procedures. And I wouldn't do it."

"I'm sorry," I repeated. "But you're here to tell me to let her have what she wants, aren't you? It's bad enough she's already interfering behind my back and has Susan nagging at me. Now you're here, and you're here to get me to go along with Joyce, aren't you?"

The greyhounds were no longer running but were at our feet, starting to shiver.

"They don't have enough fur to stay out in the cold," Owen said. "And my feet are getting numb. Let's get in the car. We can finish this discussion while we thaw out."

Sophie and Robo were still nosing through the snow with enthusiasm, so we left them to it. Owen toweled the snow off Barry and Misha and settled them on a wool blanket in the backseat of his SUV. He and I got in the front and pushed our feet close to the heater outlets.

"What do you mean by Ms. Richerson has been going behind your back?" he said as the heat began to rise.

"For one thing, this marvelous rental house Susan just happened to hear about. Fenced yard, dogs are welcome, almost unbelievably reasonable rent. And the neighbors tell me it was sold just last month and it was never a rental before. The property management company that owns it is brand new, and when I looked into the ownership of the company . . . ."

Owen held up a hand. "So Ms. Richerson arranged for you to have an affordable rental where you could keep the dogs. Is that bad?"

"I didn't say it was bad. I said it was interfering. And she bought off Erich somehow too. You know she did."

"No one can buy another person's basic rights," Owen said primly.

"Pfft." I didn't apologize for the rude sound or for my disbelief. "She wasn't letting him have a penny. He had to make do with a public defender, and he was making new threats about suing me every day. Then all of a sudden he's got a first-rate defense attorney, and what do you know, no more threats. Tell me she didn't arrange that."

"I can't tell you what I don't know," Owen said. "But if you're right, she's done you a favor."

"She has, and I'm grateful, but enough's enough. The insurance adjuster called yesterday going on about 'contributions from Ms. Richerson.' I told him to forget it in no uncertain terms, and lo and behold, here you are today. I don't want to hear whatever Joyce, the adjuster, or anyone else sent you out here to talk me into," I said, opening the car door. "Your dogs are beautiful. You can bring them out and let them run here any time you want to. It was good to see you again, Owen."

With that, I got out of the car, and whistled for Sophie and Robo. The Lexus sat there, idling, as the dogs jumped into Susan's old truck without the benefit of a towel to dry their wet legs and bellies.

I got in myself and turned the key, ignoring the sight of Owen trudging around the front of his car through the snow toward me.

He knocked on the window. I rolled it down part way.

"I have many clients who ignore my advice," he said, "but you are the first who has paid my admittedly high fees and refused to even listen to me."

I shut my eyes for a second, then met his. "If I hear you out, will you accept my decision and leave it at that?"

"Of course. Are you going to make me stand out here and freeze so that I'll talk faster?"

He emphasized his statement by hopping from one foot to the other, making me smile.

Two Rottweilers and one human are all that can fit on the seat of an ordinary pickup. I followed Owen back to his car and got in.

He might be out of the cold now, but Owen was past finessing. "Are you too angry at Ms. Richerson to allow her to . . . atone for the harm she's caused you?"

Sometimes I thought about Joyce, so eager to hear every detail of my first encounter with Jack's killer. And of me, stubbornly refusing to give her those details. Had she already heard about the killer's strange, cold eyes from someone like Marjorie Cleavinger? Was she wondering about Erich then, or was she really just looking for a vicarious thrill?

I'd never know and wasn't sure I wanted to.

"I'm not angry at Joyce at all." Hearing the lack of conviction in my own voice, I tried harder to convince myself and Owen. "None of this is her fault. She had nothing to do with any of it, and everyone knows it."

I'd forgotten how brutally frank Owen could be. He proceeded to remind me.

"Joyce Richerson was so arrogant that she thought she could buy a handsome young man and control him with her wealth. She compounded that incredible foolishness by neglecting what should be ordinary precautions for a woman in her position. She should have had a background check done on him, which would have revealed several brushes with the law in Germany and an arrest in Austria."

As he spoke, Owen dug around in his pockets, brought out two small dog biscuits, and gave one to each of his dogs. "So she brought him here, where he killed Sheffield and almost killed you. She feels guilty and humiliated, and nothing is going to stop her from trying to make things right the only way she knows how. And if you refuse to deal with her, the only beneficiary will be your insurance company."

The adjuster's babbling had made no sense to me. Not only would Owen make the situation clear, focusing on insurance let me skip over my feelings about Joyce, guilt, and atonement.

"Why is the insurance company even involved?"

"Your insurance company will use any monies Ms. Richerson pays to offset what it is obligated to pay you. Ms. Richerson, of course, wants you to benefit by a higher settlement from the insurance company because of her payment. However, if you refuse to take part in negotiations, your insurance company will settle with her. She'll pay them, but they won't pay you an extra cent."

"They can't do that," I protested. "I don't want her to pay anything."

"They can do it, and they're going to. Ms. Richerson is married to a man whose criminal acts are costing your insurance company a large amount. Even if she weren't eager to pay, they'd go after her."

"That's not fair," I protested. "She's divorcing him, and it's not her fault. She shouldn't have to pay anyone anything."

"As many people have observed, life is not fair," Owen said dryly. "The fact is if you take part in the negotiations, you and the insurance company will benefit. If you don't, the insurance company will celebrate."

My only reply was short and vulgar.

"Indeed," Owen said. "Does that mean I can negotiate with the insurance company and Ms. Richerson on your behalf?"

"It means I'll think about it."

I did appreciate Owen, for what he had already done for me and what he was trying to do, and I told him so. "Thanks for making me listen," I added. "I didn't know about the insurance, and I will think it over and let you know, I promise."

"Good," he said. "Now I think Barry and Misha might be ready for another go round. What do you think?"

"Sure," I said, smiling at him. Asking if any of his Douglas County cases had caused him to run into the man Susan insisted on calling "my lieutenant," ran through my mind, but I pushed it away. If there was anything to tell, Owen would have mentioned it.

25

AFTER SPENDING THE MORNING frolicking with the dogs, I settled down at the computer, determined to focus on client work for the rest of the day. Immersed in the intricacies of macro code, I was slow to follow the dogs when they jumped up, started barking, and charged to the front door.

The distorted view through the peephole was of Brian Forrester, juggling a large paper bag in his arms, reaching for the doorbell.

I threw open the door just as he rang the bell, then stood there, taking in the sight. The car in my driveway was his own Jeep. His sheepskin coat hung open in spite of the cold. Gray sweater, faded jeans, scarred boots. He looked as solidly reassuring as ever.

We both spoke at the same time.

"Are you going to invite me in?"

"Do we need to hide your car in the garage?"

I answered by stepping back from the doorway. He answered as he walked in. "Nope. The department may not be enthused about this visit, but they're officially neutral."

He gave me the bag. "I don't suppose you think moving in here is worth a house warming, but maybe you'd like these anyway."

Bright yellow mums filled the bag and all but spilled over the top.

"Yes, I like them," I said. "And if the new house is ever done, I'll need to start from scratch with the gardens, so every sprout will help. Come on back to the kitchen. I'll get coffee."

He sat and petted Sophie while I made coffee, taking in the modern kitchen with its granite counter tops, stainless sink and appliances, and tiled floor. Most visitors felt compelled to point out the advantages of this rental house over the home I'd lost, but the good sense my lieutenant had shown in the past was still there. He didn't comment.

"So are you going to tell me what brought the department around?" I asked. "Are you in good graces again?"

"High good graces," he said, unable to disguise his pleasure. "Kohler pled yesterday. Pled to the murder when we never came up with a scrap of physical evidence against him. And I told them the way to get him to do it."

"He confessed!" I reminded him, thumping down coffee mugs and pouring.

He just looked at me.

"All right. All right. I say he admitted he did it. He says he didn't. And I shot him."

"There's no evidence on the murder at all, and nothing that would convict him on the vehicular assault on you.

The bullets from Sophie matched his gun, but he claims he saw you run off the road, went to help and the dog came after him. He probably stole the vehicle he used to force you off the road, and we can't find it. The only good case we had was on the arson and assault at your house."

"And I shot him."

"You sure did. Poor boy just stopped by to see how you were doing, and you went crazy and sicced a vicious dog on him and shot him."

"You forgot the part where I set my own house on fire so I'd have light to shoot by," I said, unable to keep a straight face.

Brian laughed with me, but only for a moment. "He can be a charmer. Some jury might have bought it."

"So then why did he plead guilty?"

"Because of my brilliant idea. I overheard one of the prosecutors complaining about how interviewing him was so difficult because every time anyone mentioned you or the dogs he went ballistic, shouting, cursing, totally losing it."

He paused for emphasis. "I, of course, understand how you can have that effect on a man."

Another time I would have taken that bait, but right then all I wanted was the rest of his story. "So what was your brilliant idea?"

"I told them to try offering him a deal. Plead guilty to killing Sheffield or stand trial for arson and attempted murder on you at your house, and . . . ."

"And!"

"And one count of felony animal cruelty for shooting Sophie and a second for setting the house on fire knowing Robo was inside."

"Oh, my," I whispered. "That must have really pushed him over the edge."

"They tell me he actually had foam at the corners of his mouth."

"You're right. It was brilliant, but he's only pleading guilty to killing Jack, isn't he? So he's getting away with all the rest of it.

"He's not getting away with anything. When he gets out—if he ever gets out—he'll be an old man, and not so pretty. He isn't going to have an easy time in prison. With his ex-wife keeping a vengeful eye on things he'll probably serve every day of his sentence, and since he's a foreign national, if he ever does make it out, he'll be on a plane for Germany the same day."

"So it's over," I said.

"Over for the department, for me. How about you? How are you doing?" he said softly.

The nightmares of smoke and fire were down to once a week or less, and I wasn't ready to share them.

"Okay. The contractor swears they're starting work next week. Some of my things survived the fire—in the basement." I pointed to a favorite watercolor on the wall.

"I didn't mean things. How are you doing? You, yourself," he said. "You look good."

"Not covered with blood, bruises, and dirt, you mean?" I grinned at him. "We're all healed up. Sophie has a few white hairs on her face now, but we're okay."

His assessing gaze was disconcerting. It was a relief when he took his eyes off mine, looked around the kitchen again, taking in Bella on her new favorite perch atop the refrigerator, Robo flat out on his rug in a corner, and Sophie, now at my feet.

"So where's Millie?" he asked.

"She's been adopted, and they think she's a Rott-weiler Lassie."

"Good for her. And you're really all right?"

He was so serious, so intent. Making light of things again didn't seem right, and I wanted an opinion from someone who wasn't such a biased cheering section as Susan.

"The problem is that I'm going to be more than all right." I told him about Joyce and the insurance company. "So I'm going to come out ahead, and it makes me feel like I spilled hot coffee and sued and got rich. It feels wrong."

"Are you sure you'll be ahead, after all the bills come in?" he asked. "What about your business?"

As a matter of fact, my best client had taken his business elsewhere. Sorry, he said, sorry about murder and arson, but he needed help when he needed it, and I was no longer reliable.

Brian saw my uncertainty. "Tell me. If last fall the devil came along and said you could have a new house if the old one burned almost to the ground and almost with you in it, and a new car if you rode the old one down the side of a mountain and broke your collar-bone and let your dog get shot, would you have made the deal?"

"Of course not, and don't forget Sophie broke a leg in that wreck."

"I'm not forgetting. Don't you forget. You'll never be the same again. Nothing can pay you for that."

"Maybe not." I could hear the uncertainty still in my own voice.

"Look," Brian said. "If Kohler had money of his own, would you go after him? File a civil suit? Hurt him any way you could?"

"Every day of the week and twice on Sundays," I snapped.

"If it was a normal marriage, he'd have some control over some of the assets," he pointed out. "Did Turner tell you about the prenuptial agreement?"

I shook my head.

"If they divorced, he didn't get a cent. If they weren't living together when she died, he didn't get a cent. If she died before they were married five years, he didn't get a cent. After five years, if she died, he got half. Ten years, three-quarters. Twenty years, all."

Brian let his words hang in the air for a moment, then added. "She's a very wealthy woman, and they'd been married more than two years already. Maybe half would have been enough."

Just like that, he erased all my mixed feelings. Maybe I'd go see Joyce one of these days, thank her. Meeting beautiful Erich Kohler had changed both our lives.

Brian's voice brought my thoughts back. "Enough of the bad guys," he said. "How about dinner sometime? Somewhere a step up from a drive through."

"When?"

"I've got to get in to the office and push some paper today, but I'll get out of there early. Tonight?"

"I'd like that."

Maybe I would tell him about the dreams. Maybe that night. Maybe some other night. Maybe he knew ways to banish nightmares.

We talked for a while. I showed him the plans for the new house. He told me how it had been when he and his wife built the house he still lived in.

When he left I went back to my computer, looking over at the pot of bright yellow mums once in a while and smiling. Living in the rental house for months no longer seemed as bleak a prospect as it had that very morning.

The heavy weight of Sophie's head on my thigh was so familiar I didn't even look down but dropped one hand to rest on her head for a moment, then slid my fingers behind an ear, rubbing gently.

Gradually I became aware that something wasn't quite right. The head on my leg was too heavy, the skull too broad. When my fingers felt a ridge of scar tissue on the ear I was rubbing, I looked down in surprise. Then I cupped both hands along the sides of the big head.

"Welcome back to the world, Robo," I whispered.

About the Author

Ellen O'Connell lives in Douglas County, Colorado, with a motley crew of Rottweilers, Rottweiler mixes and a Morgan horse. She was active in Rottweiler rescue work for almost ten years, first on her own, then on the Board of Directors of Rottie Aid (www.rottieaid.org). At the present time, her rescue work is limited to transporting dogs for Rottie Aid, but she expects there will be other foster dogs in her future. See her website at www.oconnellauthor.com.

Made in the USA
San Bernardino, CA
24 May 2015